The Main Event

Book Three of
The Human Race

Tahnee Fritz

The Main Event is a work of fiction. Names, characters, places, and incidents are the products of the author's imagination or are used fictitiously. Any resemblance to actual events, locales, or persons, living or dead, is entirely coincidental.

For my family and friends.

Part One

The loud hum of the truck's diesel engine fills my ears and takes over my mind with the monotonous sound. I can feel it sending the craziness even further into my mind the longer I am stuck listening to it. With my eyesight taken from me for the moment, that sound is even more annoying and all I want to do is scream at the top of my lungs.

I want to scream for being thrown into the back of this truck and yell my head off for having my arms pinned tightly behind my back. I could always open my eyes and let the sunlight burn them straight to hell and that will drive the loudest of my heartbreaking screams from my throat, but it is the heartache that is keeping me quiet and unmoving in my place.

All I can think of is Ryder. I can still see him lying on the concrete with his lifeless body teasing me to believe that he is somehow still alive. I felt his chest and listened for a breath his body did not take and the only thing my mind is telling me is that death has come to him and I am trapped with the man that brought him that fate.

We left the truck stop a little while ago, maybe forty

minutes or so. It is difficult to keep track of the time when my mind can only focus on losing the only person I have left on the planet to care deeply enough about that I would die before letting something happen to him. In a way, I did die, but he is the one who is seeing the afterlife right now.

No. I can't allow myself to think that he is dead. No matter how loud I screamed his name when those men pulled me away from his body, I have to believe that he *will* wake up. If I let the hope of Ryder being alive slip from my mind, there is no saying what will happen to me. Pain and sadness are a lot for one person to bare and I need to stay strong through this.

I *can't* give up.

We hit a speed bump in the middle of the street and I bounce off the bench a bit. I hit my back against the metal of the truck and a tiny shock of pain shoots up and down my spine. Jason grunts as he hits the metal and our shoulders bump together. He sniffles and sits up straight. I almost forgot that he is sitting next to me with his hands tied behind his back as well. This seems horrible to think about, but I am kind of glad to be captured with someone I know. I haven't known Jason for long and I am sure he probably hates me right now for being stuck in this situation. But, as long as we can stay strong together, we can find a way to get out and make a run for it.

I take a deep breath and force myself to focus on other things. I strain my ears to listen to the sounds around me.

There are four other men sitting in the back of the truck with us. One sits beside me and another by Jason. Two are across from us and I hear the metal of their guns clanking as they keep a hand on them.

The one to the left across from me is scared. His teeth are chattering and he's breathing faster than the others. He fumbles with his weapon and I feel his eyes staring at me. I breathe in through my nose, letting the smell of his fear enter my nostrils. However strong the man's scent is, it isn't enough to stop the images of Ryder's unconscious form to take over my thoughts. I was hoping the frenzy would take over after smelling the flesh of the humans here, but it is eluding me and I feel like a pathetic little girl.

I don't understand why the evil thing lurking in my veins is being shy at a time like this. I need it now more than any other time in my life that I can think of. In order to save myself and save Jason, along with the rest of the world, I can't be locked up in the back of a truck only to be taken to some god-awful town which Trevor has made his home. I can't think of the sadness or the people I care about, because it is the one thing keeping the monster hidden.

It is just too hard to concentrate on anything other than wondering if Ryder will wake up or if he will be left to rot on the side of the road like thousands of others have done. The cold tears on my cheeks are stealing every bit of strength away from me and my mind can't think of finding a way out of this mess. I feel lost and confused and everything other than the badass girl I need to be.

This isn't a good feeling for me.

We hit another bump in the road. This one is not as bad as the first one but Jason's body still hits against mine. I feel his hot breath on my neck for a split second and, once again, Ryder pops into my head. There were too many nights to count where I have felt his breath on my neck. Too many minutes of my life were spent staring into his perfect eyes and running my fingers through his messy hair. I'm not ready for those priceless seconds of my life to be transformed into memories that I'll never get to experience again. I'm not ready to admit that he may be gone forever.

The truck is slowing down now and the squealing brakes sound like a box of angry mice. I force myself to focus all of my energy into my hearing so I can figure out what the hell is going on. The truck in front of us is coming to a halt as well and the engines of both get shut off.

Heavy footsteps are approaching the back of this truck. The men stomp their boots on the concrete and their guns rattle against their bodies. Voices fill the air as a crowd of people surround us. Some of the men are ordering this crowd to stay back and keep their distance from the freak in the back of the truck. Their fear and excitement drifts up my nose as I take another inhale and even that isn't enough to drive me into a frenzy.

A single set of footsteps comes closer to the truck and stops at the tailgate. The man next to me hops down, followed by the scared fellow who was sitting across from me. I feel a tug on my arm as the third man pulls me to my feet and near-ly tosses me to the street below. I stumble when I land, but catch myself and stand upright. It's hard to keep my eyes closed when I so badly want to open them and look into the eyes of those that are staring at me.

"*That's* it?" someone exclaims as though they don't be-lieve a girl like me could hold a cure so valuable.

"She doesn't look so scary to me." A younger sounding woman speaks up through the crowd.

I hear other comments like this coming from them and I grit my teeth forcing the rude retorts to stay in my mind. These people don't know anything about me or what I can do. I might not look like much, but I have done more than they could ever dream of doing.

I shake my head and ignore their words and listen to a stumbling noise coming from behind me. Jason is being thrown from the truck and isn't so easy on his feet. I hear him cry out in pain when he lands sharply on the concrete. A scuffle comes next and someone yanks Jason to his feet and forces him to stand in place.

I feel a presence standing before me. This one is tall and looming, like a statue standing on top of the world. He is thrilled with himself and the prize he obtained. I keep my eyes shut, fighting the urge to open them and stare into the eyes of Trevor. I could recognize his horrid stench anywhere.

"I hope your ride was comfortable." He speaks with a sarcastic hint to his voice.

"I hope you fucking die." I snap a response.

The crowd around me laughs and gasps at the mere thought of a girl standing up to Trevor. He is their leader, someone they are forced to look up to and depend on. He is nothing more than a sadistic murderer to me, therefore I get every right on the planet to wish him dead.

Trevor laughs along with his followers, then speaks loudly, "My people, this has been a long time coming. The cure for the undead that we have grown to fear so much is here! We can finally have order on this planet and I will be the one to lead us all to the perfect world we so desire. With this gift, this creature no man has ever seen before, I will be in control and all of you will prosper."

The crowd roars and I die a little inside as the words spill out of his mouth. My hands tug at the ropes behind my back, but they are too thick for me to break. I thought I was stronger than this. I *know* I am stronger than this but the thought of losing Ryder is eating away at every fiber of my being and I can't be the strong person I need to be.

"Bridget," Trevor directs his speech to me dragging me out of my mind once more, "why don't you open your eyes and take a look at my people."

Not a second goes by and I feel his hands on my face, placing the sunglasses over my eyes. I don't protest or try moving away from him. Sight is a priority and I allow him to grant me with vision.

I open my eyes, squinting at first until they adjust to the burning light of the sun. The scenery comes into view and I turn my head left and right to take in my surroundings. We are standing in the middle of a street with houses lining both sides. The windows are boarded up and the doors have all been enhanced to withstand a horde of zombies or vampires. A faint humming sound comes from a few of the homes, a generator perhaps, giving power to these people who I already feel don't deserve it.

The crowd is filled with dozens of men, women, and

children. All of them are staring at me and the group of fighters for which they cheer. A few of them pass me snide glances or fearful stares. One woman gives me a disgustful look, then spits at my feet. Jason is standing a few feet from me with a gun pressed against his right temple to keep him from moving. His left shoulder looks like it has been dislocated, probably from the tumble he took getting out of the truck and he stares at me with longing eyes.

I let my jaw drop as I look upon the faces of these people who think so highly of Trevor. They believe in his plans and actually *want* to follow him. How could they look up to a man who only wants horrible things to happen to the world?

I turn my glare to him and hatred fills my mind. This is the man that killed my Ryder. He took everything from me. My life, my world, my freedom. He doesn't deserve to walk this earth as a human being. He doesn't even deserve to roam the planet as a zombie or a vampire. The only type of life he is allowed to have is the one where he is rotting in the deepest pit in the worst parts of whatever hell that might exist. And I deserve the right to put him there.

My fists tighten and the rope squeezes harder around my wrists. I pull at it, willing it to snap with my mind. My hands don't break free and the monster still isn't showing herself. I feel like the helpless girl I was before I was bitten. The type of person who doesn't exactly know what to do in these types of situations. My mind is frazzled, mixed between hatred and despair. I turn to Jason and he is giving me no signs of what I should do.

I am completely frozen.

"Show us how it works!" I hear a shout from the crowd and turn my head toward the voice.

"Yeah!" many of the people cry out in unison.

Trevor steps away from me and raises his hands to calm them down, "In time all of you will see the cure in action. Once we have her in a secured location, things will begin and the world will start becoming the way we want. We can control things and we can get the riches, the food, and all the resources we will ever want with this cure. It will just take time to reveal her gift to all of you."

Another cheerful roar comes from the cluster of humans. They clap their hands together with smiles across all of their faces and they praise Trevor like he is some kind of god. He smiles and waves to his followers, taking in all of the glory they are sending his way.

His fighters are beginning to unload their weapons from the first truck and some are trying to get the crowd to head to their homes. Jason gets shoved forward and I see him begging me to do something, to end whatever hell is about to be thrust upon him. He gets closer to me, with a gun still pressed against his head and our eyes meet.

"Bridget you have to do something." Jason pleads as he is dragged away from me. "You have to get us out of here!"

I don't know what to say or even what to do. My feet are planted to the concrete underneath them unable to move. Not even when Trevor leans closer to me again and that wretched smile crosses his lips.

"You are just going to *love* the accommodations I have in store for you. My men have been busy since we found out about you and have prepared a *luxury* suite." By the way he said luxury I can tell my new living space will be more of a prison than a hotel room.

He grips my arm and we begin our walk down the street following the rest of his men. I glance over my shoulder and stare at the trucks. Part of me wishes that I would see Ryder hopping down from one of them. Even if he is just another prisoner, at least I would know that he is alive. I'd rather see him marching down the street with an army of his own, gun in hand, ready to save the day and the girl he's in love with. But that is not what I get so I am forced to face the way ahead of me.

* * *

My *luxury* accommodation was exactly what I figured it would be. A large cage about the size of a jail cell complete with a heavy duty padlock to keep the door secured. There are three walls made up of thick, metal bars which are strongly welded in the corners. The fourth wall is part of a massive brick building that used to be the town's high school and now serves as Trevor's headquarters.

I stare at this prison, eyeballing the bars as I approach it. Each one has been dug deeply into the earth and connected at the top to a crude roof made from sheet metal. The welds are strong around the roof and I'm starting to notice that I won't be escaping from this cage as easily as I was hoping I could.

Trevor threw me into my new room and the lock was instantly put in place. He left my hands tied behind my back, but at least he let me keep my sunglasses. I guess he has some sense of decency.

Jason was taken inside the school to a place my eyes couldn't follow. I'm worried about what they'll do to him or how they will potentially torture him. There isn't a doubt in my mind that they will end up using him against me to get what they want. They already have me locked in a cage, with sadness clouding the only part of my being that would aide in an escape. I don't want to think of what else they could do in order to feed their sick appetite of taking over the world.

A small crowd of Trevor's followers have grouped together to gawk at me. Their eyes are constantly judging me, the freak in a cage. I've been put on display like I'm some kind of animal and they are waiting for the main event. The part in their life story where they see something simply remarkable that they could only wish to see it again.

I scan their clean faces. The men are neatly shaven, wearing unstained shirts and jeans with no holes. The women all have their hair done nice and perfect without a strand out of place. Some wear dresses while the younger ones wear jeans and t-shirts. This place seems like a normal town without the worries of zombies or vampires roaming the world beyond it.

I'll give Trevor a point on this one. He at least knows how to take good care of his people. They look fed and well rested and they don't appear like they ever worry about the apocalypse. He has kept these few dozen humans alive and I am forced to respect him for that. The human race needs to survive, regardless if a man I want to stab with a dull and painful knife is behind some of it.

I back up to the brick wall of the school, distancing myself from these prying humans. The bricks are rough against my hands and my hoody sticks to them in a few places, catching on one of the many holes it has acquired. There are blood stains all over my clothes and holes from where I was shot and hurt over the past few days. I look like I belong in the wild to live off the land, yet these people ogle me like I'm some sort of miracle.

I can see the wonder and amazement in their eyes as they stare at what they believe is the savior of humanity. They are utterly excited to see their leader's plan coming into action and they certainly cannot wait to see what I can do.

The smell of fear catches my nose and I glance to the few who are frightened of me. The ones who can't bring themselves to even look my way. They avert their eyes as though I'm a gory monster waiting for my next kill. Seeing their fearful faces leaves me with a feeling of shame and disgust growing through me. They think of me as a freak and I can't blame them.

I scan a few more faces and spot a young girl around ten

who keeps her eyes on the bars instead of looking directly at me. She is clutching onto a stuffed dog with a missing ear. Her father stands behind her with his hands on her shoulders and a look of despair across his face. His eyes meet with mine and I can see sadness behind them as he stares at me. He reminds me of my own father. The way he is standing guard of his daughter, keeping an eye on the threat locked in the cage before him. That's exactly what my dad would do, only he would pull out his gun and shoot the threat to end it.

The little girl's mouth is moving, but her voice is being overtaken by the crowd around her. I focus my attention on only her, forcing my ears to hear her voice above the others as she speaks in a soft tone.

Her father leans down, getting his ear closer to her lips to hear her speak, "Why are they so mean to her, daddy?" she asks. "Isn't she something good?"

"I don't know, Sarah." Her father replies. "These things just happen."

She isn't afraid of me. That brings an iota of relief to my unbeating heart. I hate the idea of bringing fear to the eyes of people who should see me as something good. If I ever get the chance to get out of this place, I'll remember to take that small family back to Des Moines with me. At least I'll try convincing them to go with me. The life of a traveler is not good on little girls like her.

A few people in the crowd are stepping aside, letting Trevor walk between them. He approaches the cage door and lets that evil smile pass my way. He wraps his fingers around the bars and leans closer.

"Tell me," he begins, "how does this cure of yours work? I have a few subjects I would like to test it on immediately."

"Why don't you come in here and I'll show you firsthand how it works." I pass him a snide smile.

He brushes my suggestion off his shoulder and asks, "Do you have to bite them? Do you let them bite you or do you need a syringe to take the cure out of you? Just tell me how this works and I will be a more pleasant host."

I keep my eyes focused on the tree not too far from my cage instead of the man standing before me. The leaves have already changed colors for the fall and some have started drifting to the ground. They are in a sloppy pile at the base of the tree. Winter will be here soon and with that even more death and ruin will come to the humans. More people die in the winter because the cold slows them down and they just freeze to death.

"If only I hadn't killed your boyfriend back there," Trevor gets my attention and I turn my eyes to his, "I could use him to get whatever I want from you. I saw the way you looked at him, the way you cried for his lifeless body at the gas station. He was more than just a boy to you."

I keep my mouth closed and grit my teeth. I can't let his words get to me. I can't let the mere thought of Ryder cause me to break down. Looking weak isn't ideal at a time like this. I just need to keep myself calm, force the rage in my heart from escaping through my mouth, and stay focused.

"No comment from the smart ass." Trevor states with a smile. "Maybe the boy was a nobody after all."

Okay Bridget. Don't listen to him. He doesn't know a damn thing about Ryder or your life or *anything*. He's a maniac who can't get his head out of his overzealous ass to see how demented his plans of world domination truly are. Let him think what he wants. Let the anger and hatred build so when the time comes, I'll have the power to take him down in one swing.

I don't normally have these little pep talks with myself, but it felt needed today.

Trevor turns back to me and leans in, "You see these people out here? You see the looks on their faces? They are waiting for *your* cure. They *want* to see what you can do. Why don't you give them what they came here for? Let them see the show."

I look around at the people standing within twenty feet of

me. They are simply voyeurs expecting something that will change the world. I'm sure some of them deserve to see what I have to offer. Maybe they've lived good lives and had no choice but to join Trevor in this little town. Maybe they want the same thing I do, a world without madness. Then I look back to Trevor and his men standing around him. He doesn't deserve anything from me. Not even an answer for his many annoying questions.

He waits for my response. Several long seconds pass and his face scrunches into anger. His cheeks get flushed with red and his knuckles turn white as he grips the bars.

"The cure ain't real!" I hear a man's voice coming from the crowd and a few people turn to walk away.

"I can assure you that the cure is real!" Trevor shouts, "I will get her to show all of you what she can do. You will be surprised by the life she is able to breathe back into the un-dead." Trevor faces his people and shouts at them.

I can't help but let a little smile come to my face. His people are turning against him because he can't do the one thing he promised them. These people came to see the cure and he apparently didn't expect me to not cooperate. This small accomplishment is just enough to mask some of the depression flowing through my mind.

He spins around and glares at me, "I'll get you to show me the cure. I can promise you that."

"Good luck." I say and he rushes away from the cage and heads for the school.

The rest of the crowd has gone already. A few still look over their shoulders, passing me one final glance before heading to their homes. Some are shaking their heads as they walk away. They are disappointed at the thought of seeing something so rare, yet having it ripped from their fingertips. The only two that remain are the little girl and her father.

Their eyes are glued to me and awe is written on both of their faces. The girl, Sarah, clutches the stuffed dog as well as her father's hand and wants to get closer to the bars. I take a breath, letting her sweet child scent fill my nose. She is so innocent and curious about me. Her father is as well and he moves right along with her to get closer.

The guards have moved on to more important things. One lights up an old cigarette and starts a conversation with a tattooed woman leaning against the wall by the doors of the school. None of them bother to pay attention to the two people approaching me.

"Why would they do this to you if you're not the cure like Trevor says you are?" the father asks quietly so only I can hear.

I take a few steps away from the brick wall toward him and reply, "Why would he do this to me even if I *am* the cure?"

The man raises his eyebrows and asks, "Good question. Are you?"

I shrug, unsure if I should let this man know the truth about me, "Maybe I am, maybe I'm not. As long as I'm stuck in here the rest of the world will never know."

"But they should know." His daughter speaks up and I look down to meet her gaze. "Everyone should know. It's good to have a cure."

"Like it was good to have the cure that created the vampires and zombies? Maybe this new cure is just as bad as that one." I reply, sounding harsher than I meant to.

Her father takes her hand and gently forces her away from me, "Whatever you are, maybe you deserve to be in there. How could you tell a little girl something like that?"

"You try having your entire life ripped away from you and see how you fucking feel." I retort with anger to my voice.

He scowls at me and doesn't bother responding. I watch as he pulls his daughter away from the cage and they head for the street nearby. There's no sense in stopping them. I can't convince them that I don't belong in here. I can tell the little girl wants to believe that I am a good thing, but I have no reason to show them that I really am. No one in this place deserves to see me as anything but the harsh, sad person that Trevor has turned me into.

The good Bridget, the one whom certain people of the world have come to rely on, she is dying a slow death. She has nothing left to live for except the bitter future that awaits her while she's trapped in this cage. Depression has set upon myself and it is erasing the nice girl I used to be. I guess losing the only person I had left to love was the one thing to suck every ounce of energy and hope away from me.

Despite the cure, I have absolutely nothing left to live for anymore.

* * *

Hours have passed. The world outside these bars drifts by me and there's no stopping it. The sun fades below the horizon and stars have overtaken the sky. Not a sound can be heard or a light can be seen in this little town. The people have barricaded themselves indoors for the night. I could hear the locks of the houses near the school and the doors slamming shut so nothing can get inside. This place still reeks of humans and could draw a crowd of any creature this way, but so far I haven't seen a single one of them.

The brick wall of this old high school is not comfortable to lean against at all. At least the grass is soft enough for me to sit on. I haven't moved from this position since the last person disappeared into the school.

Those people in there are watching me. A camera is positioned at the top of the steel door and it is aimed right at the cage. The red light above the lens tells me that someone, somewhere in that place has an eye on me. There aren't really many places for me to go being stuck in this cage.

Other than the loneliness, this town is infuriatingly quiet. I can't hear crickets chirping or bats flying through the air or even a damn rabbit scurrying through the grass. This place dies at night and joins the rest of the world in the constant fear of facing a vampire or zombie. I hate the quiet, now more than ever. I can't stand thinking about my past or asking myself a million questions that will never have an answer. My mind won't stop focusing on anything other than Ryder and it is draining every part of me that I wish to remain strong.

I lean my head on the bricks of the building and feel the sharp edges against my skin. I can't see the sky from where I am sitting and I would love to get lost in the stars right now. They might be enough to take my mind off the constant madness I'm enduring. But there is nothing to help keep certain things from popping into my head and adding to this already ruined evening.

I failed with my life. I am one of the millions of people unlucky enough to walk this earth as a failure. The one person I had left on the planet to care about, the *only* thing that really mattered to me is dead and I'll be stuck knowing that I failed him. I couldn't be there for him when that bomb fell and took the very breath from his body and I couldn't hate myself more for letting it happen.

How can I live with that thought always on my mind? How could I possibly go through my life knowing that I'll never be happy again? That I'll never find peace or safety in the hands of Ryder again?

Without Ryder, I really don't have much left to live for. Sure I have the cure to distribute to the world and an entire race of people to save, but what's the point? When this is all said and done, and humans have a place back at the top of the food chain, what's left for me? An endless life filled with regret and hatred and the constant judgment from the rest of the world?

I'm sorry, but that's not a future I consider something to look forward to.

Something hits my cheek and I open my eyes. Something wet is drifting down my face leaving a cold streak along its path. I blink another tear and shake my head from side to side. I feel like an idiot crying out here in the middle of this stupid cage while the people here are safe and sound in their warm beds. I guess it doesn't matter how I feel anymore. No one is here to comfort me or take the bad feelings away. Everything that once brought fear to my life can make its way back and take over. Ryder isn't here to stop it and Jason will never be good enough to even try.

Another tear slides down my cheek and I wipe my face on my shoulder to get rid of the evidence. I might be part of the undead monstrosity that roams the earth, but sadness can still find a way into my mind. It will always be here to destroy me, to make things much worse than they already are. I want to stop thinking about everything. I want my mind to shut down like it has in the past and never let me think of these painful thoughts again. It can take me to a place where I can be happy and maybe allow me to see the people I care about.

I would love to see my dad one more time. He could talk some sense into me and get rid of the misery I feel. He would tell me that even though things look bleak beyond repair, that I will find a way to end this. Maybe if he were here he would end it all for me. He could take his very own gun, press it to my head, and I would be more than willing to let him pull the trigger. He did it for Charlie and Maggie, he should be here to end my suffering just like he ended his own.

But he's not here.

He will *never* be here.

I keep my teary eyes glued to the dark world in front of

me. The wind is calm and the eerie silence would send anyone into a slight panic. There is a darkness taking over my
life as well. A darkness that I might never break free of.
Without anyone here to care for me, I have no way of finding
a light at the end of this tunnel I have to call life. I have no
family to guide me back to the world I once knew.
I think back to those people I've known since birth.
Every second of their lives were wasted because they met an
end too early. Everything we have ever done as a family was
for nothing. All of those ridiculous moments of laughter and
happiness, the clever sayings and songs my mother made up
to make us feel better. She got it all wrong. That ridiculous
lullaby she used to sing to us every night of every *damn*
week. It's not true anymore.
She should have sang it differently.
"You hear that mom?" I say, knowing no one will ever
answer. "You're stupid song is a fucking joke. Nothing is
going to be alright. I'll never get to sleep at night. I don't
want to think about being in bed, because everyone I care
about is fucking dead." I don't bother singing this new *anti*-
lullaby, it feels better to shout it with all of the anger that
burns through me. "I would love to forever close my eyes and
forget your stupid lullaby. Because nothing will ever be
alright. You're all dead, sweet dreams, and goodnight."
I don't know if my mom is watching me right now. I
don't really care if she or any other member of my deceased
family is watching this. I *hope* they hear me, hear my pain
and watch my suffering as I rot in this cage for the rest of
eternity. They'll never be here to help me end this life of
mine or help me get out of this mess. I'm stuck and it's my
fault. I'm the only reason I'm here. I could have changed
things. If I never went with George or his sister to their village, I damn sure wouldn't find myself in this situation right
now. Ryder would still be alive and I wouldn't have to be so
miserable about his death.
I never should have left the city walls. Dwayne would

have been fine without my help to find that village. They would have found it on their own and bring the people back to safety. Who cares if the cure would never have gotten discovered. The human race has lasted this long without it, they could last a few more years until they figured something else out. But no, bad things *had* to happen. I *had* to let myself get bit and let everything go to hell from that moment on.

I wipe another tear on my shoulder and go back to staring at the quiet town. The house on the other side of the playground is boring and white. The blue trim around the windows and the awning does nothing to add any spice to the building. The humans inside are probably sound asleep, snoring under a mound of blankets without a care in the world. Trevor will take care of them. He will provide them with a life filled with possibilities because he has the cure. They'll never have to worry about the girl in the cage as long as they get what they want.

Those people will never have to worry about dealing with sadness like I have to and they'll be able to die happy as humans instead of a freak like me.

* * *

A cold mist has spread throughout the town. My clothes are damp and a few strands of hair stick to my face. Tiny droplets of water cover the lenses of my sunglasses which makes it difficult to see, but I've been through worse things.

The ever-annoying Trevor is pacing back and forth right

outside the cage. For the past two days, he has done this and I never bother to give him my attention. He hasn't said a word to me since he came out here this morning and the only look I get from him is the same evil glare I've grown accustomed to seeing.

I stand with my back pressed against the brick wall behind me. There are four guards with rifles at the ready and their eyes glued to my every movement. I can smell the tension and sweat protruding from the pores of their skin. The salt of their luscious, pink flesh is enticing and I am currently devouring each one of them with my eyes. I'm sure their blood, skin, and bones taste fantastic.

I grit my teeth and quickly close my eyes, forcing that side of me to stay inside.

A crowd of around twenty of Trevor's followers have decided to join us. They keep their distance from the cage, afraid to get too close to the freak on the other side of the bars. I've heard that word being uttered from quite a few of these people. They might not know what I am at the moment, but they still want to believe that I'm different enough to be a freak. Their words are merely empty air to me. Nothing they say can drive me further down this winding road of depression, especially when my thoughts are doing a great job at it already.

I take another whiff of the air, smelling their precious aromas as they watch me. There's something else on the air in this town. A smell that I shouldn't be noticing this close to a lot of human life. I can recognize that dead stench anywhere, even without being this new creature that I am. Trevor must have his *chosen* ones locked away somewhere. The ones he deems fit enough to join his army once they receive the cure.

I'm sure the ones he has picked out are big, muscular beasts of men who look like they could destroy a normal person with their bare hands. That's what he's looking for anyway. The best of the best who can handle their own when they are up against an enemy. I bet I'll see them soon enough, but it can wait.

Trevor stops pacing, lets out a sigh, then adjusts the zipper on his black, leather jacket. It is a bit crisp this morning. Most of my audience have put on long sleeve-shirts or light jackets to keep warm. I'm fine with my blood covered hoodie to keep the chill away. It's served me well in the past.

"Are you going to do what I ask today?" he says with an early burst of anger. "Are you going to show us how the cure works?"

"That depends," I say, feeling my eyes burning with rage and sadness, "are you going to let me test my bite on you?"

His smile widens, "You are so funny this morning. I forget what a devilish little bitch you can be." He wraps his fingers around the steel of the cage and leans closer, "I'm sure you're pretty hungry, right? If you're anything like the zombies out there you're always hungry. Why not end that pain and let me feed you and you can show us the cure? I have plenty of zombies or vampires to choose from."

I keep my glare on his and reply, "I'm not hungry enough for that shit."

Trevor leans his head against the bars, annoyed with my lack of obedience. A gun hangs at his waist with a long knife in a holster right beside it. If my hands were free, I could get that gun and this would all be over in just a few seconds. I could end his annoying existence and perhaps get myself out of this mess in the process. Either by freeing myself from the cage or getting shot so much that I actually die to the point where I won't be coming back. No matter what would happen, I'd be better off dead than locked in here.

Trevor finally opens his mouth and speaks slowly, "Do you know what they are doing to your friend in there?" he smiles and looks me up and down. "Of course you don't. But they are torturing him, beating him senseless until he begs us to kill him. He keeps his mouth shut because of you and I'm finding it hard to understand why he thinks you're worth it."

"Go ahead, do whatever you want to him." I shrug. "Why

don't you just feed him to the zombies while you're at it? Or perhaps let him turn into one again. He already knows how to live that life."

Trevor darts his eyes to mine and I realize I just gave myself away. If he and the rest of the people out there believe my words, then they now know that the cure is real. Or at least they can start to believe that it's real.

"What did you say?" Trevor asked, pulling himself away from the bars of the cage. "Your friend in there *used* to be a zombie?" he turns to the crowd and waves his arms around like he's just discovered the holy grail. "Why, that must mean the cure is real. She just needs to show us how it works. Who else feels the same?"

His audience shouts out demanding that I show them the cure. Their eyes are filled with a strong desire to see it up close and personal. I don't understand why someone would *want* to see that. It's disgusting to watch a zombie tear into a human being. Their intestines fall out of their stomach and there is always so much blood and gore flying through the air. I might not be *that* bad when I bite into my victims, but I'm sure it's not very pretty to witness either.

I scan my eyes over each and every one of these people. Some of them actually seem to be nice, innocent beings. The kind that have no purpose being here other than to stay alive. Maybe I should show them the cure. It wouldn't be such a bad idea to give them a tiny amount of hope for their race. I could get Trevor off my back about the topic and end the hunger building in my stomach. No one I care about is here to stop me or tell me that I'd be doing the wrong thing by show-ing these people what they came here for.

"Trevor!" I speak up. "You want to see the cure?"

He spins around, eyes lighting up as he looks to me and says, "What else are we waiting for?"

I take a deep breath, already hating myself for allowing these words to come out of my mouth, "Bring me a zombie."

The smile grows, stretching from ear to ear on his hideous face. He nods to one of his men, who suddenly disappears around the school building. His followers have grown quiet, speaking soft whispers amongst themselves. A few more have even joined them and I recognize two of the faces walking this way.

Sarah and her father stand away from the others to get a good view of the show that's about to begin. That little girl will get to see just how evil this new cure will be in the hands of a madman. Trevor will use it for power and control. Her life will be even less glamorous than it already is and she'll be forced to grow up with him for a leader. Zombies and vampires might not be as overwhelming in his idea of a future, but the world will be worse off and more humans will die due to the unending war Trevor will force upon the planet.

I turn away from her and wait for the guard to come back with my meal. I hear the groaning and the struggling of one man against the pull of the zombie he's dragging behind him. They come into view, walking around the corner of the building. A dog catcher's leash is wrapped around the neck of the zombie cutting into his skin. The metal pole is barely long enough to keep the creature's arms from reaching the man holding onto it.

I sniff the air and a familiar frenzy begins and the sadness, along with my painful memories, are starting to drift away. The blood of that undead monstrosity is more than inviting and my mouth is watering at the thought of tasting it. I lean away from the brick wall wanting nothing more than to rip his head off and eat until I'm overstuffed. The zombie isn't too far gone either. His skin will be tough at first, but my teeth can break it.

The people in the area gasp and cover their eyes at the sight of such a beast. They have spent so many years in fear of those things and in just a few minutes they'll have another thing to be afraid of. Something that will never be understood or explained properly. I might have the cure for every nightmare these people have come across, but in the manner I plan on showing it to them, it will be less than pretty and I pray they hate me for it.

Trevor orders another, younger man to unlock the padlock of the cage when the zombie gets close enough. The lock clanks against the bars and the door swings open. They quickly shove the poor zombie inside with me, then close the door and lock it once again. With the leash now removed from his neck, he is free to move around and reach his arms between the bars, trying to grasp at the humans nearby. They laugh at his attempts and tease him as he begs for their flesh.

I take a step toward it and stare at the holey shirt on his back. Blood stains the tattered fabric and his pale skin shows through. His shoes are missing and his jeans are muddy and torn on the bottom. He doesn't pay any attention to me, doesn't turn around or even bother smelling the air for my flesh.

I look past him and notice the surprise written on Trevor's face. He has no choice but to believe everything he's heard about me. The zombies don't care for what flows through me and he is seeing it up close and personal. The whole damn crowd is in shock by what they are witnessing and I'm standing here with a grin on my face and hunger growing inside of me.

The frenzy in my stomach is taking over and I feel the monster coming to life, driving my sad thoughts even deeper in the blackest parts of my mind until I can no longer recall them. I clench my hands into fists, tugging at the tight ropes that bind them. This will be difficult to do with my hands behind my back. In one quick movement, I use my arms like a jump rope and bring them to the front of my body. A hushed gasp fills the air and the sound of guns being aimed are quick to follow. I pass them an annoyed glance and shake my head.

"I'm locked in a cage you morons. What do you expect I'm going to do?" I say in a harsh voice I don't recognize.

I get no answer, just the slow lowering of their guns as

they shake my words off their shoulders.

I move to the zombie. My only care is showing these pitiful people what they came here for. I lift my arms, grabbing the back of the man's shirt and yank him away from the bars. He's heavier than I expected and hits the ground with a loud thud. A low growl escapes his throat, evil fills his black eyes and he leaps into the air, springing at me with all his might. He wraps his arms around me and pins me against the bars of the cage. There isn't enough room in here for me to do anything and this damn rope on my wrists is constricting most of my strength.

This zombie's moans fills my ears as he presses his body against mine and reaches through the bars once again. His real prey is out there taunting him with every scent they create just like they are taunting me. His neck is close to my face and I close my eyes letting the frenzy take over my mind. I open my mouth and clamp down hard on his skin. A shrill scream upsets my ears and he rips himself away from me, letting a small chunk of his skin rip away from his neck.

I swallow my bite and wipe the blood from my face and stare at the confused zombie. No longer does he bother fighting for the humans out there. I am his focus and his lifeless eyes cannot figure me out. He growls again and rushes at me. This time I'm quick to get out of the way and I grab onto his shirt once more. He claws at my arms trying to reach for my face and neck. I keep out of his reach and lift my right leg to his chest. The force of my kick sends him crashing into the bars behind him.

He slides to the ground in a disheveled state and his head bobs back and forth like a ragdoll. I dive through the air, landing on top of the big zombie. Once more, I clamp my jaw against his neck at the same spot I got the first time. I feel his hands digging into my back and his legs flail as he tries to get away from me. I hold onto his shirt and let the disgusting juices flow down my throat. The blood oozes from the wound, sliding down my chin and I hear cries of disgust coming from my audience.

My hunger pains are slowly fading. The frenzy is getting the relief it so deserves and I can feel my strength returning to me. The ropes don't feel as tight against my wrists and the cage doesn't seem so small anymore. I close my eyes and allow myself this tiny moment of joy to consume me.

The world vanishes and a black cloud takes over my mind. It doesn't last more than a minute. The haze slowly clears and a face comes into view. A face with dead eyes and blood in the corner of his mouth. Confusion takes over as I stare at this familiar face. The tiny frenzy took away my memories of him, but they are slowly coming back. Ryder stares at me with dead eyes and a pale face. Just like the last time I saw him, I have no idea if he is alive or dead, or perhaps both.

That's when it hits me. The sadness comes back and the frenzy dissipates into tiny fragments of the only part of me that seemed to erase my despair. I let go of the zombie, spit his flesh from my mouth, and thrust myself away from him. I open my eyes and flush the image of Ryder from my head. I can't bear the thought of him running through my mind like he is trying to tell me something. I don't want to see his face or deal with the pain from the sadness his death is causing me.

I get to my feet and dig my fingernails into the palms of my hands. I press my body against the bars and force Ryder and everyone I have ever cared about from my mind. I need to stay focused. I need to keep myself from thinking of them. They're never coming back to me and I can't let them live in my mind anymore.

My eyes turn to the man lying on the ground. His body is motionless and his eyes are closed. The mark I gave him on his neck still drips with blood, but it won't be for long. That inevitable gasp will soon fill the air and Trevor will have his cure and my life will still be over.

The man's chest is the first thing they notice. It is slowly moving up and down, sucking in tiny breaths. His right hand twitches and his eyes flutter open revealing the bright blue irises. The gasp comes next, followed by coughing and he rolls onto his side. He closes his hands around the blades of grass and rips them from the ground as the pain of becoming human takes over.

"Holy shit." Trevor exclaims. "The damn cure *is* real!"

I ignore his comment and stay focused on the man at my feet. He lifts himself to sit up on the grass and his eyes turn to me. They are screaming with fear and I slowly wipe the blood from my chin. I can still taste his zombie flesh on my tongue, but seeing him as a human has me craving for him all over again.

"Where am I?" he asks, his voice is filled with terror.

I lean down and say quietly, "In a place worse than hell."

He scrambles backwards to get away from me and I hear the lock on the cage door rattling. His eyes dart toward the man opening the door and his face flushes with panic. Trevor orders his men to get this newly cured human away from me. Two of them rush inside and yank the poor soul from the ground and force him out of the cage.

I wasn't lying to him. Being in a place controlled by Trevor is a fate worse than death in my eyes.

* * *

The man I cured had served in the Marines for fifteen years before he was honorably discharged. After that, he took up wrestling as a hobby and began teaching it at the high school in his home town. He's got the muscle Trevor is looking for and the ability to take a man down with his bare hands. His mind just isn't in the same place as Trevor's. He's kinder and knows how the world should be handled. I think that's why he is being locked in the school instead of being allowed to roam outside with the two others I brought back.

Trevor was so thrilled after he saw the cure that he brought me two more around noon. They made for a decent lunch and I felt the same, memory-erasing frenzy take over my mind again. It lasted for a few brief moments while I attacked the zombies. Then another flash of a dead Ryder, as well as the rest of my family, interrupted my gorging and I ripped myself away from the meal. The memories and images are getting worse and the sadness is getting to be a distraction that I cannot run away from.

Such is my life now.

Anyway, these two new guys are much more suited to Trevor's liking than the first. One is a short bald man with a tattoo of a dragon covering most of his back. He served time in the Iowa State Penitentiary for murdering his wife and the man she was in the process of sleeping with. He got lucky when a few of the guards were bitten and he was able to make an escape. The other guy is a massive black man with his hair in extremely tight braids on his head. He never spent any time in jail, but he's been in more fights than I can count. By how big his arm muscles are, he looks like he could kill a man in one punch.

That has been the majority of my morning and afternoon. I listened to Trevor interview these two guys and explain to them his plans for the world. I saw their eyes light up when they heard that they would have a part in his plan of absolute control. They were more than eager to join his army and were instantly given weapons and a warm meal. They will be cherished like everyone else on Trevor's team.

Once all of his minions are cured, it won't be long before

his new army is up and walking around, terrorizing the streets and taking what doesn't belong to them. I am now a part of that simply because I gave in and showed him the cure. I can't honestly say it was a bad thing. For those few minutes of devouring my prey, I was able to have glimpse of a life without painful memories and flashbacks. I actually preferred having that frenzy taking over my mind. It erased certain things from my head and I was able to feel peace while I ate.

If only there was a way to make it last more than a few minutes. I could really use a break from all this.

The sun has gone down and it has been dark out for nearly an hour. My sunglasses hang over the collar of my hoodie and I lean against the wall of the school staring through the bars at the guards pacing on the grass. Most of the people have gone inside to hide for the night. The few that are left outside are nervous and afraid. The rifles are rattling in their shaking hands and they reek of fear. Trevor is out here with them, standing tall and proud of his accomplishment for the day.

He turns toward me with a smile on his face. The chilly air is creating a slight fog from his breath when he exhales. He pulls the hood of his jacket over his head and folds his arms across his chest in an attempt to keep warm.

"Hard to believe another winter is right around the corner." His eyes meet with mine as he speaks, "Can you even feel the cold since you're dead?"

What an odd question, "Not really." I reply, giving in to his small talk.

"Yeah, I guess you wouldn't." he says.

The snapping of a stick echoes through the playground and the guards surrounding Trevor whip their guns around and aim for the invisible creature sneaking up on them. I turn my eyes toward the sound as well and don't see a thing. It was probably an animal or a ghost or maybe a vamp trying to sneak in on its prey. I can only hope for the latter.

"I trust you'll be this obedient for me tomorrow. There

are others I would love for you to cure." Trevor states.

I shrug, "I'm pretty full. I think you'll be alright without my help."

He laughs, "I do enjoy your smart ass comments every once in a while."

"Don't we all."

He moves closer to the cage and leans against the bars, "You know it really isn't so bad on my side of things. You'd get to be inside in a room with a cozy bed and warm sheets. I'd make sure my men treat you fairly and give you whatever makes you happy."

I glare at him and say, "You killed the only thing that makes me happy, so you can keep your worthless shit to yourself."

He shakes his head and glances to his feet, "I do apologize for that. Things should have gone down differently between us right from the beginning. You should have joined us when I gave you a peaceful offer."

I roll my eyes, "The type of peace you have to offer isn't something I want to be a part of."

"I don't understand why you wouldn't want any of this. My vision for the world is great. The cure will go to those who deserve it, those who can contribute to the rest of the world and my people will have a better life. *You* could even have a better life. You could live like a queen in a world created by us both."

"I take it you would be the king in this twisted scenario."

He smiles, "Who else would there be? I'm the only one who can control the world I plan on creating with you. Why wouldn't you want to be with a man like me?"

I can think of a million different answers to that question, "You're not a man. You're just a pathetic excuse for a human being who was never granted the privilege of living life as a zombie or a vamp and allowing me the pleasure of ending that pitiful existence."

The smile drifts from his lips and he grits his teeth, "You

should be careful what you say to me. If you recall, I have your friend locked up inside and my men are more than eager to do what I say and beat that boy senseless."

"Go for it." I reply. "If you think that will hurt me, you are mistaken. You've already destroyed me to the point of no return and there is no bouncing back."

"There is always a way to hurt a person. I just have to find another weakness of yours and go from there." Trevor states. "Unless you decide to join me. I will always welcome you with open arms."

"As unappealing as your offer sounds, I am *always* going to pass." I reply.

He smiles and leans away from the cage, "One day, dear Bridget, you will see that my way of things is best for the world. People need order and I can give them that. I can see a leader in you as well, you just won't let her out." He turns to his men and motions for them to follow him, "Let's get inside boys. It's getting late."

I listen to their footsteps crushing the grass as they walk to the door of the school. Trevor taps his knuckles on the steel door and a faint beeping sound responds a few seconds later. The latch gets released and they pull the door open and disappear inside.

Once again I am left alone in the quiet night air to think about everything I don't want to think about.

* * *

With dawn came a thunderstorm that forced the small town to stay indoors. Lightning brightens up the sky, cracking against the grey clouds like a whip against a slave's back. The roof over this pitiful cage serves no purpose in a storm such as this one. The rain is blowing in through the bars, soaking my clothes and hair. I put the hood over my head even though it does very little to keep me dry. On the plus side, it's cloudy enough to block the sun and I don't need to wear my sunglasses. They are dripping with water as they hang over the collar of my shirt.

The door to the school has stayed shut since Trevor vanished inside last night. No one has bothered to come outside to check on me nor have they dared to face the storm. Of the few houses nearby, only one has opened their front door and they only did so to catch some of the rain water in a pot. That woman glanced my way for a split second, then went back into her house to disappear.

I feel like I'm the only person left in this place. The storm took the other people away and left me to wallow alone in my never ending hatred and sadness. There is no one here to talk to, no one to simply be around for company. I'd even be fine with one of Trevor's men out here to keep an eye on me. Anyone would be better than the constant loneliness of this place. I only need one single person to help take the memories out of my mind.

I lean my head back against the school building. My knees are brought up to my chest with my bound hands wrapped around them. My clothes are soaked and water drips from the end of my nose and the tips of my hair. This is the first kind of shower I've had since I became this way. It doesn't make me feel any cleaner or less dead, only wet. Nothing like that night with Ryder at the hotel in Hatfeld.

That night was beautiful. It was the first night I stepped out of my comfort zone with a complete stranger and allowed him to discover a side of me no one has ever known before. I think I actually fell in love with him on that very night.

I grit my teeth, squeeze my eyes shut tight, and bang my head against the brick wall. Why did I have to bring up that painful memory? My mind could have kept its damn mouth shut and let me just deal with the fact that it's raining and I'm wet. But no, I *had* to force myself to think of this rain as a shower therefore making my mind drift back to that night alone with Ryder. The first night I spent with him that *actually* meant something more to me without even realizing it.

I'll never have a night like that again. I'll never get to stare at his half-naked body as rain water washes away the sweat, grime, and worries from his day. There will never be another moment where it's just the two of us alone in a random room so we can share more than just intimacies.

That's what my life is from here on out: a series of nevers. The people in my family are dead so I'll *never* know what that type of love feels like again. I left my life back in the city so I'll *never* have that kind of safety again. The love of my life is probably still lying dead at that gas station and I'll *never* get to hear his voice again. I'll never get to touch him or feel his skin against mine. That's the worst of all this. Ryder was the only person in the world who had the power to make the worst situations seem not so bad and I could move on with my life.

There is nothing now to take the worst of things away from me and I have completely crashed to rock bottom.

A crack of thunder resonates all around me and I squeeze my eyes shut tighter. The sound doesn't frighten me, just the sheer emptiness of all that surrounds this place has me shivering. I was never good at being alone. Those few days after my dad passed were some of the worst. With my memory filled mind being my only friend and the obnoxious questions that will never be answered, being alone has become one of my worst enemies.

"I've tried telling you," a quiet voice catches my ear, "you're never really alone."

I know that voice. It was the only sound I heard during the terrible transformation I endured.

I pull my head away from the wall and open my eyes. I scan the school yard and the interior of the cage from left to right. No one stands beside the wilting tree and the playground is barren. I am the only thing in the cage and the doors to the school haven't been unlatched.

I *heard* the voice though. His tone is so familiar to me. No matter how many years go by I'll always recognize my own brother. He *has* to be here. He *needs* to be here to show me what I'm supposed to do in order to get the hell out of here. But Charlie's ghost is not paying me a visit this morning. My mind didn't shut down and I'm not going any crazier than I already am. I got my hopes up on seeing my brother and my eyes are heavy with tears.

"Charlie?" I call out, begging for an answer, despite the emptiness around me.

The rain bounces off the bars, cascading down from the broken gutter hanging over the edge of the school. It splashes into a building puddle in the grass near the cage. Lightning takes over the sky letting a barrage of thunder follow in its wake. There is no sign of my brother and there never will be.

I roll my eyes and let my head rest against the building once more. I'll always be longing for my family to show up when I need my mind to shut down. They'll never be there. Just the familiar voices I'll be stuck hearing for the remainder of time and they'll slowly be breaking me down until I'm nothing but a bag of undead bones. I close my eyes again and stare at the blackness before me.

"How can you let the greatest love story I've ever seen come to an end?" a female voice takes over and I open my eyes quickly.

The same result as before fills my vision. I'm alone without my sister, but I hear her words echoing through my mind. It's not like I meant for this to happen. I did my best and tried getting to safety. The bastards here had other plans and destroyed my only hope.

I don't bother closing my eyes to wait for the next voice to fill my ears. I don't need to hear my mother telling me that I'm failing at everything I have set out to achieve. I don't need her judging me right now. I just need to stop hearing my family's voices if they aren't going to be with me long enough to have a conversation.

Actually, the voices can just stop altogether. They are only annoying reminders of people that *used* to be in my life. Horrible recollections of a past I no longer want to relive. My mind can erase any part of them from my history, completely destroy those memories so I no longer have to torture myself with the images of my past. I never want to see their faces behind my eyes, no longer want to hear their voices ringing in my ears, and I especially don't want to miss them anymore. Missing people hurts too much and it's less painful to be angry with them instead.

"You hear that family," I say out loud, "I want to forget you. Each and every one of you can leave my mind forever. I don't need you anymore."

The rain muffled the sound of my voice but if they are really here, as Charlie has claimed, they will hear my every word. Maybe they will listen, most likely they won't. I'm hoping that my words have made them angry enough to at least turn around during this part of my life. They can sit on the sidelines, watching something else for a change, until I'm dead and can join them once and for all.

In some ways, that's what I'm really waiting for. Now that I have no one left to live for, Trevor can come out right now and forget all about taking over the world. He can put his small little handgun right to my head or my heart or whatever damn part of me that will forever end my suffering and pull the trigger.

Maybe then will I find peace throughout this world of utter chaos.

A squirrel scurries through the grass, running to the tree

to my right, totally taking my attention away from my mind for a brief moment. This one is different than any other squirrel I've ever seen. It has a fluffy white tail instead of a grey one. That tail sticks out in the dark world the storm has created and appears to brighten up the path the squirrel takes to the tree. I focus as it climbs halfway up the trunk then stops before it reaches a branch. It clings onto the bark and whips its tiny head in every direction. The moment its beady little eyes meet with mine, it stops moving.

This creature stares at me with such focus, that its tail stops twitching and it isn't breathing as fast anymore. I don't know if this is some kind of sign from the people I want to forget or if this damn squirrel is just afraid because it knows what I am. No matter what it is, I wish it would leave me alone and go back to its home in that tree. It serves no purpose to stare at a worthless freak locked in a cage, yet it keeps its eyes locked on mine until a loud clap of thunder startles it enough to get it to move again. It disappears in a small hole above one of the large branches and is gone.

I shake my head and turn my attention away from the tree. If the little thing was close enough, I could have made a nice snack out of it, regardless if it was a sign from my family or not.

* * *

The rain lasted for two days and I was left out here alone and soaking wet. Only one person poked his head outside to check on me. He didn't really need to since there is a camera pointed right the cage, but at least the kid asked if I was okay when he came out here. I didn't have the words to respond, but a simple shrug from my shoulders gave him enough of an answer for him to go back inside and report to Trevor.

During those long two days, I have barely moved from my spot against the wall. My legs are stiff and my arms ache every time I move them. My clothes are soaked and the sun is busy hiding behind a few clouds to dry them. Trevor brought me a snack this morning once the rain came to an end and I was actually eager to give him the cure. I didn't have to move very much in order to bite the guy's leg and get my nutrients. Once he woke up as a human, Trevor took him inside the school and I have not heard from him since.

His men are still hanging around with their guns as they keep watch for zombies. This place is relatively quiet and free of those things. Other than the ones Trevor is saving for his army, I haven't seen a single zombie roaming the streets. This is actually a safe place to call home. There might not be any walls to completely fortify the residents from any oncoming threat, but they are doing a bang up job at keeping the monsters at bay.

A few people from the town wander across the school yard making sure they stay in small groups. Some of the younger ones steal a quick glance in my direction and a look of sorrow forms on their faces. I don't need their pity. I don't need anything from these strangers other than for them to leave me the hell alone.

Of course, I can't even get that.

Two familiar faces are strolling through the grass, coming my way. The stuffed dog is clutched in her small hand and she holds onto her father's fingertips and walk towards me. I take in their scent when they get closer and relish in the sweet aroma. They smell clean, lacking that sweaty, dirty stench that comes from the guards standing nearby. The blood flowing through their veins is fresh and intoxicating, exactly like every other human being within smelling distance.

The little girl inches her way closer to the bars of the cage, but her father forces her to keep some space between her body and my prison. He's worried about me getting my hands on her. After giving them a disgusting show of what I am capable of doing, I'd be worried too.

"I'm glad to see you survived that storm we got." The father states.

I shrug, "You're probably the only one."

He shakes his head, "I'm sure there's someone else out there who's glad that you're alive."

"There is no one and I'm not alive. My heart doesn't beat anymore." I reply.

A frightened look crosses his daughter's face and she hugs the stuffed dog even tighter against her chest. She looks away from me, staring at the tree and watches the white tailed squirrel perch on one of the branches. It has been sitting there all morning and I would love if it got closer. That thing has been annoying me and I could use a warm snack instead of the zombies.

"What's your name?" the father asks.

I turn my eyes to his and reply, "Why do you care?"

"I don't know. You're an important person to the world right now and I want to know your name." he says.

"Bridget." I say as I roll my eyes.

"I'm Phil and this is my daughter Sarah." He says and I pull my head away from the bricks behind me.

It has been quite some time since I've heard that name. I wanted to forget it. I still want to forget it. It is associated with someone I can never see again and now I am tortured because this man has the same name as my own dead father.

Why the hell does he have to have the same goddamn name? What reasons could this man possibly have for coming here and torture me with this? He and his scared little girl need to leave me alone just like everyone else on the planet.

"You okay?" he asks.

"Why are you here?" I snap.

"Sarah wanted to see you today." He says.

I shake my head from side to side, "Quit with the bullshit. Why are you *really* here? Did you come here to torment me or get me to believe that everything is going to end up alright? Or are you just here to criticize me because my life didn't wind up turning out the way you wanted it to?"

Confusion crosses his face and he opens his mouth to speak, "What are you talking about? We only came here to see that you were okay. Sarah and I could see you from our window and watched you through the storm." He motions to a small window at the very top of one of the houses across the street from the school. "Despite the fact that you are not the nicest person in the world, we were concerned for you."

The more he talks, the more his voice is gradually changing into my father's tone and all I can think of are the many lectures I would be getting if he were really here. The more I stare at the man's face, which is younger than my father's, the more I see the similarities between them. The same eye color, the same hair color, the same concern in their voices. I don't need this. I need to forget them and focus on ending this situation.

"You shouldn't have come here. It's a waste of your time and my fucking day." I argue.

Phil let go of his daughter's hand and steps closer to the cage, "Listen, I don't know what the hell has gotten you so pissed off about us being here, but you need to stop it. You're in a bad situation and you don't need to make things worse by yelling at two people who might care about what happens to you."

I want him to stop talking, to stop saying words that my own father would say to me. I close my eyes and listen to him speaking, sounding more and more like dad with every passing second. It's killing me as my dad's face flashes through my mind and the craziness is really taking over.

"You need to understand that you can't let yourself go

through this alone. You have to accept other people in your life no matter how hard it is going to be. You don't need to be alone when others are willing to be here with you, Bridget."

That took things over the top. He spoke my name and it was clearly my father's voice shooting into my ears and I can't take it.

I rip open my eyes and let the anger surge through me as I shout at him, "Just leave me the hell alone, dad, I don't need you in my life anymore!"

Phil stammers back a pace or two. His eyes scream confusion as well as his hands he has raised in surrender. A few of Trevor's goons caught this part of my tantrum and they turned the barrel of their guns toward me. Sarah grabs her father's hand, holding on tightly, and awaits whatever fate is about to greet me.

I stare at his face. Those brown eyes that don't belong my father anymore, they are different now, just like the rest of his face. I can no longer see the resemblance nor can I hear my father's tone when he ushers his daughter away from the cage.

They head back for their small house across the street and leave me alone with whatever this emotion is that has taken over me. It doesn't feel like rage or contempt. It isn't sadness or despair either. This is much more powerful than any of those feelings, even if they are all balled up into one.

This gut wrenching pain that is coursing through me, this terrifying sensation that is taking control is the worst form of guilt I have ever felt. It's more painful than when I changed into this monstrous creature that I have become. It's scarier than the mere thought of being alone for the rest of my life. It builds up in the back of my throat, forcing a few small tears from my eyes and they drift down my cheeks. But I can't take back what I said. I can't go back in time to stop myself from screaming at my father to leave me alone.

* * *

I feel like I'm losing my mind. I mean, it's already been lost a long, *long* time ago, but I feel like this time it's truly gone. After seeing my father's face and hearing his voice in that man a few days ago, I can't shake this feeling. Everywhere I look, I see them. In the faces of the citizens in this community, in the eyes of the people who gawk at me on a daily basis. Even in the damn zombies Trevor brings me to cure. Once they wake up alive, all I see is my family staring back at me.

Their voices terrorize me. They scream at me every time I hear someone speaking nearby. There is pain to their words and sadness in their voices. I can't beg them to leave me alone nor can I will them to show their dead faces. I'm stuck in this limbo my mind has created and I'm slowly slipping into the madness of the world before me. The *only* time I feel peace at all, is when the tiny frenzy takes over as I lose myself in the bite I place upon a zombie.

That feeling is the only thing that makes me feel less insane and every time it occurs, I want it to last forever. I feel better when my mind is completely blank.

I see Trevor out there with his men. His numbers grow by the day and his army is becoming stronger. I am the one responsible for everything that's happening outside of this cage. As those men train in the school yard, gaining their strength after being a zombie for god knows how long, I can feel myself changing. The monster is getting darker, I can feel it growing deep in my gut and there's no stopping it. Don't get me wrong, I want the monster to come out and show her devilish face, but I fear she might want something different than I do.

The frenzy I feel when my mind erases the memories is the monster showing itself, but something happens and it goes away just as quickly as it arrived. It wants to be out, I can feel it, but it wants complete control. As much as I want the memories to disappear and my mind to be rid of the sadness, I don't know if I can allow myself to lose to the creature I never wanted to become in the first place.

I am losing this war with my mind and things are only getting worse.

Trevor's army is growing by the day and the word about my cure has spread. Close to three dozen people have made their way to this town to catch a look at me. They set up their camps in the empty field by the rusted playground equipment. I can hear their voices of praise as they chant my name over and over. Their beady eyes light up whenever they turn my way and they thank god for the miracle that I am. One family even arrived with a zombie of their very own. Their son, *I believe*, and they begged Trevor for the cure. What kind of leader would he be if he didn't show some kind of compassion toward his followers? He gave the boy my cure and that family became whole again.

That happened yesterday and I am still hungry for the undead. I have never been more disgusted with myself and it's all because I gave Trevor what I swore he'd never see. I just can't help it. The hunger is too much to handle and I like the fraction of sanity I feel when I suck their flesh and blood down my gullet. It's the after effects that just drive me insane. Maybe one day I'll get this figured out, but I don't see that day coming any time soon.

I stare at the people across the yard. They have a few fires lit and meat roasting over the open flames. The sun is making its descent and the stars are starting to shine. Trevor is inside the school enjoying his feast with his expanding army. He keeps bothering me about curing a vampire. As much as I would love to slip into that state of unconsciousness, now is not the best time for that to happen. There is no saying where my mind would take me or what would happen while I am asleep. I will unfortunately have to stay awake in order to maintain some iota of control in what is going on here.

A loud, cackling laugh breaks through the silence and I turn my eyes to a small family sitting away from the majority of the crowd. Five of them are perched on the grass around a fire, roasting some kind of meat on a stick. I sniff the air and it smells like pig. Those people look like they are trying to keep to themselves and not be annoyed with the constant chatter of the others. The mother and father sit between their oldest daughter and son while the youngest daughter sits alone and stares at me.

They look so familiar, almost like I have run across them at some point during my travels. I squint my eyes to focus on each of their faces in hopes of putting some clarity to how I know them. One by one their features become clear and my jaw drops in shock and disbelief.

There is a reason why I recognize this family.

They are *my* family.

My mother and father are sitting alongside Maggie and Charlie. Even me, the way I looked six years ago when all of them were still alive and happy. When I *had* a family to watch out for and care for and worry about. A family that I loved more than anything else in the world. All of them are staring at me with hatred behind their eyes right now. The younger version of myself looks especially pissed off. How can I blame her? Look what she's become. A pathetic excuse for the savior of the human race who's only reason to live is giving the cure to a lunatic.

"What?" I say, snapping at the family who can't hear me. "Did you expect this not to happen? This is your fault after all. You all left me here to suffer in this life and look what you did to me. I'll die in this cage because of you."

The only response I get is the deathly stare and angry glares coming from each one of them. Why would they answer me. I want them to go away and leave me alone so I can stop thinking about them. I deserve no answer from them and I could care less to hear their voices.

"Are you okay in there?" a deep voice steals my attention away from the family.

I turn my eyes to a tall man wearing thick, brown overalls and a black jacket to keep warm. He stands just on the other side of the cage door with a pistol in his left hand showing no sign that he would ever shoot me with it. His voice sounded concerned but his terrified eyes don't match his expression.

"Who are you talking to?" he speaks again.

It never occurred to me that someone else would hear my little rant just now. I don't care that he heard me or if he thinks I'm crazy for talking to people that have been dead for a few years. This one man's opinion doesn't matter in the slightest.

I look past him and squint at the family. Something is different about them. For starters, it isn't my family anymore. Just a simple group of five relatives that are entirely different from my own. My parents' faces have disappeared and my brother and sister can't make me feel bad anymore. The younger version of myself, the less badass Bridget, is gone and she can stay gone. The world has no use for her kind.

The man by the cage rolls his eyes and walks away without an answer from me. I have no intention of giving him the privilege of hearing my voice tonight.

I think of my past self. There were so many days I spent wasting time in school and hanging out with friends who I will never see again. I should have been preparing my life for the apocalypse. I should have forced myself to be ready for this future. If I could go back in time, I would tell myself to be ready for the shit storm of a life that's waiting right around the corner. I'd know what to expect and the world would have an even better version of the cure than what I am now.

Instead, I'm stuck wasting my time and tears on people I'll never see again. That's no way for me to live.

* * *

Sleep has yet to find me and the night is dragging by slower than molasses. Many of the people by the fires have crawled in their tents and not a sound can be heard but the silent snores escaping them. The air is quiet and I hate it. I want the sounds of the people talking, the quiet laughter as they listen to a bad joke, and even the crying of a tiny baby. Any sound is better than the war going on in my head.

I close my eyes and try thinking of anything other than the silence. That doesn't leave me with much to think about. There are too many memories that I don't want to sift through anymore. Too many faces I don't wish to see behind my eyes. I don't want to feel the sadness I get from thinking about them. It hurts so much and I hate myself for allowing this type of pain to enter my life.

I was perfectly fine a few weeks ago. Things made sense and a good part of the world mattered to me. I loved thinking about my past and my family and I hated the days when their faces didn't pop into my head. My old family photo album holds so many pictures of a life that I'll never be able to have again. I don't even think I could look through it anymore now.

I guess losing too many of the wrong people has left my mind changing for the worst and I just want to give up the part of my life that actually meant something. If I could forget that I ever had a past that was close to perfect, it would be much easier than dealing with the crap that life lead up to. It would be easier to stop thinking about the people I can't have anymore. It would hurt a lot less and the sadness would go away. Giving up never used to be in my nature, but when you have nothing else to hope for, maybe it's time to give it a try.

"You don't have to give up, Bridget." I hear a voice and I am terrified to open my eyes.

It's a voice I never thought I would hear again and he had to show up now. It's painful to let that soothing tone of his words fill my ears after so many days of not hearing him speak. My hands are shaking and a warm sensation is filling my eyes. A single set of footsteps follow his words and I know he's close by. I can feel him sitting down beside me and feel the warmth of his body and breath on my skin. He might not be real, but my mind is finally shutting down enough for me to believe that he is.

I take a deep breath and force my eyes to open. The world beyond this cage has vanished. The fires are gone and the people in those tents have disappeared. There is nothing here to distract me from spending this short moment with someone I know is disappointed with me. I can see it on his face and hear it in his words as he speaks.

"Why do you want to give up?" he asks again.

"Charlie." I say, wishing he was someone else.

When he spoke he sounded like our father, but my mind deceived me just like it has done millions of times in the past.

He keeps a stern look on his face, "Yeah it's me and you obviously don't have an answer for me."

I grit my teeth, fighting back the tears as I think of something to say. This was never a conversation that would pop into my head because it was much too painful to think about. Yet, my brother is here with me and I am speechless.

He sighs and looks me up and down, "You have grown up so much since the last time I saw you. I can't believe what you've become." He doesn't sound very proud of me, not like he did when he watched me turn into this.

A tear falls from my eyes and I feel it splashing against my cheek. This isn't the warm and loving visit I thought I'd have with him. My mind gave me a wonderful feeling when it shut down and let me talk to Maggie and my mom and the first time I saw Charlie. This time I feel nothing but sadness and disdain.

"I didn't want to leave you the last time we met like this. I wish I could have spent more time with you and give you the advice to help you out, but I couldn't and I'm afraid I don't have any to give you right now." He says.

"Then why are you here?" I ask, still whispering.

He shrugs, "To say goodbye."

I lean away from the wall and shake my head, "What are you talking about?"

"You are giving us no choice. All of us, we have to leave." He replies.

"So you're just going to die on me again?" I shout. "Why would you do this to me? Why would you even bother to visit me just to torture me like this?"

I can tell by the look on his face that his next words are hard for him to say. He can't look at me, he stares only at the grass under his feet. His hands are clasped together and his lips are stuck in a frown.

"You give us no reason to watch over you anymore. Your main goal right now is giving up and living in this hell you've brought to yourself." He says without looking at me. "You want to forget all about us and go through a life where you wish you never had a family. You *want* to give up."

I sit away from the wall and shake my head furiously from side to side, "I'm not giving up on you. I just can't stand thinking of the memories anymore. The very thought of everything hurts and it is driving me crazy. If I go on like this any longer, there will be nothing left of me but the empty shell of the girl I used to be. You have to understand how much it hurts to have you stuck in my head."

"And you think it doesn't hurt any of us to see you like this? To see our only living family member give up and let those men out there win?" Charlie argues and leans closer to my face, "I have seen you fight your way through the worst possible situations and you never once thought to give up. You risked your life for a group of strangers on more than one occasion. What happened to the sister I once knew? What happened to the Bridget that wanted a future for the human race?"

I swallow the lump in my throat and stare him in the eyes, "All of those things happened a lifetime ago. I'll never be that person again. The Bridget you used to know is dead. You'll just have to accept that."

His eyes are red with tears. His cheeks are flushed with sadness and hurt. I'm not his little sister anymore and I never will be again.

"I don't understand you. You *want* to live like this?" he asks as a tear falls from his dead eyes. "You always hated seeing those creatures locked away for amusement and now you are the animal in the cage for the world to see." He stands and moves away from me, his hand gripping one of the bars, "How could you give up like this?"

I keep my glare focused on his face, "It's easy when you have nothing left to live for."

He shakes his head and stands, gliding toward the bars of the cage, "You are carrying the very thing that could save the world. Is that not something to live for?" he shouts at me.

I shake my head, "It isn't when I have no one to love or share life with."

He turns around and gives me that look of utter dis-appointment, "The world would love you for giving life back to it. None of us want you to give up on it. You think Ryder would want you to do that?"

I clench my jaw shut, trying not to think of Ryder. His death is still too fresh in my mind and even more painful than losing my family.

"I know you love that boy and I know you love him more than life itself. Just because he and I aren't with you right now, that doesn't mean you should give up." He states, then turns back to the world beyond the bars.

"Trevor wants the cure and has a plan for the future. I don't have one anymore. There is no other option for me than to let him have what he wants and give up on everything else." I argue.

I hear another sigh escaping him and he doesn't bother looking at me when he says, "If you think you have no other choice in life, then neither do we and you'll just have to accept it. Goodbye Bridget."

I let him leave. I let him die right in front of me one more time. There's nothing I can say that would stop him anyway. He and the rest of the family have already made up their minds. They want to leave and never look over me again, why should I stop them.

There is a vast amount of anger surging through my veins. Anger toward the world and especially the one person I needed to show up tonight. If my father had been the one to reach out to me, he might have been enough to change my mind and get to want to go on. But he will never show up for me and I will always be stuck hating myself and the world I am forced to live in.

I stare between the bars of the cage and the world outside is coming back from the darkness. The fires are glowing brightly and the outlines of Trevor's men are taking shape. I stay on the ground, my hands holding me up as I lean forward on my knees. The pain from my despair is gone and all I can feel is anger for the world right now.

I'm tired of this sadness that is constantly dragging me down. This hatred toward my life and all of my failures is sickening. I shouldn't have to deal with this anymore and maybe I don't have to. Maybe I *could* change this part of myself that wants to give up and let the weak part of me die. I can no longer deal with the hardships this life continues to throw at me and I don't feel like I should have to anymore. I could end the sadness and forget about everything that drives me insane.

My family wants me to accept that they are gone forever, well here I am calling upon the very part of my being that is capable of accepting anything life throws at it. The part of me that I am still terrified of setting free. I am sure she is controlling and will go about this life so much differently than I had ever planned.

I don't have a reason to keep her from having her own life anymore. Ryder is gone and the depressing part of me will never accept that or anything else that goes wrong while I'm trapped here. There is only one thing I know I can do that will take the pain away and replace it with something that will make things easier to manage.

"You hear this monster," I speak quietly to myself. "You want a life of your own? You want to come out a play until the end of time? Then do it. I'm giving you the permission you need to erase the weak segments of my brain and replace them with what you know it needs to have in order to make it through this and survive. I'm allowing you to take over."

I stop talking and stare straight ahead of me for a long moment. The wind picks up and the leaves rustle on the ground nearby. The guard in front of me zips up his jacket to cover his shivering neck, then blows his steamy breath into his hands.

That's the only thing that is happening though. I still feel like the crumby, annoying Bridget that can't seem to let things go. It must take something more than just me telling my monster to take over. Trevor might have just the thing to help coax her out.

* * *

The sun is shining high in the sky above. Only a few white clouds are floating in the late Autumn breeze and I can hear the children across the yard trying to guess which animals they look like. I stand in the middle of the cage and stare at the humans who are laughing and having a grand old time. They live like their lives are meaningful in a world filled with so much hatred and death. If they could spend a day in my shoes, their minds would change pretty quickly.

A new herd of people have made their way to the small community and I watched them set up their tents alongside the others. About fifteen newbies are over there, staring at me whenever they get the chance. I can hear them talking to the others who welcome them to the group. They say how grateful they are for finding this place and how they already feel safer just knowing the cure lies in this very town. They don't bother asking why it's locked in a cage or why there aren't zombies lined up to receive a new lease on life. All they care about is feeling safer by following Trevor on his path of destruction.

Speaking of the man, he's been pacing around the school yard for an hour arguing with some guy with a Mohawk styled haircut. I haven't really been paying much attention to what they are saying. I just know it's about me and how the man with the Mohawk believes I should be taken to a more private location. Trevor is still hoping I'll switch sides and he won't have to worry about moving me at all.

I've actually been waiting for them to stop talking so I

can get Trevor's attention. I need something that only he can bring me and I don't want to wait too long. Ever since I gave myself permission to let the bad side take over, I can feel it bubbling in the pit of my stomach as well as the back of my mind. It just needs a little push in order for her to completely take over and erase myself from a life I don't want.

It sounds horrible, I know it does. Giving up never seems like the greatest thing on the planet but I feel that I could benefit by letting the monster take over. So what if I lose a part of myself in the process and I can never actually bounce back from it. Maybe that's what I want. I mean, who would honestly want to come back to a life they know they'll never be happy with?

Not me, that's for sure.

Trevor gets one last, loud word in the argument and the Mohawk goes inside without a question. He glares at me as he waits for the lock on the door to be released, then he goes inside and out of my hair.

Trevor looks frazzled as he runs his hands over his bald head. He lets out a sigh and I take a step closer to the bars of the cage. He slowly spins around and our eyes meet. I stare at the man who is responsible for everything that's going wrong with me. The horrible thoughts, the maddening sadness that will never end. It is all his fault and now he needs to fix it.

Slowly, he saunters through the grass and stops a few feet from the cage, "You look like you have something on your mind."

I shrug, "Maybe I do."

"I hope it's not something you'll regret." He states.

"No." I say, confidently. "I just need your help with it."

He raises both eyebrows out of surprise and says, "Oh really? What could you possibly need my help with?"

"I want a vampire." I say and the surprise leaves his face.

Trevor inches closer to the bars and keeps his voice low so the crowd of followers cannot hear our conversation, "What the hell do you want a vampire for? I thought you said it was dangerous if you bite them?"

"It's not dangerous. I just fall asleep for a few hours and I need that right now. I need to clear my head permanently and wake up as something I know you'll like much better than this pathetic mess standing in front of you." I reply.

"And just what do you think you'll wake up as?"

I lower my eyes and glance to my feet for a second. I don't even know if this will work and I have no idea what the hell I'll wake up as if it does. Either way, I know the sleep I get from biting a vamp will grant me some time to be away from the world and have some amount of peace. Who knows, maybe I won't wake up at all and I'll be at peace forever.

Finally, I look back to Trevor and stare into those big, brown orbs of his and say, "I'll wake up as something who wants the same things you do. Something that won't fight or try to escape. She'll *want* to join you and help you take control over the world with the cure." I'm not sure if that's true, but he might give me what I want.

He nods his head and says, "That would be a nice thing to have right about now. I don't want you to be locked in this cage out here forever. It would be beneficial to my people if they saw you as an ally instead of a threat. But, how do I know that I can trust you?"

"You honestly have no reason to trust me, but I just want a vampire. I need it." I say.

Again, he rubs his hands over his scalp and turns away from me for a moment to think. He stares up at the sky, watching the clouds soaring through the air above. Then he turns to the houses across the street and the few people tending to yard work and getting ready for the winter. Both of us look to crowd of people living in tents across the school yard and his growing army of used-to-be-zombies as they patrol the area. They don't see me as anything other than a freak in a cage and he wants them to see me as a savior like they see him as one.

He slowly spins around and tilts his head to the side,

studying me. I stand still, not giving him any body language to judge or read upon. He has heard my simple demand and I know a part of him wants to see a vamp get the cure. Trust will always be an issue, but soon it shouldn't matter. He takes a deep breath and exhales slowly, then walks to the cage. His fingers wrap around the bars and he stares intently at the sunglasses covering my eyes.

"If I do this for you, you *will* be on my side no matter what you wake up as. You will see things my way and do things the way I want them to be done. Do you understand?" Trevor demands.

I slowly nod my head in agreement and say, "Completely."

"Then I will bring you a vampire tonight just after the sun goes down. You will cure it and give me what I want so you can have what you want. We both win in this situation." He states.

"That's all that I want." I say.

"Good." He says, then releases the bars and turns away from the cage.

He strolls to the door of the school and taps on it three times. I hear the beep coming from the latch being released and he grips the door handle. Before he goes inside he passes me a long look of glee. The smile on his face tells me that he knows he has truly won the war between us. He gives me a wink of his left eye, then walks over the threshold and disappears inside.

If things finally work out the way I need them to, this war between us has only just begun.

* * *

Night fell and the sound of bewilderment has filled the voices of the crowd that is slowly making their way toward the cage. They all wonder about the show they are going to witness. The rumors that have gone through the small camp across the school yard have all been true. The few that have heard the story know that I will pass out a few seconds after I let the luxurious sweetness of a vampire's blood flow between my lips. Some don't believe that will happen, but they are curious to see the show regardless.

Trevor has not come out with my meal yet, but he has extra men on guard tonight. Vamps are pretty strong, no matter how detained they might be, they can still break through anything. A rope wouldn't hold it very well and neither would one of those dog leashes they bring the zombies out with.

I stay put in the middle of the cage and stare at the faces standing a few meters away from my prison. The guards are making sure to keep them back in case things go wrong. A smart idea, but I have seen plans like this fail before. It was a mess back then and I can only imagine how it will be now.

There are two faces amongst the crowd that I am currently staring at. The father, Phil, shakes his head at me. Sarah has her hand wrapped tightly around his and she is still holding onto that damn stuffed dog. It would be weird to see her without it though.

The way Phil is staring at me, I can tell he's disappointted. I doubt he has heard my reasoning for this or if he even knows the full story of it all, but he is still upset with me. I'm sure if he had the chance to get closer, he would lecture me just like my own father did when I was a child. Probably tell me how I'm making a horrible mistake and taking the wrong path and blah freaking blah. I've had enough lectures for one lifetime.

I've had enough of everything for a million lifetimes.

Finally, the door to the school squeals open and the entire crowd shifts their attention to the people stepping foot outside. A large man comes first, dressed in a black sweatshirt and dark jeans. He has a rifle tight in his grip as he leads the way for a tough looking woman to follow him. Her clothes are baggy and messy, matching the ratty mop on top of her head. She looks nervous and walks quickly to get out of the door and away from what is coming behind her.

It stumbles outside with a bag covering its pale face. The black sack is tied tightly around its neck and its hands are chained with thick metal behind its back. I'd like to meet the person who got close enough to the vamp to do that. I'm sure it wasn't an easy task.

Trevor follows the beast through the door with part of the chain in his hand like a leash. The vamp isn't even trying to get away, but I hear it gnashing its teeth and sniffing the air for the flesh it will not be tasting tonight. I take a big whiff of the air and instantly feel a familiar sense taking over. My hands are shaking and my mouth is watering as they bring my feast closer.

The crowd might be gasping in terror and backing away from the creature they've feared for the past few years, but I am enjoying this moment. I stare at the thing as he glides through the grass with such ease that he's barely walking at all. The paleness of his hands and arms are bright with the moonlight cascading down upon him. My lips are quivering and I move closer to the bars. I wrap my hands tightly around the cold metal and devour this creature with my eyes.

The dead blood under his skin is enticing and I simply cannot wait to try a taste. From what I remember about biting Katie back at the village with Adam and everyone I used to know, a vampire's blood tasted like complete shit, but for some reason I am craving it this very instant. I need to have it and I need to feel the texture of it flooding my tongue and dripping down my chin. I can fight through whatever hell the flavor of it might bring me and force myself to fall into the slumber I so desire.

Trevor pulls the vampire closer to the bars of the cage and a young boy moves to the padlock with a key in his shaking hand. He fights with the lock for a moment, then it comes undone and holds the door closed.

"How long does this take, Bridget?" Trevor asks me before I am allowed to eat.

I take a moment to think, to remember what happened when I bit Katie. I passed out within minutes after the blood hit my stomach and woke up the next morning in a daze. The girl, however, woke up sooner than I did and was even more herself than before.

"All night. You'll have to keep an eye on him and be there when he wakes up, just like the zombies." I reply.

"And you?" he asks.

I shrug and shake my head, "Just keep me in here until I open my eyes."

"I can do that." he states, then motions for the boy to open the door.

The vampire gets shoved forward, but before he steps into the cage, he digs his feet into the ground and stops moving. He's stronger than Trevor or any of his men and the crowd is backing further away.

"Smell...dead blood." The vamp says, his voice is quiet under the sack over his head.

I move closer and stand right before him, "Of course you smell dead blood, you idiot. Don't you want to try some?"

"No." he replies, then takes a step backward.

He pulls on the chain and fights against Trevor's hold on him. The guards step in with their guns aimed for the vampire's heart and I wait for the blasts to fill my ears and take away the thing I need most right now. They are willing to take away my chance of finding peace and there is no way in hell I am letting that happen.

The vamp fights blindly against the chain and his teeth snap open and closed with the bag getting sucked into his mouth. He digs his feet into the ground, trying to go for the meal that's closest to him. People are starting to scream and shout for the fear that this thing might get loose and attack them all. Their shrieks are deafening as well as an aide in the frenzy building even faster in the pit of my stomach.

I take a step out of the cage and the world slows down for me. Every movement the humans make appears to be going in slow motion. I take another step and the vamp is within inches of my reach. He digs his feet further into the ground, pulling against the chain being held by Trevor who is starting to lose his grip. His fingers are straining against the sharp steel, cutting into his skin until the blood loosens his grip completely.

The instant that chain falls from his hands, I leap through the air and tackle the vicious vamp to the ground. He might be strong, but at certain times when my monster is at its highest point, I can be stronger. I pin the thing to the grass, straddling over his midsection, then rip the ropes from around his neck and pull the bag from his head.

He's much older than I am and has definitely seen his fair share of fights. His forehead is covered in tiny scars and one is sliced across his hazy left eye. His nose has a piercing with a metal spike sticking out and his black hair looks dull and lifeless. He fights against me and shouts at me with muffled groans of hatred. I tilt my head to the left and stare into his eyes. He gnashes his yellow teeth at me, frightening the humans standing within a few feet of us.

I grab hold of his throat and tighten my hand around it. I lean closer to his neck and take in the sour scent of his dead flesh. I lick my lips, then bite down hard, splitting the skin to let the juices flow. I suck in his blood, fighting through the horrid taste covering my tongue and close my eyes.

Here's to the moment when my life stopped making sense. The times when everything fell apart and I found no way out. Here's to the people that I have to accept are dead and I'll never get to see again. There is no part of me that can survive long enough to deal with the fact that they are gone.

The longer I hold my bite on the vamp's neck, the more weight is taken off my shoulders. The sadness is starting to disappear and my mind is fading to black. The memories aren't trying to fight their way into my head and take over my every thought. I can breathe without the hatred clogging my throat and already life seems easier. I just need more of this blood to make the rest of my life go away.

I keep my teeth clamped against his skin and feel the vamp's twitching body slowing down against my grip. My head feels light and the world appears to be spinning underneath me. My entire body is shaking and goose bumps take over my skin.

The vamp stops moving completely and I take one last, long sip of his blood. I open my eyes and pull myself away from him. The crowd looks shocked as they watch the red stuff dripping from my chin. They are spinning faster and faster as I stare back at them. Trevor's face is a messed up blur and I fall to my side away from the body of the vamp. I try catching myself but my arms give out and I hit the grass with a quiet thud.

I can see the stars and the moon high in the sky above me. They are spinning in rapid circles. They don't really look like the tiny dots of lights that they are as they move quicker and quicker, becoming one white line that eventually fades into the blackness that is overtaking my vision. The world outside of my head is gone and I only see the dark land my empty mind has created for me. I allow myself to slip away from the world of the living and rest peacefully so I can wake up as a completely different creature.

* * *

Stars fill every corner of my vision as I take a look at the place my mind has sent me to. It seems like I get sent to beautiful places when I'm unconscious and this starry night just about tops the flowery meadow in which I spoke to my mother on that first little trip of mine.

I thought I was really dead that time, but I know I'm lying on the grass in front of whoever has been chosen to watch over me until I wake up. There's no saying how long that will be, so I'm going to revel in the magnificence of this comatose moment.

Everywhere I turn I see millions of bright dots floating against the navy blue canvas. I don't recognize a single constellation or any order these stars might be in. They appear to be moving slowly through the air and stop when I take a step forward. Once I stop moving, they glide once again and their game brings a smile to my face.

I glance to my feet and take another step. The floor is solid yet it ripples as though I'm walking on water. The stars reflect off the shiny surface, but my image does not. I don't create a shadow in this world of mine nor do I even feel like I exist here. I feel like a ghost banished to this place because I chose to give up on a life I can't handle anymore. I'm not the first person who has done such a thing, but I'm sure the others like me didn't wind up in a land full of stars inside of their wicked imagination.

I take a few steps forward smiling at the constant ripples under my feet. This place is peaceful and relaxing to a certain point. Sure, it's completely lonely and barren of any and all other forms of life, but it's the calmness of this place that makes me feel a lot less sad about things. I can breathe easier here and not think of the people that have ruined my life.

The stars float slowly through space when I stop moving and I try concentrating on the direction they are heading. Each one is drifting to a different place that I cannot dream to follow. There is one that catches my eye, it's moving faster than the others leaving behind a tail of white stardust in its wake. My eyes follow it until it disappears in a flash of colorful light far off to my left. The silent blast illuminates the darkness and I shield my eyes from the bright colors taking over.

It lasts only a few seconds, then everything fades back to the slowly moving stars and the small waves under my feet. I keep my eyes focused on the spot where the shooting star landed and see a figure walking toward me. The dark shadow blocks out some of the white speckles as it moves. It walks on two legs and I see their arms swaying back and forth indicating that it is clearly a human being. Living or non, I won't be able to tell until they get closer.

The figure moves swiftly and comes into focus. It's a woman with flowing brown hair as wild as the look in her eyes. Her clothes are black and menacing, different than the filthy attire I am sporting. She stands taller than I do and has a much stronger desire in those metallic silver eyes than I could possibly imagine. She approaches me and I stare at her face like I am looking into a mirror that shows the future.

I know that devilish grin, that pale skin that used to be a light tan color during the summer months. Her hair is a bit more wild than mine and she doesn't have the striking resemblance of a zombie like I do. But here I stand, staring at a version of myself I can only recognize as the monster hiding deep inside of me. The very creature I have fought so hard to keep hidden from the world and she is finally showing her face.

"I wish I could say that I'm happy to finally meet you, but a part of me doesn't want that." I speak and she tilts her head to the side in a confused manner.

She doesn't respond or open her mouth to speak. That grin is plastered on her face as she glares at me. She floats over the water-like floor until she stands inches away from me, then she moves her face close to mine. Our noses are almost touching in this surreal moment and I feel her eyes piercing into my very soul. She lifts her right hand and my left one moves at the same time without my command. Our palms press together and I feel an odd force flowing from her body into mine.

I keep my eyes focused on hers and slowly things begin to change around me. The world lights up and I recognize the inner makings of Des Moines. I look around my home and notice that everything has changed. The houses are burned to the ground and people are running frantically through the streets. Gunfire echoes in the distance and a loud blast fills the air. I look to the explosion and see a massive hole in the wall surrounding the city. An army that cannot be controlled runs through the gap, chasing after the people who live in peace behind that wall.

My jaw drops as I watch the massacre of the humans I helped to keep safe. Their blood sprays through the air, staining the concrete of the street they were just running on. The army, dressed all in black, advances through the wall with such force, they rip through the place like tissue paper. A tank is following them and I recognize the man standing on the very top of it. He wears an accomplished smile as he takes over the city and gains control over a good majority of the surviving country.

I turn back to the monster version of myself and the smile has faded. I don't know why she chose to let me see this. If this is a part of the future where Trevor wins and gets the world he wants, then it is something I can't let take place. Trevor will destroy everything that is good and safe on this planet and leave nothing but charred remains of what could have been. He won't give the humans a life they deserve, only the life of a slave under his ruling.

I close my eyes and shake my head from side to side. Our hands peel away from each other and mine falls back to my side.

I can't let Trevor take over. I can't let him win. There has to be something for me to do in order to stop the destructive madness.

I feel her hands grab my shoulders and a strange sensation fills my body. My arms and legs are tingling in the way they would if they were asleep. My hands are shaking uncontrollably and a coldness is taking over. She moves in closer to my ear and her warm breath caresses my skin.

"You are not strong enough to win." She whispers and I drop to my knees as all of my strength has been sucked away from me.

My energy is gone and my legs no longer work the way I want them to. I keep my eyes closed tightly and my upper body lies on the suddenly frozen floor. Ice is forming where is lay and a light fog emanates out of my mouth as I breathe. I can't stop shivering or keep my teeth from chattering. I fold my arms over my chest, but nothing I do can fight the coldness rapidly taking control.

Her footsteps flood my mind and I open my eyes a slit to see her stepping in front of me. Slowly, she kneels to the icy floor and stares deeply into my eyes. She gently places a hand on my shoulder and even more of my strength gets stolen away from me.

"You wanted this, remember?" she says and I feel my lips moving along with hers. "You wanted to forget everything and give your life to me. The sadness cannot hurt us anymore."

"N...no." I stutter. "I ch...change my mind. I want to go back."

She smiles and shakes her head, "It is much too late for that. I am in control now and nothing will stand in my way."

I can't move my head or say anything to stop this from

happening. My mouth is glued shut and my heavy eyes fall closed once more. The monster leans forward, balancing herself against me. I feel her lips press against my forehead and my shivering comes to an abrupt end.

Part Two

The sound of birds fill my ears. Their monotonous chirping is like an ice pick to my brain and I grit my teeth as I listen to that annoying sound. My hand moves around on the soft grass, feeling every blade for the first time. The morning dew soaks my skin and the cloth of the hooded sweatshirt on my back. I take a deep breath, the first of many in this new form and I slowly open my eyes.

The sun is blinding, burning my eyes like a fire poker fresh from the flames. I seal my eyes shut and remember that I need something to shield them from the sun. I feel around on the grass and the collar of my shirt until I find the sunglasses I need to protect my vision. As I move my hands, I realize they are bound at my wrists. The worthless girl I once was did not have the strength to break through the rope. I tighten my hands into fists and pull them away from each other until I feel the rope begin to fray and inevitably snap.

I finally find the sunglasses on the grass a couple feet away from me and slide them over my face. They still burn when I open them, but the feeling fades quickly as I take a look at the world I have been waiting to see through these eyes.

The colors are brighter and the air is just as crystal clear as I have been lead to believe it was. Seeing things through that pathetic girl's eyes could never live up to the magnificence that lies before me this very moment.

I sit up and stare at the humans standing just on the other side of the cage I am trapped in. They hold weapons as they walk back and forth across the grass like they are guarding me. Their pink flesh looks appetizing and I sniff the air to get a better feel of what they would taste like. It is sweet and salty, the blood under their skin is warm and thirst quenching. Those humans are weak compared to the beast that I am. I could take one of them down in seconds, then quickly move on to the next one in line.

But that isn't the plan.

I need to get out of this box and free myself of the prison that girl let them throw us in. She should have let me out *days* ago. I could have gotten us out of here faster than she could have dreamed and we would be well on our way of having everything I have ever dreamed of.

"She's awake." A woman's voice catches my ears. "We should get Trevor."

I turn my head and stare at the woman with long, black hair. She has it braided down the center of her back, swaying against the leather jacket she's wearing. Her brown eyes turn to me and I focus on the scent of the beautiful brown skin she's hiding under all of those clothes. Her neck is beckoning and I want to taste her flesh so badly. How the last version of myself went so long without biting into a human, I will never understand.

An older man with grey hair and a fat gut sticking out of the bottom of his shirt walks past the bars, heading for the door of a brick building. He's sweating through his clothes and that gnarly stench isn't as appealing as the rest of these humans. I grit my teeth and curl my lips back in disgust as the man disappears inside.

Slowly, I pull myself to my feet, letting the stiffness of

my arms and legs fade as I move them. It feels good to stand on my own instead of relying on that crutch to carry me around. I take a step closer to the bars and lift my fingers to touch the cool metal. It's rough against my skin and I smile as I wrap my fingers around the bar as tight as I can.

"Shit, she ripped through the ropes." I hear a man's voice this time and I move my eyes to his.

He is a boy more than a man. He is shorter than the woman and doesn't quite know how to hold the gun he's trying to aim at me. His hands are shaking causing the metal of the weapon to reverberate against itself causing another annoying racket to fill my ears. I snarl and look away from him. All of these repetitive sounds are enough to drive anyone insane. I can see why she wanted me to take over.

A squealing sound rips through the air and I whip my head around to see the cause. The door to the brick building is opening and a few men come waltzing happily outside. I recognize the one in the lead. He has a particular bounce in his step as he approaches the cage with a smile on his face and a slice of white bread in his left hand. His eyes light up as he sees me standing.

"I'm glad you chose to come back to the land of the living, Bridget." He speaks and his voice is more than familiar. "I see you didn't waste any time snapping the ropes on your wrists. I hope that isn't a sign of something bad you're planning."

I tilt my head to the side and allow the slim smile to cross my lips. This one smells tastier than the humans who surround him. He has a certain stink to him that reeks of destruction. The way he stares at me, willing me to see things through his eyes, and another familiarity rushes through my head.

I feel a strong hatred for this man. He has wronged me in a way that is not forgivable. Revenge is the thing that makes his flesh more desirable to me, but I cannot let that craving for him show just yet. This will take time. I need his trust before I allow myself to taste his flesh.

"Bridget?" he speaks again, noticing my lack of conversation, "Did you get the rest you needed in order to wake anew and see things my way for once?"

I ogle him from head to toe then back to his eyes and say, "I believe I have done just that."

The smile widens across his face and he tosses the last of his bread to the grass, "I have to say that is great news, but I'm still having trouble trusting you."

I shrug and keep my own devilish grin plastered to my face, "Maybe I was wrong about you. You want a world to follow you and believe in your visions for the future. I want the same thing, only better." I might be lying, but this man cannot see that at all.

He takes a step closer to the cage and asks, "And what about the past? Have you finally forgiven me for the incident with that boy?"

"What boy?" I say.

He throws his head back in laughter, then he speaks, "Oh I have to say that I love how you are thinking today." He moves even closer to the cage and wraps his fingers around the bars, "I hope that maybe one day you will forget all about boys and focus on finding yourself a man like me to have by your side."

Our eyes stay locked in a laser beam of focus. I feel his fingers gently rubbing against my own and his heavy breathing is disruptive. He smiles and winks at me and I know I have gained his trust. It happened much faster than I thought it would. He's a bigger idiot than he lets on to be. Then again, I am giving him exactly what he wants to hear. He wants me to be a part of his plan for the future he wants to create.

The smirk remains on his face and I watch his hand dig into the front pocket of his slacks. A key jingles as he pulls it out and walks to the lock on the cage. Here comes the real freedom I have been waiting so long to obtain. The time for me to do what I need to do and live the life I was created for. He pulls the lock from the latch and pushes the heavy door open. He steps to the side and I slowly cross over the threshold.

I stare at the faces of the men around me and take in their wonderful scents. All of them fear me and that smell is overpowering. A jolt of hunger stabs me in the stomach, but I hold back what my instincts are telling me to do and walk calmly into the open air. I might be craving their flesh and bones, but I can control this far better than the old me ever could.

Past this small group of humans is an even larger crowd starting to form. Their frightened eyes gaze upon me and I simply let my grin pass over each one of them. If I could read their thoughts, I would see that they are all wondering when I am going to make a break for it. It would be so easy to leap over these people, rush through the crowd that would part at the mere sight of me, and head for the vast world that awaits the monster I have become.

I cannot do that. Not only does my reasoning have to do with the many guns being aimed for my head and heart, but I have something I need to accomplish before I can depart from this place. There is a task which I cannot leave undone and it involves this man I hate so dearly.

I turn to face the one I recognize as Trevor and wait for his next words. He walks to me and reaches for the ropes still dangling from my right hand. He quickly unties it and tosses the frayed rope to the ground.

"Let's get inside, shall we?" Trevor suggests. "The room I have prepared for you is much better than this cage."

He strolls away from the metal building and I allow my feet to glide across the grass and follow him to the door of the school. The scent of human flesh grows when the door opens and another, equally intoxicating aroma drifts up my nose. There are undead souls in here somewhere and I am dying to find out where.

* * *

It is warm inside the brick school building and the smell of human flesh is mixed in with the scent of zombies. I can also detect a faint cleanness to the place. I hate to tell them that they can scrub and clean all they want but that amazing aroma of the undead creatures will always be soaking into the walls as well as their clothes.

The lights are dim down this first hallway and the old classroom doors are shut tight except for the one right by the entrance. I look through that open door and spy a wall filled with television monitors and a generator under the barred window to power it all. A man and a woman sit side by side, staring at the screens and acting busy as their boss walks by. The screens show various parts of the town and even one aimed at the empty cage outside.

Trevor leads me through the hall and his minions stay a few paces behind us. Some of them stop following and take their coats off, then disappear into one of the classrooms. I glance into one of them and see dozens of dark colored coats hanging from hooks on the wall. Beneath the coats is a vast array of weapons ripe for the picking. Pistols, rifles, automatic machine guns, and swords of many different lengths fill the shelves and the floor and the men simply add theirs to the pile. One man, a large guy with arms as big around as a tree trunk, stands guard of this room with a rifle strapped around his back. I pass him a sly smile and he raises an eyebrow out of sheer confusion.

I turn my attention back to the path ahead and follow Trevor around a corner. He points to a large room and tells me it is their cafeteria. Tables are setup and a few people are seated together eating the last morsels of their meal. The kitchen is right off that room and the smell of meat fills my nose. The dead, charred meat isn't as appetizing as the living flesh all around me. I think I'd prefer something a little more rare in my diet.

We turn down yet another long, echoing hallway, passing by a few more rooms with closed doors. Two men dressed all in black stand watch outside of one with a bloody handprint on it. The window has been blacked out and I stop walking and stare at the smear on the wooden door.

I breathe in the smells coming from the other side of that door and fresh blood is strong in there. It's not masked by the skin encasing it nor is it dead. Something is happening to humans inside this room and I can't help but wonder what that something is.

"I have an extra room setup for you at the end of the hall. Mine is right next to it and I'm sure you'll be comfortable there. Of course, I'll have to keep an eye on you until I can fully trust you." Trevor states as he keeps moving.

My eyes are glued to the door behind the guards. They stand firm as I glance to each of their angry faces. Their fingers rest on the trigger of their handguns and they act as though they are prepared for anything I could throw at them.

Trevor's footsteps stop moving and I feel his eyes on me. He backtracks down the hall and stands at my side.

"This room isn't for you." He says.

"What's in it?" I ask.

"Just my little prison for people who tend to get out of hand. Nothing you need to concern yourself with." Trevor replies. "C'mon, your room is a little further down the hall."

He waits for me to turn away from the door before he starts walking again. His boots click against the old marble under his heavy feet. I am much lighter on mine as I walk, mastering the craft of sneaking up on my prey.

He takes me to a door at the far end of the hallway. It's black and the window on the door is tinted dark as well. He pulls a small key from his pocket and sticks it in the door-knob, then pushes the heavy door open.

This old classroom is dimly lit, but I can see everything perfectly. A mattress lies on top of an old wooden bed with mounds of pillows and blankets piled on it. The windows are boarded up completely to block any amount of sun or moon-light to shine through. The teacher's desk is shoved against the wall under the white board and a row of flickering candles are placed neatly with wax dripping onto the desk.

I step into the room and take everything in. It is so com-fortable in here and is more suited to a creature as great as I am than that wretched cage outside. If I am to be the cure for the humans I so desire, then I deserve to live in luxury.

I move further in to the room and spin around. My eyes catch a tall wooden cabinet with the doors hanging open. Shirts and jackets dangle from hangers and jeans are folded on one of the shelves above them. Three pairs of boots and one pair of tennis shoes line the very bottom of the wardrobe and the smile grows wider across my face.

"There is a shower down the hall with warm water. In the morning I'll have one of my guards walk you down there." Trevor mentions from the doorway. "As you have noticed, there are clothes in the closet. Mostly things we have scav-enged out here but all of them are in good shape with no holes. You can finally change into something a little less dead looking."

I smile at that thought. I don't understand why I ever thought it would be a good idea to stay in the same, bloodied clothes for more than a day. This soiled outfit should be burned and replaced with one a bit more suiting.

I turn to Trevor and he smiles at me. For a man that creates a lust for revenge deep inside of me, he sure knows how to make a girl feel welcomed. I am finding it difficult to see the reasons why I have chosen to hate him when he is giving me all of these nice things. I just cannot fight the feeling the old me has left behind. It is the one thing she has managed to keep inside this head of mine and I can at least humor her by letting the hatred linger until I find a way to deal with it.

"I'm really glad you've decided to join me." He says, leaning against the frame around the door. "You have no idea what this will mean to the world now that you have made the right choice. I hope you enjoy this life as much as the rest of us do."

"I have no reason not to enjoy this life." I reply.

"And you'll give me the cure to build the army I want and have the world I deserve?" he asks.

"That is what you desire, so it shall be done." I say.

He smiles from ear to ear, showing off the white teeth behind his lips, "You really are a miracle, aren't you?"

That is how people see me? All this time I was forced to stay hidden from the world because the old me was terrified to let me out, yet I am a miracle to these humans. If only I saw this sooner, I wouldn't have had to stay in the deepest parts of my mind, watching through the eyes of a girl who could barely control this gift that I am. She should have let me out much sooner and because of her failure to do so, this world was unable to see just how truly great I am.

"You have no idea just what kind of miracle I can be." I say, with the devilish grin creeping across my face.

He nods and says, "I'll leave you alone to relax and get cleaned up. I'll come by a little later to check on you."

I don't bother replying to his chatter and he leaves the room in silence. The door closes and I am left alone to relish in this master suite he has given me.

* * *

Morning came and just as Trevor had promised, there was a man waiting outside my room to escort me to the showers down the hall. The water in my shower was warm and inviting. I washed away every ounce of deadness on my skin. Blood and dirt runs slowly down the drain and I dry myself off with a large blue towel that was left out for me. I wrap it around my body, then glare at the pile of my old clothes wadded in the corner of the room. I grimace and turn away from them.

I walk through the halls wearing only this towel. Water drips from my hair, splashing onto my shoulders and gliding softly down my back. The guard passes me an odd look as he walks with me to my room and I simply smile in return. He opens the door for me and closes it tightly once I am inside.

The large, wooden closet catches my eyes and I stroll across the floor to it. I pull the door open and admire the apparel Trevor has left for me. I pick out a few things that will be fitting, then close the door.

I let the towel fall away from me and slip into a pair of tight, black-colored jeans. Next, I pull a low-cut black shirt over my chest and the soft fabric clings to my skin. Over the fresh pair of socks on my feet, I slip into black leather boots with silver buckles on the sides of them. They are a little snug, but I smile at them admiringly.

This dark outfit of mine would only be complete with the leather jacket that was hanging at the very back of the closet. It hugs my body, showing off every curve and adding to the menacing appearance I am hoping to show the world. Finally, I turn to the mirror leaning against the wall beside the closet. I stare at the side view of myself and grin, then slowly walk to it.

My hair is still damp in places and I run my fingers through it to smooth it. The wavy mess on my head is soft to the touch, matching the silkiness of my milky white skin. I lean closer to the mirror and fall in love with the metallic silver of the eyes staring back at me. They are simply breathtaking. It is a shame that I am only limited to the night hours to reveal them to the world.

I stroll away from the mirror and head for the desk at the front of the room. My sunglasses are sitting on top of the structure and I grudgingly take them from their place. I carry them with me to the door and reach for the knob.

The door to my room was left unlocked, but my escort remains standing in the hall to wait for me. He tightens his grip on the small pistol in his hands when our eyes meet and he shudders at the sight of me as I step through the doorway.

The morning sun is shining through the windows at the top of the walls, casting bright rays of light to bounce off the marble floor. I sigh as I slide the shades over my nose to hide my precious eyes from the sun's harmful beams.

We pass the two men standing guard at the door in the middle of the hall and I feel their eyes inspecting my body. I wish I could see what is really going on inside that room. The smell of blood and anguish is strong in this section of the hallway. I begin to wonder if Trevor is holding prisoners in there to torture them for disbelieving in his ways. He does seem like the type of man to go out of his way to whittle a man's life down until there is hardly anything left.

I turn the corner, brushing that whole prison room off my shoulder and the guard leads me to the cafeteria. He holds the door open for me, then heads for the line of people standing by a table filled with food. Trevor had asked me to meet him there once I was finished pampering myself and I scan the area for him.

I step into the large room and study it for a moment. The sun is shining brightly through the barred windows and the hum of a generator radiates from a small closet in the far left corner. A group of three men and four women are seated at one of the tables eating scrambled eggs and sipping from water bottles. Each of them pass me awe-filled glances when I walk by, but they keep their words to themselves.

Trevor is standing around a taller table by one of the windows that overlooks the street in front of the building. Two men stand with him and they step aside so I may join them. I stand beside a man with a ridiculous hairstyle and he runs his hands over the strip of long hair going straight down the center of his scalp. He steps to my right and glares at me while Trevor smiles and checks me over, giving me a nod of approval.

"I'm glad to see you took advantage of the apparel we have here." He states. "You look much better than the bloody mess you were earlier."

"It feels good to change into something more suiting to me. I plan making a lot of changes from now on." I reply.

"Good to hear." He says. "I have breakfast waiting for you outside. Two zombies, one male and one female. I believe the woman used to be a nurse before she was bitten. Her scrubs give that away and we could use someone in the medical profession. The man will be another nice addition to my army."

I smile and nod, my mouth already watering at the thought of the meal awaiting me. There is just something about their grotesque flavor that gives me the satisfaction I need to continue on and the strength I need to take down a dozen more. A shudder runs up my spine just thinking about the taste that should soon be enveloping my tongue.

"What about the vamps in the basement?" the man with the Mohawk asks. "When are you going to cure them?"

I turn my hungry eyes to his and grit my teeth. Being the very core of this creature that I am, I know every tiny detail about myself. I know what is good for me and what is not. The blood of a vampire is not even the tiniest bit appetizing to me. With just one taste, I will slip into an unconscious state and I do not have the time nor the patience to deal with that.

"Bridget?" Trevor's voice catches my ears. "The man asked you a question."

I snap my head toward him and reply sharply, "I cannot bite them."

"Yes, I know this, but we need to find a way to cure them too." Trevor replies.

"If you can't bite the fucking vamps, then what good are you?" Mohawk snaps.

I devour this man with my eyes as he scoffs at the mere thought of me. There is something about him that is irritating. I would love to rip his damn head off and see what drives him to be so annoying. He stares at me with those senseless blue eyes, that out of style Mohawk on his head, and a look that screams how worthless he is. If I weren't trying to fit in with Trevor and this group, I'd happily take this man out with my bare hands. I think I would even smile while doing so.

Finally, the third man standing with us speaks up and suggests, "Neil might be able to come up with something we could use to shoot the vamps from a safe distance. Would that work?"

Trevor rubs his chin and raises an eyebrow, "That's not a bad idea. A dart gun might actually do the trick. We can drain some of your blood, just enough for a few darts, and shoot them into the vamp cage downstairs. It's brilliant!"

"What if that don't work?" the annoying man speaks, making me want to kill him all the more. "What if that only kills them instead of bringing them back?"

"It will work." I bite my tongue and keep myself from saying what I truly want to say. "I don't need to bite them in order for the cure to work. Are you that big of a fucking moron to understand that all it takes is a little bit of blood in order for them to come back?" I guess I am not so good at holding my words in after all.

Mohawk clenches his hands into tight fists and keeps his

steely glare fixated on me. I can hear his heart racing and smell the tension on his skin. He might not be afraid of me while he is surrounded by his peers, but leave me alone with the man and I will show him the true meaning of fear. I would grant him a death so swift, he will fall before he has the chance to beg for mercy.

Another shiver of delight passes through me as that image plays through my mind.

"Alright, we've got a plan. Bridget will go to the science lab and meet with Neil. If anyone can figure out a way to get her blood into a dart gun, he's the man for the job. Then we'll get the guns ready to go and get to curing some vamps." Trevor orders, then faces me, "I'm so glad that you made the decision to join me. So far it's turning out to be quite the asset."

I smile and keep my eyes on the Mohawk and reply, "In time you will see that I am more than just an asset."

* * *

After my morning meal, I was escorted down another hall to an old science lab by the bodyguard Trevor assigned to me. This guard is a massive fellow with a truckers' hat on his head to cover the bald spot between his greying hair. Without his hat on, what few hairs are left up there look like a horseshoe. I can see why wants to keep that covered.

He brought me to a large room that stinks of chemicals. Three fluorescent lights flicker on the ceiling which casts enough light to see through the boarded up room. Eight rows of tables are set up neatly for the class that used to take place here and a few wooden stools are pushed under the tables.

A short man wearing a white lab coat stands by one of the tall tables. His dark framed glasses stick out on his pale face and his red hair is a tangled mess on his head. The odor emanating from his skin and clothes tells me that he hasn't bathed in a while. Considering that this place is equipped with running water, it is actually surprising that he doesn't take advantage of it.

This man is older than I am, probably in his early forties. He looks up when the door behind me closes and the guard stands watch next to it. Quickly, the scientist drops what he is working on and steps around the table and stands in the aisle. His gawking eyes look magnified through the glasses and they move up and down my body. I can tell he is thrilled to be meeting a creature as unique and amazing as I am. The grin on his face is practically screaming with astonishment.

"You must be Bridget." He states with excitement in his voice.

I nod, "You must be Neil."

He rushes down the aisle towards me and says, "I am indeed." He takes my hand and shakes it quickly, although I did not offer it to him. "It is such a pleasure to meet you. I have heard and seen the wonderful things you are capable of doing. I've been looking forward to studying your blood ever since you got here but Trevor hasn't granted me the pleasure of doing so until now."

"That Trevor is such a card, isn't he?" I reply, not hiding the sarcasm to my voice.

He seems taken aback at my comment and says, "I guess so." He then spins around and walks to a table with a cardboard box in the middle of it. "They brought me this just a moment before you walked through the door. It will take some time and concentration, but I will be able to extract your blood and fill all of these."

I follow him to the table and peer inside the box. Covering the bottom of it are a few dozen empty syringes that will were made to fit the dart gun resting on the table beside the box. I stare at the tiny needles at the very ends of them and smile just thinking of how easy it will be to cure the vamps. So long as I still have the privilege of killing the zombies, then this life will be a piece of cake.

Neil proceeds with taking a few of the darts from the box and sets them neatly on the table, "Tell me something, what's it like?"

I raise an eyebrow and ask, "What do you mean?"

He chuckles and says, "You are the only known member of the undead that still has the capability to speak and remember who you are and what you are meant to do. What is it like being a creature so different that you can actually save the world?"

I pass him half a smile and run my fingers through my hair. I like the way he smiles at me as though he truly believes I am the savior of all mankind. I get that look from a lot of people around here, but this man seems obsessed with it.

"It is actually quite amazing." I reply and his smile grows wider, "I can do things I never thought were possible; jump higher, run faster, see for miles, and hear things across a crowded room. I can fight a zombie and not get a single scratch that won't heal. And believe it or not, I feel more alive now than I ever have before."

"Hmm, I wasn't expecting that for an answer." He states.

I shrug, "I was not expecting an interview."

"Is it ever lonely?" he asks quickly. "I mean, I'm sure you had to leave a lot of people behind when you were bitten, don't you get lonely and miss them?"

"Not anymore." I answer simply.

I have no reason to feel lonely or sad about anything anymore. That was the old me. She couldn't handle this life or the task she was given and that's why she passed everything along to me. She knows I can deal with things without a problem and let her live in peace with the people she chose to forget. I might not know who any of them are or why she chose to care about them so much, but that's not why I'm here. I am the monster she was afraid to let loose and I am the one here to live the life I was meant to have.

"You seem so different than what I was expecting." Neil finally opens his mouth again. "From everything Trevor has told me about you, I thought I would meet this girl stricken with loneliness and hatred. You are more put together and I can see just how strong you are. I guess I just don't understand why you don't have anyone to miss."

"There is no point in wasting energy on the useless act of missing or thinking of people that are dead. In order to be strong, one must forget the past and allow themselves to transform into the creature designed for the sole purpose of staying alive. Memories and sadness only get in the way."

He lowers his head and says, "That's not always true. Sometimes it's the memories of our loved ones that *help* us stay alive."

"Not for me."

"I understand." He says and starts to fidget with the darts on the table. "Don't you want to be a normal human being again though? Wouldn't you ever want a cure for yourself?"

I cock my head to the side and say, "A cure for me does not exist and I would not accept one."

"Why wouldn't you accept it?"

This man is getting on my nerves with all of these questions, "Because I do not need one. I am perfect as this being and I would not change my life for anything." I snap, hoping to end the interrogation.

"I see," he says and goes back to focusing on the darts, "I'm sorry I brought that up."

He doesn't seem so interested or excited about me anymore. Whatever stories he's heard of me belong to the weak person trapped inside the deepest, darkest pit in my mind. A place she will never escape from.

Neil stops fidgeting with the needles and darts and looks back up, "Can I ask just one more question?"

"What?" I snap.

"Will you show me your eyes? I've heard they are mesmerizing." The smile across his lips is forced but I hear the sincerity in his voice.

I nod and reach for the sunglasses on my face. I slowly slide them down my nose and away from my ears. I fold them neatly and set them on the table beside the darts. His eyes open as wide as they will go as he stares at the silvery hue of my irises. He looks like a kid in a candy store and his parents are letting him pick out whatever he wants. I am probably the rarest candy on earth and he will never see anything like my eyes again.

"Beautiful." He whispers, "Simply remarkable."

He leans forward and examines my eyes up close. I can smell the sweat and see it beading on his brow as he moves his head closer. Beneath the sweaty exterior of this man, I can smell the blood flowing through each and every vein below that skin. My hands shake as I stare at the pink flesh that would be so easy to break through and devour. He is so close to me, it wouldn't take much effort at all to bring him down. I clench my hands into fists and fight through the hunger I must save for the undead.

Neil backs away from me and smiles. He turns around and pulls open a drawer from the table behind him. He comes back with a pair of latex gloves and an empty syringe, "Let's get started, shall we?" Neil states.

He stretches the gloves over his hands, one at a time, then snaps the latex against his wrist. He plunges the air from the syringe and reaches for my arm. I lift the sleeve of my leather jacket, showing off my pale skin and blue veins. His eyes light up and he carefully slides the needle into my skin. I don't feel a thing but I can see the crimson cure being sucked from my arm, filling the thin vial.

This small amount of red stuff is what the world is waiting for.

* * *

Neil filled enough darts to take care of the vamps in the basement of the school. It took him a couple of hours to get the darts ready to go. He chose to test one on an old mannequin that was stored in a closet. The cure was released into the soft material the thing was made of and it seemed to work perfectly. We just need to test it on the real thing.

While sitting in that classroom with Neil, I suffered while he told me his life story. Apparently he used to be the Chemistry teacher at a high school a few towns over. He never had a family, which meant it was easier for him to cope through the loneliness of the apocalypse. Trevor found him about a year ago, wandering through the streets practically begging to get himself killed. He made himself comfortable in the school, keeping to himself in the lab and doing his own experiments. He begged me to let him examine the cure under a microscope. I reluctantly agreed simply to end his annoyance.

He decided not to join us on our trip to the basement. As much as I could tell he wants to see how the cure works, he was afraid to be that close to the vamps. Your typical human, afraid to face something they don't understand.

We strolled through the tunnels under the school until we came to a dead end. There are six of the pale faced creatures locked in a cage. Trevor found the darkest corner in the darkest tunnel to keep his blood thirsty prisoners. The sunlight can't get to them down here no matter where he chose to keep them, but he wanted to be certain.

I stand before the vampires and listen to their hungry groans. They growl and reach their arms through the bars for their prey. Their hazy eyes are begging for the humans to come closer and they gnash their teeth at Trevor. He smiles and puts a dart in the gun, then locates the perfect specimen to test it.

The one he has chosen is a middle aged man missing his shirt. His pale chest glows in the dim candle light and his greying hair blends in with his skin. He has both of his arms outstretched through the bars, trying to reach for the nearest human. There is a few feet between us and their hands so the living are safe.

Trevor raises the weapon and looks through the scope to get the perfect shot. He lines it up with the vampire's throat and pulls the trigger. The blast bounces off the walls, screaming into the ears of the humans around me. They quickly cover their heads with their hands and fight the deafening sound.

I stare at the vamp with the dart sticking from his neck. I can see the blood seeping into his system until the small vial is drained. Still, he stands with his arms reaching for the meal he will never have.

"How long does this take, Bridget?" Trevor asks, a hint of anger in his voice.

"His vampire body will die in a moment. It will take time for his human form to wake up, but he will be cured." I reply.

My eyes stay glued to the vamp and I await the effects of the cure to take hold of him. There is something familiar about watching this creature and staring into his eyes. The dull haze of them is like any other vampire on the planet, but watching the dead life being taken from him feels like déjà vu. I might never figure out why this is familiar, but I am positive it has something to do with the life I threw away.

A gargling sound comes from the vamp's throat and he starts clawing at the dart in his neck. I feel the same scratches on my own skin although nothing is behind me to cause it. I close my eyes and shake the feeling from my head, but it remains there to torture me. I grit my teeth and clench my hands into fists. These feelings aren't meant for a creature as great as I am.

I open my eyes and glare at the vamps before me. They take no notice of their fallen friend as he lays on the floor waiting to wake up human again. I think it's about time the rest of them join him.

I snatch the dart gun from Trevor's grip and take one of the darts he has in a pouch around his waist. I slide it into the barrel and take aim. The woman I choose has long black hair and looks to be no older than I am. I aim for her throat and pull the trigger, then take another dart.

The humans cower with their hands over their ears as I take the final shot getting the last of the six vamps in the throat. His friends are lying at his feet and he is completely oblivious to what is going on around him. He begins clutching at the dart until it falls from his skin and hits the floor at his feet. Seconds pass and he is toppling over the bodies and landing on top of them with his eyes closed.

I lower the gun and let the smile creep across my face. Shooting these damn things seemed to do the trick and get rid of that obnoxious feeling roaming through me. I feel more like myself again and less like I am reliving a memory I cannot recall.

Trevor pulls himself together and I hand him the gun. He takes it and stares at my handy work. Each vamp has been injected with something that will change the world and they have no idea. As far as they are concerned, they were just killed and waiting to enter the world of the permanently dead.

It is just that easy.

"So," Trevor sighs, "we just wait?"

I nod, "That is exactly what we do."

"Got it." he replies.

I stare at the lifeless forms locked behind those bars and feel nothing for them. No mercy, no hatred, and especially no envy. They will wake up as a weak human being with a beating heart and an aroma that will drive any zombie or vampire hungry for their flesh. They will have to go through their days fighting to survive in this hellish world.

I don't understand why anyone would want to live like that.

I am proud to be what I am. Proud to be the freak those humans will see me as and damn proud of what I can do to them if they get in my way. The old me never saw it like that. She wanted to help them and give them a better chance for the future. Sure, the cure can do that and with my help the world will go back to the way it was before the zombies and vamps came around.

That is only if I *want* to help them. Right now I am simply playing Trevor's little game and he believes that he is winning.

* * *

The vamps that were cured woke up when the sun went down. All six of them opened their human eyes and stared at a world they had not seen in a while. They were confused and scared, but every last one of them was grateful to be alive again. They shared their stories of being bitten to the crowd in the cafeteria as Trevor's expanding army rejoiced and welcomed their newest members.

I stand in the corner of the room and stare at the faces surrounding the tables. The six *ex-vamps* sit together and laugh their cares away, acting as though nothing terrible had ever come to them. The man with the Mohawk sits alone and glares at me while a few others are busy getting drunk off moonshine and old liquor. I was offered to consume the beverages with them, but I happily refused. Human refreshments will do me no good. They are like a poison and I will not allow myself to fall ill to it.

I lean against the wall and take in the praises and cheers as these people rejoice in their new lives. Each one of them welcomes me into this group of unruly misfits and looks forward to the future we will all create together. Trevor has it carved into their minds that they will have complete control over the world and get to do whatever they want under his ruling. He believes that once he rises, the humans out there will have no choice other than doing what he says in order to get my cure. I will let him believe this for now, but it is *my* cure in the end.

"Here you are!" Trevor exclaims as he approaches me, his breath stinks of liquor. "Why aren't you celebrating with the others?"

"Doing what I am meant to do is nothing for me to celebrate." I reply coldly.

He seems confused for a moment, then brushes it off and leans against the wall beside me. He takes another swig from the bottle in his hand and nearly finishes it. He looks out to his people and smiles. More of his followers are elsewhere in the school or outside patrolling the small community, but his favorite people are right here in this room.

"You have truly outdone yourself today, Bridget." He states with a smile. "I couldn't be happier with how things went downstairs. I can promise you there will be more of that."

"Glad to hear." I say.

He nudges me with his shoulder then says, "I have a surprise for you. Something to show you just how much I appreciate the gift you've given me."

I turn my eyes to him and say, "What surprise could you possibly have for me?"

His grin turns sly and he pulls himself away from the wall, "Follow me, my dear."

He leads me through the doors of the cafeteria and I follow him down the hall. He stammers as he finishes off the alcohol and tosses the glass bottle to the floor. It doesn't shatter, but it clangs against the tile and rolls away from him. He takes me down a familiar path until we are standing outside the door to my room. It's closed and a guard is standing watch by it. I raise an eyebrow and cock my head to the side.

Trevor spins around and speaks with a slur, "Your surprise awaits you, dear sweet Bridget. Inside this room you will find your reason to celebrate."

He is completely drunk right now. He holds onto the wall to maintain his balance as that annoying grin is slapped across his face. Unless there is a delicious meal waiting for me inside of my room, there is no surprise he could give me that I actually want. Although, I will humor this man and grant him the thanks he believes he deserves.

The guard moves aside and I reach for the doorknob. I twist the cold metal in my hand and push the door open. Candles have been lit on the old desk and a few are scattered about the rest of the room. I sniff the air and take in the scents around me. Beyond the strong liquor pouring out of Trevor's mouth, there is a separate human odor in the room. It is strong and filled with fear and wonder. There is a familiar tinge to it and I slowly spin on my heels until I catch the cause of the aroma.

"I'll leave you two alone." Trevor says and the door closes behind me.

I walk further into the room and this strange man lifts his head. His dark hair covers his ears and part of his forehead. A bruise is healing on his left cheek and he stares at me as though he knows me. The look in his eyes tells me that we have met, I assume before the weaker Bridget allowed me to take over. Whoever he is, I must admit he looks rather tasty.

His pink flesh is inviting and the blood under that skin is warm and smells sweet. His dark eyes are appealing, matching the clean clothes on his back. He pulls himself to his feet and allows me the pleasure of checking out the rest of his body. His muscles are just the right size and he is a few inches taller than I am. There will come a time in my existence where I will be granted the privilege of devouring as many humans as I can, but I believe this one will be saved from my wrath.

"Bridget?" he questions, his deep voice is soothing to my ears.

"You know who I am?" I ask.

He nods, "Of course I know who you are. Don't you recognize me?"

I walk closer and remove the shades from my eyes. I pin him against the wall and take another whiff of his luxurious aroma. There might have been a time in the last version of my life where I did know this man. I came to life without those memories so he is nothing more than a man of my desire.

"It's me," his voice is shaking, "Jason."

"Jason." I repeat, slowly.

His eyes go sad and he asks, "What did they do to you? Why don't you remember me?"

I pass him a smile and shrug my shoulders, "She couldn't handle the sadness anymore."

"Who are you talking about?"

"You know," I step backward away from him and motion to myself, "the girl who was *supposed* to save the world. She couldn't take the depression that she allowed to enter our mind, so I stepped in and made things better for her. That past is gone now and I only see the present and the future I will make great. I am the monster she wanted to keep hidden from the world."

Jason scrunches his eyebrows and scowls at me, "Why would you want to do that? Why would you want to forget about the people you care about? Your family and friends? Ryder?"

"You did not listen." I say, moving toward him again, "*She* was the one who wanted to forget."

He looks down at his feet, ashamed of me, "I just don't understand. The Bridget I know wouldn't want to forget anything. Especially not Ryder."

I shrug once more and say, "Well, that Bridget is dead. She will never resurface so long as I am around."

He shakes his head and runs a hand through his soft hair. He mentioned someone named Ryder as though he should be important to me. That name does not ring a bell or draw up a face in my head for me to think about. I only see blackness when I close my eyes and that is how it needs to remain.

Jason lets out a sigh, then opens his mouth to speak once more, "So, if you're not the person I used to know, what is *your* plan? I know what the old you wanted to do and I'm sure that ship has sailed. So, what are we going to do to get out of here?"

I raise an eyebrow and say, "Where would we go?"

"To the city." He states as though this is obvious. "Our plan was to get to the city and let the government know about the cure. You wanted to save the world with it."

I take a short moment to consider his idea, then say, "Is that all?"

"What do you mean, *is that all*? You should be all over saving the world and finally bringing an end to the zombies and vampires." He states.

I shake my head and shrug my shoulders. Jason seems aggravated and confused with me now. He looks to his feet, passing his eyes over the different shades of marble on the floor. His eyes turn up to the ceiling and he rubs his face with his hands. As though he has just come up with the perfect plan, he looks at me with hope in his eyes.

"There was something else you were planning." He says.

"What would that be?"

"You wanted revenge on the man that hurt you the most in the world." He replies and steps away from the wall.

"Trevor." I whisper without taking any time to consider it.

"Exactly."

"But why?"

He takes another step closer, "Because he hurt you. He killed somebody you love."

I raise an eyebrow and ask, "Ryder?"

"Yes." He answers, taking yet another step. "You two were in love, yet you were torn apart because you couldn't touch or kiss him after being bitten. You were afraid you were going to hurt him and Trevor came along and killed him."

That would explain the severe demand for revenge I feel every time I look at Trevor. I feel it coursing through my veins every chance our eyes meet. I picture myself ripping him apart limb from limb and leaving him to rot on the street like the disgusting corpse he deserves to be.

While I was lost in that magnificent thought of destroying Trevor, Jason has moved closer to me. He places a hand on my shoulder and looks me in the eye. I feel the warmth of his skin and it ignites a new feeling in my unbeating heat.

"You *can* kill him, ya know." He suggests. "You can end his life and get us out of here. We can get to Des Moines and go on with saving the world."

"Is that your plan?" I question.

He nods, "Yes, but it could be *our* plan."

I smile and place my hand on the back of his neck. There is some kind of passionate attraction drawing me to want him.

Not to bite into him or drink his blood, but physically want him. I move my head closer to his until I can feel his hot breath against my cheeks.

"*This* is my plan." I whisper.

Before he can stop me or speak his words of protest, I press my lips against his and let the craving desire take over. I put my hand on his waist and force his body against mine. Our tongues caress one another and I feel both of his hands on my shoulders. I hold onto him and shove him backwards until his back meets with the wall and our kiss grows more intense. A flutter of emotions fill my mind and all I can think about is Jason. His thick black hair, his moist lips against my own and those mysterious hazel eyes that drive me to crave him all the more.

Wait a minute.

That last thought is not accurate.

I stop the kiss and open my eyes. He opens his as well and they are not the hazel shade that corrupted the blackness in my mind. They are dark enough to be black like the very soul deep inside of me. Why would my mind allow me to think of the wrong thing?

I step away from him and shake my head. He is frozen against the wall, his arms up in surrender and an expression of fear written on his face. His lips are quivering and he slowly wipes my saliva from his mouth on the back of his hand.

"Wh...what's going to happen to me?" he stutters. "Am I going to turn into something like you?"

I glare at him, still trying to get past why my mind fucked up, "No, you idiot. You are still going to be the same human being you have always been."

"But you, the old you, was afraid that she would hurt humans if she touched them like that." his words are slowly erasing those hazel eyes from my mind.

Again, I shake my head, "It doesn't work like that. She was just too stupid to let me out long enough to let her see it.

I am the cure and I know how it works and exactly how to use it."

"Are you sure?" he asks, his fear is quickly fading.

I smile and nod my head slowly, "Why? Are you afraid that you enjoyed my kiss?"

He swallows hard, but doesn't respond. He merely stands there, leaning against the wall and doesn't reject me as I inch my way closer to him once more. I run my fingers through his soft hair and he places a hand on my waist. He wants this just as much as I do.

* * *

Jason is still sleeping in the bed beside me. His snores are quiet and his breathing is calm. He probably just experienced the best sleep he's had in years thanks to the hell outside. This might not be his ideal place to live for a while, but I am sure he can't complain with his head buried in comfortable pillows while lying under a thick blanket to keep him warm. As long as he stays with me, I will make sure he gets to live in comfort right by my side.

I sit up in the bed and look over my shoulder. His eyes are closed and he lies on his stomach with his arms tucked under the pillow. He refused to get intimate with me last night, other than the mind-blowing kissing that sent a spark shooting through my veins every time our lips met. He said it was too soon after Ryder's death to do anything more than that. No matter how many times I tried to convince him that he was part of the old me, Jason still couldn't bring himself to share long moments of intense passion with me.

I turn away from him and sigh. As much as I craved him last night, I could feel something holding me back. Whether it was his words of persuading me that it wasn't a good idea or if some part of my subconscious was trying to tell me something, I could feel an annoying pinch in my head keeping me from gaining what I desired. I can guarantee that it won't happen again and I will get what I want.

I slip into my leather boots and zip them over my jeans. Then I stand from the bed and stretch my arms over my head, listening to my elbows cracking. I roll my neck, hearing the same popping sound, then take a step away from the bed. My shades are sitting neatly on the desk by the door and I gracefully take them and slide them over my nose. I grab my jacket that was hanging on the doorknob and put it on and zip it up about halfway.

Before I leave the room, I take a long look back at Jason. He hasn't moved since I woke up and he is in such a deep slumber it is not likely that he'll wake up any time soon. As much as I would love to have him explore this place with me, I feel the need to be on my own.

I grip the knob and quietly pull the door open. I step into the silent hallway and close the door without making a sound.

This part of the school appears to be empty. The guard that normally stands outside my room is gone. I stroll down the middle of the hallway and pass the room that smells of blood. Only one man stands by this door and he looks tired. There are dark purple bags under his eyes and he yawns as I pass by him. I smile and shake my head as I keep my feet moving in the direction of the cafeteria.

Voices are starting to flutter in this part of the school and all of them are coming from the cafeteria. The scent of eggs drifts up my nose and I grimace. Humans might enjoy that taste, but no part of that yolky odor is appealing at all to me.

I walk through the open doors and spot Trevor sitting at

one of the tables closest to the windows. The man with the Mohawk sits across from him, devouring the meal as though it is his last. Three young women dressed in low cut shirts and skin tight jeans sit around Trevor, drooling over his leadership. The bleach blonde massages his scalp while he takes a drink of water. A brunette is practically sitting on his lap waiting to feed him his next bite and the youngest of the three stands behind him rubbing his shoulders.

I stare at the smug look on his face. He appears to be a man who has everything he truly desires. The girls surrounding him, this mansion of a home made from an old school, and the love of all those people camped in the grass outside in the cold. He has the power to lead his army, the army that I gave him, and take them to the farthest corners of the globe and gain absolute control all because of me.

Trevor eyes me as I stand near the wall closest to the door and I pass him my most devilish grin. He might not understand all of my capabilities or even want to understand them, but I can see that he enjoys having me around. All he cares about is that I obey him and give him the cure he feels he deserves. He might not know about the secrets roaming through my mind or the demented thoughts I sometimes think of whenever I look upon his hideous face. I can't quiet grasp why I am so vengeful when I am near him, but I love the feeling. It is one of the best, most strongest parts of my being.

The rest of these people don't bother glancing my way or giving me one of the many praises that I have grown used to since I was brought inside. It is nice to be appreciated sometimes, but that can get distracting and I don't go for that.

"Good morning." Speaking of a distraction, Neil is walking up to me chewing on a piece of toast.

I play nice and smile right back, "Morning."

"Did you sleep well?" he asks, then acts like he's confused, "Or do you even sleep? I guess I don't know too much about you. The zombies just slow down, they don't really fall asleep and as far as I know, the vamps simply keep moving and hunting."

"I sleep." I say quickly, getting him to shut up.

He smiles and says, "Good. People deserve sleep. It gives us time to unwind and think about things.

"I take it you had a lot to think about last night." I say.

Neil takes another bite of bread, then speaks with his mouth full, "I did think a lot, but I didn't get much sleep because of it. I just can't rack my brain about what makes you tick. I studied your blood under a microscope dozens of times yesterday."

"What did you find?" I ask, genuinely curious.

"You are very similar to zombies and the vamps. The cells are dead and the blood doesn't move. It just sits stagnant in your system yet it somehow has the ability to reproduce itself. I'll need stronger equipment to get to the bottom of things, but I'm going to find out everything I possibly can about you." Neil rambles on and on, not giving me anything worth listening to. "Maybe one day, after some testing and experiments, I can find a cure for you. Of course, I would need a bigger sample and you would have to be willing to be a part of the tests, which we won't know if they would be fatal or effective. I believe it would be worth..."

"Who said I wanted you to find a cure?" I ask, interrupting him. "I never asked you to look into something like that especially when I don't want to be cured."

He raises an eyebrow and shakes his head, "I'm sorry, I just thought you would want to be human again once the world is cured. I mean, I would want that more than anything."

"Well, I'm not like you. I enjoy this life and everything I can do with it." I snap.

"But, don't you want the life you used to have? There has to be someone out there that you care about enough to want to go back to your old life. Living as a dead creature, doomed to wander the earth for God knows how long, that's not what us humans were meant for. You should want a cure for yourself." Neil insists.

I pass him an annoyed smile and say, "I don't want a cure. I wasn't meant to live as a *normal* human that is why I was given this life in the first place. I was not strong enough to fight the pain before this and now I am. There isn't even the slightest part of me that wants to trade what I have now to live as a pathetic human being."

Neil looks shocked at what I've just said, like he has never heard someone say that they are happy with their life. He should get used to hearing it from me because the part of me that may have wanted a cure is gone.

He finally nods his head and accepts my answer, "Fine, I'm sorry I ever brought up the subject. I'll just leave you alone until Trevor sends you down to my room."

I shrug as he walks away from me and turn my attention to the window. My hand is shaking as I stare at the bars protecting the glass from the outside. My fingers on my right hand are twitching and I glance down to see it. I ball it in a tight fist, then grab onto it with my left hand to stop the shaking.

There is no reason for me to feel anything other than glee for my current state of being. I love what I am.

I grit my teeth and turn my attention back to the man who drives the revenge out of me and the shaking slowly goes away until my mind is completely blank once more.

* * *

After breakfast and the grueling moments I spent listening to those girls swoon over Trevor as he pulled himself away from them, he decided that we would go outside and visit with the common folk. He told me that even more people have flocked this way since I was brought into the school. I guess once they heard that I was willing to give up the cure, they eagerly volunteered to follow Trevor wherever he may go.

Stupid humans. They will never learn.

The sun is hidden by a few clouds this morning and there is no breeze to bring a chill to the air. It is warmer than it has been and many of the people have shed their heavier coats for the day. The thick fabric and the cold air conceals their scent, so I am finding my own joy in this warm day.

As Trevor had stated, the crowd doubled over the last ten hours. Tents and other manmade shelters have completely covered the school yard. Some have even taken over the lawns of the nearby houses as well as barging into the homes for shelter.

The larger men have joined the rest of Trevor's army. They are being taught how to use a certain type of gun underneath a tent close to the school building. The women are busy cleaning clothes and making breakfast for their families and loved ones.

I stare at them in awe. They are living right on top of each other in this small area of space. It's as though they believe being this close to the cure will grant them the ability to use it whenever they please. Maybe they think it will land right in their laps if they close their eyes and pray hard enough. Like I would ever do something as ridiculous as give these random people a gift as amazing as what flows in my blood. Trevor is lucky to have what I chose to give him so far.

I follow him and the few others who walk with us. I step foot on the grass outside and instantly feel hundreds of eyes upon me. People have stopped what they are doing, turning their heads to eyeball the current savior of mankind. Their jaws drop and they ask various questions if I am really the cure or if I'm really what they say I am. I actually wish there was a zombie or a vamp right here so I can show them the gift they have been longing to see. That would be a satisfying reward for all of us.

Trevor and I walk on. Unfortunately there are no zombies lurking through this crowd or vampires hiding in the shadows.

The people move out of the way and back away from me when I get too close to them. Fear protrudes from their pores and is written on their faces when I glance to them. Some try to hide their disgust when they get a glimpse of my pale skin and demonic appearance.

They think of me as a freak of nature cursed to walk the earth as one of the undead. At least I am a freak who serves a purpose. Those zombies and vampires out there, they are good for nothing other than providing me with a snack. I need them around in order for these people to need me. If those creatures are gone I will be useless, but I could still have some fun with my life. Humans will always be here to taunt, to sneak a quick taste when I want one. It would be so easy too.

I smile and let out quiet laugh thinking about how these humans see me and everything I could do to them if I were given the chance. My smile confuses the few standing closest to me and they quickly retreat only forcing my smile to widen.

Trevor is leading me to an area in the grass he has covered with a large canopy to block the sun. There are a few folding tables set up on the grass that people are gathered around. A few of them are the vamps I cured, trying to learn new ways to fight and take down an enemy. They are uncoordinated and clumsy, but they still try. At another table, a muscular woman is showing three small children how to load a gun and aim properly. I guess it's good to get them started while they're young.

I stand at one of the metal support posts and watch as the crowd moves away from me. I fold my arms over my chest and stare at them with defiance in my posture and a smirk on my face.

A young girl and her father approach me, getting closer than any other person has dared since I came out here. The little girl holds onto a stuffed dog like her life depends on it and the man keeps a strong grip on her shoulders in case she chooses to stray too far from him. He stares at me in shock, with his mouth hanging open and shame in his eyes. They move within a few feet from me, then stop and stare, waiting for me to acknowledge them.

"Can I help you?" I ask, giving them what they want.

"What are you doing, Bridget?" the father asks. "Why did you choose to join him?"

I run my fingers through my hair and say, "I take it you know the old me."

He passes me a look of confusion and says, "What do you mean?"

I shrug, " Exactly what I said. You clearly aren't here to see me when you expected to see the weak thing I *used* to be. I hate to tell you that she's gone now."

"So your plan worked then." He states and lowers his eyes. "You wanted to make everything disappear, I guess it worked."

I smile and say, "Of course it worked. You think she could keep me locked away from this world forever? I am the main part of her life, the only part that means something to the world she planned on saving."

"So you still plan on giving the cure to those who need it?" he asks.

"What does it matter to you? You aren't sick or dying or part of the undead and neither is your daughter. Why do you care who gets the cure?"

"Because humans deserve it. I know you used to think

the same thing. I know you wanted it and wanted to be out of this place more than anything. When you first came here, I knew you were scared and sad, but you still refused to give Trevor what he wanted."

The man moves closer to me and keeps his voice low so only I can hear him speak. "Whatever this is that you have become, I know you still want the same thing. You don't want that man to get what he wants when he has hurt you in a way that can't be undone. You want the revenge I know you deserve so you can get out of here. Think about it and you'll see that I'm right."

I smile and tilt my head to the side. I like this man. He speaks his mind and says things that really get on my nerves, but I like that.

I lean closer to him and see his grip tightening on his daughter's shoulders, "You're right. As annoying as you may be right now, you are right about revenge. I don't know why I want it so badly, but I could rip into him and tear him to shreds with my bare hands and stand up with a smile on my face."

"Then why haven't you done that yet? He set you free and you can do whatever you want. Why not get revenge?" he asks.

It is getting difficult to understand this man's motives in coming to speak with me. At first he seemed upset and pissed off that I have changed enough to join Trevor and his men. But now, a mere few seconds after his arrival, he seems like he *wants* me to kill his leader. I can see it in his eyes the longer I stare at him and I know he wants something more than just an answer from me.

"I don't think you fully understand the situation that's going on here, guy." I reply. "I think you should consider taking your daughter and your life back into whatever shelter you call a home and let me deal with things as they commence. Trust me," I put my hand on his shoulder and he shudders in fear, "things will transpire that no one can control."

I take my hand from his shoulder and he quickly backs away. He lifts his daughter in the air and carries her through the shelter and disappears through the crowd. It feels good to strike fear into the hearts of those that care for the person I used to be. Something about it just makes it more meaningful to know that she is stuck in the prison of my mind and forced to watch as I run this life.

I take a deep breath through my nose and close my eyes for a short second. The voices are loud around me, blocking out any other sound that could possibly be heard beyond the school yard. I smell the sweat of their skin and the stink of their breath of those that stand nearby. It is strong, but not nearly as strong as the sweet aroma drifting up my nose and steadily getting stronger. I take another inhale, basking in that wonderful scent, letting my taste buds come to life for the meal they are about to devour.

A shriek of death and the sounds of gunshots quickly fill the air and I open my eyes. The small crowd under the canopy goes dead silent as those around them begin to run toward the street behind me. They shout inaudible words of terror for the monsters that are running after them.

The woman at the table with the children is quickly ushering them to run to their families and find safety while she handles the oncoming threat. I spy a few men grabbing swords and knives, preparing themselves for a fight. I look around for Trevor. He has a small pistol in his hand and stands behind a few of his men as he walks with them in the opposite direction that the people are running.

I lower my eyes and feel the hunger spreading through my body, taking over every inch of my very being. It makes me feel so alive and stronger than I could ever dream to be. I let my lips upturn into a devilish grin, clench my hands into fists and take one last inhale.

It's time for me to do what I was made to do.

* * *

I let the panic and terrified shrieks fill my ears as the ever familiar frenzy rises inside of me. I feel every inch of my body craving those wild beasts and the scent of them electrifies my taste buds. People sprint past, paying no attention as I slowly walk toward the threat instead of joining the cowards who choose not to fight. They run to their shelters and hide with their loved ones and pray that everything will work out for the best.

In a world like this, nothing ever does.

I inch toward the parking lot of the school and the crowd of humans is getting thinner. The groaning from zombies has overtaken the screaming and I let a tiny smile cross my lips. I stare ahead of me and keep my eyes peeled for that first zombie to come into my line of vision.

And there she is, lumbering across the parking lot, bumping into a rusty minivan with her arms outstretched for the humans just out of her grasp. Her black hair is long and tangled, thinning at the top of her scalp. The dress she is donning is tattered by her ankles and holes reveal a very pale and veiny stomach.

I turn toward her and roll my neck, listening to the muscles pop and pull against me. I clench my hands into fists and take a long whiff of my future meal. I lick my lips, then let my legs do the work for me. I feel like I'm flying over the pavement as the world whips by in a quick blur. The faces of the people still running for their lives are nothing more than a peach colored blob in my peripheral vision.

My left hand grabs the collar of the female zombie and I stop her dead in her tracks. She howls at me and claws at the leather on my jacket, never piercing the material to get to my skin. I stare into those lifeless, black eyes and slam her body against the minivan parked behind her. Another growl escapes her throat, but I'm quick to muffle that annoying drone. I clamp my jaw down hard enough to break the skin on her neck and let that amazing flavor cover my tongue and drift down my throat.

She claws at my back and kicks her feet in the air in some ill-mannered attempt at getting away from me. I feel her blood sliding out of the corners of my mouth and down my chin, soaking through her grimy dress and the collar of my shirt. I take enough of her blood and flesh until I can no longer feel her struggling. I pull my head away from her neck and let go of her clothes. She falls to the ground with her body smacking against the concrete like a sack of potatoes.

I take a quick look around me. More zombies are piling into the parking lot. Guns are being fired from a few of Trevor's men, but none of them have an aim good enough to hit them in the head on the first shot. A nearly rotten one hits the grass as a bullet shoots through what is left of his stomach. Another bullet sprays his brains through the air and he smashes his face on the curb.

A shrill scream enters the air behind me and I quickly spin around. A male zombie has a young woman pinned against a tree. All she has is a long stick to protect herself with and that is less than useless in a situation such as this one. I dash across the lot, clearing the distance in just a few seconds. I charge at the zombie right as he grabs onto the stick and I tackle him to the ground. The woman screams once more then makes a mad dash out of this hell hole.

I pin this zombie to the ground and stare at the glossy black orbs against his pale face. His teeth are green and rotten, matching the yellow color under his fingernails. His skin is scabbed over and stinks of decay, but I still find myself grabbing his wrist and biting into it until I can taste the cold liquid that is his blood.

The seconds tick by and I let the dead zombie's arm slip from my hand and land on his stomach. Two more of them come stalking close to me, giving me no time of day. I reach for the ankle of the one closest to me and he trips over his feet crashing to the ground in front of him. The other zombie takes a bullet to the back of her head, while I dig my teeth into the flesh of the boy. He wriggles and squirms against my grip, but soon succumbs to my cure working it's magic.

A gunshot echoes around me and I feel a slight pinch in the back of my right leg. I release my grip on the zombie and wipe it's blood from my chin and mouth. Slowly, I pull myself to my feet and spin around facing the man with the Mohawk. Smoke is pouring from the barrel of his handgun and he wears a smile as though he is pleased with himself.

"I am very sorry," he states with much sarcasm to his voice, "you sort of blend in with these bastards so you can understand my confusion."

His aim with the gun is still at me and I can sense that he wants to pull that trigger one more time. I wipe more of the oozing blood from my mouth and take a deep breath, filling my nose with his scent. He raises the gun, aiming more for my head and just before he pulls the trigger, I leap through the air and land on the pavement behind him. I latch my grip onto the back of his denim jacket and throw him to the ground at my feet.

The gun flies from his grip, landing out of his reach and the wind gets knocked out of him. He coughs and gasps for air while turning onto his side to breathe more easily. With my left foot, I slam it against his stomach, pushing him onto his back where he belongs. I kneel down beside him and grab the collar of his jacket pulling his face closer to mine. His struggled breath is hot against my cheeks.

"You must forgive me, but you blend in with all of the other pathetic humans running around here." I whisper in his ear.

I bring my lips to his throat and sink my teeth into the warm flesh that has been taunting me for what feels like years since I became this way. I can feel his screams escaping his body as his blood oozes out of him and fulfills the hunger I have for humans. Words cannot explain the smoothness of his blood as it flows down my throat. The warm texture and the sweetness of his flesh is more succulent than I have ever dreamed it would be.

I rip away a chunk of flesh from his neck and his screaming grows muffled and faint. The weight of his head is increasing, but I hold him still. His arms have stopped flailing and he no longer tries fighting me off. I bite through the muscles and veins of his neck and let the sweetest taste in the world drift down my throat.

The minutes tick by and I finally let the Mohawk's head hit the ground when I release my grip. I stare at his lifeless form for another moment, watching the blood seeping from the wound on his neck. It is a gory scene, but I cannot keep the smile from my face. I can't shake the feeling of relief from my body. I finally had the privilege of tasting something that felt so forbidden to me. Those zombies and vampires had it all figured out right from the very beginning. Why chase after something dead when the blood and flesh of the living is much more rewarding.

The dead man on the ground before me never moves again, proving to the world that what flows through my veins will have no effect on human beings. They will not change into what I am nor will they suffer through life as a member of the undead. They will simply be dead and nothing more.

I get back to my feet and take a look around. The panic has died down and the gunshots have come to an end. People are no longer running in terror and I stare at the many zombies who have perished at the hands of Trevor's army. The three that I bit into aren't even a handful in the small mass that came after the food source in this community.

Footsteps approach me from behind and I slowly turn around. Trevor stands on the grass by the parking lot, a gun hanging from his grip and blood stains on his coat. The blood doesn't belong to him, but it still looks appetizing. The few men and women that have crowded around him stare at me with fear in their eyes and guns raised at my head and heart.

Trevor steps onto the pavement and nods to the bloody mess on my face. I wipe my chin with the back of my hand, not bothering to get every ounce of the crimson juiciness.

"Do I need to worry about you, Bridget?" he questions.

I step closer to him and hear the familiar sounds of guns cocking all around me, "You should always be worried about me."

He raises an eyebrow and says, "What's that supposed to mean?"

"Only what your mind wants you to believe." I grin.

He raises a gun and shouts, "Quit playing this damn game and promise me this will never happen again!"

I tilt my head to the side and allow my eyes to pass right through him. I can swear to him a million times that I will never touch the blood of another human being. It will be a massive lie, but a lie is what he wants to hear.

Finally, I smile and say convincingly, "It won't happen again."

"Good." He says, then lowers the gun, "Get back to the school so my men can clean up your mess."

Trevor turns his back on me and the wind brings his scent to my nose. I take a deep inhale and allow his sweet flavor to drift up my nostrils. Even with the guns aimed for my head and chest, I still want that blood beneath his skin to caress my tongue in a way that will ignite every sense in my body and bring an end to the revenge that I crave.

* * *

I stroll through the halls of the school with my head held high as some human blood remains on my chin and neck. I knew from the moment that liquid caressed my tongue that no other taste on the planet would ever measure up. It was like a forbidden fruit and I was lucky enough to steal some of its sweet nectar. My mind has been in this euphoric state and not even the eyes of the people around me can snap me out of it. In fact, they are making the feeling spread throughout my body.

I stare at the frightened people scattered around the building as I head for my room. All of them are panicking and fearful for their lives. Not only from the threat that just raided their precious town, but for the beast that now roams the halls in the very building they are meant to feel safe in. Their terrified glances cannot keep the smile from my face.

Some of these people move quickly, with guns in their hands as they head for the crowd outside to help maintain order. They keep their distance from me, pressing their bodies against the wall so they do not come within arm's reach. I think it is quite humorous how these people are so afraid of me, yet they know nothing about me at all.

I spot a small group of them, young and crying, crouching in the corner just before I turn down another hallway. Five of them are hovering together, too afraid to look up. One of them does and his eyes meet with mine. I lick my lips, tasting the blood still lingering on my skin, and pass him a devilish grin. He whimpers and wraps his arms around his friends even tighter. Tears are flowing from his eyes as he buries his face with the group and I keep walking.

I make it to my room and push the door open. I step inside and close it quickly. The candles are lit on the desk, but they are steadily getting shorter the longer they burn. They will soon be nothing more than a puddle of wax and a black dot where the wick once burned. I turn my head to my bed and spot the figure sitting upon it. His hair is a mess and a bruise has taken over his left eye. A small trickle of blood is oozing out of the corner of his mouth and he dabs at it with a grey rag.

I lean away from the door and stare at his face. Somebody hurt him while I was away. I will have to find that person and deal with him for marring something that belongs to me, but for now I can only focus on the sweet liquid slowly oozing from the cut on Jason's upper lip.

I glide across the floor, moving closer to the bed until he looks up and lowers the rag to his lap. He stares at the blood on my face and hands and worry quickly writes itself across his face.

"Are you okay?" he asks, clearly unknowing of what happened outside.

I inch my way to him, my eyes are focused on his lips and I say, "Never better.

"What happened outside?" he asks.

"Zombie attack." I say, creeping closer to him.

"I thought that's what was going on. I heard the commotion and tried running to help, but some guy hit me to get me out of the way." He replies.

"That's unfortunate. You'll have to show me who he is and we can deal with him together."

He raises an eyebrow and cocks his head to the side, "Why are you staring at me like that?"

"Like what?" I ask, just a few more feet to go.

He stands from the bed and backs away from me, "Like you want to rip me to pieces."

I shake my head, "You must be shaken up from the whole ordeal. I'm fine."

He keeps backing up until he hits the wall behind him, giving him nowhere to run without me catching him. The blood is still by his mouth, beckoning me to come closer and closer until I allow it to engulf my tongue in that mouth-watering liquid. I move quicker than he notices and I pin him against the wall. Fear takes over his eyes and drenches his skin in that sweet sweat on his brow.

His fear smells delicious.

"Please, if you're going to kill me just make it quick." Jason pleads.

"I would never kill you." I whisper as I stare into his teary eyes.

"Then what are you doing?"

His lips are quivering and his hands are shaking. He holds his breath while I move my lips closer to his. I close my eyes and bring my mouth to his. His lips are moist from the blood on his cut and his entire body is tense from our en-counter. I stick my tongue out and drag it from his chin, then back to his lips, licking every last ounce of blood from his face.

I pull my head away from him and allow him to breathe again. His body relaxes, but there is still a trace amount of fear in his eyes. I don't want him to be afraid of me. I want him to enjoy this and crave me just as much as I crave him. I want him to be a part of the future I plan on creating with him by my side when I save the human race.

"I promise that I would never kill you." I say quietly, breaking through the silence taking over the room.

He slowly nods his head and stares down at the floor. His hands are shaking and he shoves them into the pockets of his faded jeans. There is something on his mind that doesn't have to do with the attraction between us. I step closer and run my fingers through his hair and down the length of his face.

"What's the matter, Jason?" I say quickly.

"What are we doing here?" he replies with a sigh.

I raise an eyebrow and say, "I don't understand what you

mean."

"I mean, why are we still here? We need to find a way to get out of here and get back to the city. We have to get back to the original plan of giving the cure to someone who will use it wisely."

"You think we have strayed from that plan?" I ask.

He nods and says, "Yeah, we've been stuck here for a few weeks now and we have our freedom. We can leave any-time we want."

I take a step away from him and stare into his wonderful, dark eyes. He seems passionate about the words he is saying. The look in his eyes is sincere and I feel the need to say what he wants to hear.

"Who's to say that isn't part of my plan?" I say and his eyes light up.

"It is?"

I shrug, "Let's just take this time to enjoy the small luxuries that Trevor wants to bestow upon us. Things will transpire and the world will be able to feel safe again."

He nods and says, "Can you promise that?"

"Of course I can."

He smiles and brings his hand to my chin. I feel him wip-ing away some of the excess blood that remains on my skin. His fingers are soft and soothing and he caresses my face so gently, never taking his eyes off of mine. I lift my right hand and pull the shades from my face. The sun cannot get to them in here and I want to see him fully.

"You really have changed, haven't you?" he questions.

"Only for the better." I reply.

He puts a hand on the back of my neck and forces his lips onto mine. The fear he once had of me is gone as he massages my tongue with his. I feel his hands rubbing up and down my back, feeling every inch of me through my clothes. I move my hand to his waist and feel his smooth skin under his shirt. He pulls me closer and our bodies finally touch.

I wrap my fingers around his shirt and hold on tight. We

move away from the wall and he gently pulls me towards the bed with our lips still sealed together. The want for him is growing stronger by the second. My breathing has gotten faster and there is a tingling sensation flowing up and down my spine. We topple onto the bed and Jason lies on top of me.

He breaks our kiss and stares intently into my eyes. He runs his fingers through my hair and caresses my cheek with a smile on his face.

"Ever since the day I met you I've wanted to be with you." He says quietly.

I smile in return and say, "Good things always come to those who wait."

He slowly lowers his face toward mine until our lips touch once more. I close my eyes and let the emotions run through me, taking over every inch of my being. He runs his hand down my side then gradually goes under my shirt, feeling my soft skin against his rough fingertips. Just as he is about to graze his fingers over my stomach, a sound in the hallway interrupts us.

Once again, he pulls himself away from me and both our heads turn toward the door of the room. Footsteps are quickly approaching from the other side until they stop completely. Next, a loud banging fills the room as a fist hits against the door over and over.

* * *

I stare at the locked door and listen to the banging of the

fist on the other side. The man yelling at us to open the door is not Trevor nor anyone that I recognize. He sounds angry though, there is much hatred and fear in his voice as he screams profanities at us. Jason stands a few feet away from me, waiting for the door to burst open or me to be unwise and open it myself.

"Open the damn door!" the man shouts again. "You need to pay for what you've done you fucking freak."

A louder sound hits the door next and the whole thing vibrates. They are trying to kick the door in. I have a feeling I know why this man is angry with me. He most likely saw what happened outside with that Mohawk man and I can only assume he doesn't want to risk something like that happening again.

There are other angry voices filling the hall beyond the door. Men and women both are shouting, cursing my name and the very thing that I am. The cure means nothing to them right now. All they care about is destroying a monster like me and ending a threat that could easily rip this place apart.

They kick at the door again and it shakes uncontrollably in the frame. The hinges are old and rusted, it wouldn't take much to break the lock and burst inward at us. I turn to Jason. He is standing tall with his hands clenched into fists. Behind him are the boarded windows that prove to be of no use. It would take some time to pull the nails out of the wood in order to get through and by then the angry mob in the hallway could very well be inside with us. That would be dangerous for us both.

"C'mon out, beast!" the man shouts and kicks at the door.

I would prefer to be called something a little more suiting to my nature. A beast makes me sound like an animal and a monster is something of nightmares. I can't be called a zombie or a vampire, but I deserve to be called something other than the names they are shouting through the door.

"Bridget," Jason speaks up, "what should we do?"

I look back to the door and take a step forward, "Maybe we should give them what they want."

I move closer to the door and reach for the knob as they kick at it one more time. I feel the cold metal in my grip and hold it firmly. All I need to do is twist my wrist and the lock will be set free and the door will swing open. They will get what they want and face the thing that ended the life of a human being. I just need to turn the doorknob.

I listen to the sounds coming from the other side of the door before I turn the knob. They continue to shout at me and bang their fists against the walls and the door itself. Beyond their voices, I hear more footsteps rapidly approaching the scene. More people to add to the mob.

"What the hell is going on here?" Trevor's voice shouts, barely loud enough to carry through the angry yelling.

"That *thing* you brought here needs to pay for what it did to Randall." The shouting man speaks, mentioning the guy with the Mohawk.

"Yeah," the mob shouts in agreement, "The bitch needs to die!"

"Listen to me!" Trevor yells over them, "I saw what she did out there and how she killed Randall, but I am not going to kill her because of it. She is our cure, our future of surviving this apocalypse. One human being is not reason enough to kill her."

I keep my hand on the doorknob and listen to them speaking about me. Trevor has a way of talking sense into his followers and I am positive he can get these people to back away from the door. From the smells coming from the other side, there are too many humans to try to fight through and get myself and Jason out of here alive. I cannot risk his life for this.

"Who the fuck cares if she is the damn cure!" one of the mob members shouts back at Trevor. "She is capable of killing us and we all know she wants to. We can't let this thing walk freely amongst us knowing at any second one of us could be next."

"How are we supposed to sleep at night if she could be planning to snack on our children?" a frightened woman adds to the argument.

"I get it, believe me I do." Trevor replies, "But the cure is important. If we as humans plan on having any future at all she has to stay alive."

I wish I could see through this damn wall to get a picture of what they are doing out there. My hearing only allows me so much and right now it is not good enough. I hear them talking, arguing about my fate in this world, but it is not theirs to decide. That belongs to me only.

"You're wrong Trevor." The man who was kicking at the door retorts. "Humans can survive without a cure. We will find a way to take down the zombies and the vamps without adding another threat to the mix. That thing in there needs to die."

His words are followed by some kind of commotion. Feet are scuffling against the tiled floor of the hallway. They are shoving each other about because of a ridiculous argument. I hear something metal clanking together and a gunshot erupts through the air in a split second. The crowd goes silent and a body thuds to the floor right on the other side of the door.

"Anybody else want to fuck with me today?" Trevor shouts. "Anyone else care to risk our future because one man got killed out there?"

Another gunshot echoes around us and the smell of human blood drifts up my nose, igniting my senses. My mouth is watering and my hands are shaking. I could use another helping of that magnificent taste. It would make up for being so rudely interrupted a few moments ago.

I keep my hand on the door knob and slowly turn it until the lock clicks and the door opens. I let it swing inside the room, revealing a stunned crowd standing in fear. Two bodies lie dead at my feet and the blood of the men is pooling around their heads, completely wasted on the dirty floor.

Trevor stands with a gun in his grip at his side, glaring at the people who want to kill his most prized possession. His more loyal followers stand beside him, aiming their weapons at the unruly crowd in case they get out of hand once more. Women are shaking and crying on the shoulders of the men holding onto them. I catch a snide glare from an older woman to my right and turn my eyes to hers.

Her grey hair reflects in the sunlight and her aging eyes stare daggers at mine. Her lips are pursed together and I know she would just love to see me with a bullet in my head along with the two men on the floor. I take a step through the doorway and the crowd gasps and backs away. A few of them even take off down the hallway toward the nearest exit.

I smile and return her glare. She doesn't wince or back away at all. She keeps her position and refuses to move, even as I get even closer to her.

"You are not afraid of me?" I ask and more of them hide away in fear.

"Why on earth would I be afraid of a pathetic monster like you? You kill humans for no reason and yet you are allowed to stay alive." She replies.

I shrug and say, "I am the one who is going to save all of you. I am allowed to do whatever the fuck I want."

She takes a vengeful step toward me and says, "You are going to die a horrible death and when you do, not even burning in hell will grant you the torture you deserve for what you've done." The old woman spits at my feet, then gets dragged away by one of Trevor's men.

I never thought that killing one measly human would have this type of hateful effect on people. That man with the Mohawk deserved to die and I was the only one who could see it. I don't deserve anything but praise for ending that life.

"The rest of you get the hell out of here." Trevor orders and the crowd disperses quickly.

My hands shake at my sides as I stand frozen in the doorway. I have done nothing wrong. This is what I was created for. To be the savior of these people. To bring an end to not only the zombies and vampires, but also the lives of those that don't deserve to walk the earth with the rest of us. These angry people are more than wrong about what they think of me.

I finally turn my eyes away from where that woman was standing and spot Trevor's men dragging her down the hallway. They stop outside the door that is constantly guarded and stinks of blood. That door gets open for a brief moment and the woman gets thrown inside. She screams and shouts, then the door slams shut in her face.

Trevor comes to my side and places a hand on my shoulder, "Don't listen to anything those people say. I saw what you did and I have no intention of killing you. You are much too valuable for that."

I look up at him and can't think of anything to say. I can only stare at the smile looming on his face. His grip on my shoulder tightens and he guides me back into the old class-room, then gently shoves me inside.

"I will, however, need to keep an extra eye on you in order to keep my people happy. You'll understand that this door will be locked from the outside from now on." Trevor states, then backs away from the doorway. "Just consider yourself lucky I'm not taking that boy away from you."

As he shuts the door in my face, I feel the revenge rising in the pit of my stomach. It is a strong feeling, stronger than the hunger I have for humans that constantly burns inside of me. Stronger than the need to get the hell out of here and much stronger than the craving I feel for Jason.

This severe hatred I feel for that man has just grown from simple revenge into the need to destroy him.

* * *

The day goes on as it would normally do. I can smell the men standing on the other side of the door with their guns as they keep guard. We are trapped in here. Jason can try prying the wood away from the windows as long as he wants but it will never break free. His fingers are bleeding with splinters from trying and he has gotten nowhere.

I stare at the door, my feet are planted to the floor in front of it. Jason sits on the bed tending to the splinters on his hands and wincing every few seconds from the pain of pulling them out of his skin. His blood might smell enticing, but I would much rather taste that of the men outside of this room. It would be more satisfying to end their lives than just get a taste from someone I plan on keeping around for a while.

"Bridget, you can't stand there all day. They aren't going to let us out." Jason calls from across the room.

"You should never doubt things when anything could happen." I reply.

He scoffs and says, "Well, that *anything* could happen right about now. They could come through the door and say screw it to the cure and kill both of us."

I ignore him and keep my gaze on the door. My hands are tucked into the pockets of my leather jacket and my shades hang over the low-cut collar of my shirt. Of all the gifts that I have, there is nothing for me to do from inside this room that will be of an advantage. They have that door locked up tighter and stronger than I can get through. There is no way out through the ceiling for me to jump through and the heating vents have all been sealed off. I feel like a worthless human trapped in here.

It is not a good feeling for me to have.

"Will you please just come sit with me?" Jason asks.

I slowly nod my head. There is no reason for me to stare at a door I cannot get through. I turn on my heels and saunter across the room to the bed. I sit on the mattress beside him and watch the blood dripping from his fingertips as he picks another splinter from his skin. There are tiny scratches all over his hands from prying at the wood over the windows.

The longer I stare at the blood on his hands, the more I think of that room down the hall. There are people in there, no doubt they are being tortured and beaten. The scent of blood is far too strong to assume otherwise.

"Where did they keep you before you were brought to this room?" I ask.

His hands stop moving and he stares at the floor. His lips are quivering when he opens them, but he takes a moment to think before he speaks.

"Umm," he begins, "they had me locked in a room not far from this one."

"The one down the hall with the two guards?" I ask.

He nods, "Yeah, that one."

"What did they do to you in there?"

He swallows hard and says, "I, umm, I don't want to talk about it."

I take one of his hands and hold it tightly in mine, "Please," I say and he slowly turns his eyes to mine, "tell me what happened."

He lowers his eyes and nods, "That room used be a large storage room for the science department or something. They had a huge refrigerator for the animals they would dissect and other things." He explains. "There were three other guys still alive in when they took me there. They were hanging upside down from the ceiling with chains around their ankles. All of them were naked while a man stood behind them with a chain in his hands and a whip hanging from his waist."

I knew it was a torturing room. Trevor never struck me

as the type of man to not have something like that here.

"They forced me to take my shirt off, then tied my wrists to a hook hanging from the ceiling. They hit me a few times with a whip, trying to get me to blab about you, but I always kept my mouth shut. So they forced me to watch the other people get beaten and there was so much blood on the floor. They brought in a zombie on a leash and let it feed on one the prisoners and they laughed about it as we screamed." He holds my hand tighter, reliving the nightmare that happened only a few days ago. "They would let the zombie get so close to me that it almost scratched me, but they never hurt me like they did the others.

"Trevor would come in sometimes and try to get me to tell him things about you, but I never did. I planned on dying with the secrets about you, because they don't deserve them. But when he brought me here and told me how things have changed, I knew that you gave him what he wanted. Part of me was grateful to be out of that room, but you weren't sup-osed to give up and let him take the cure like that."

"That was the old me. *She* was the one who gave up, not me." I say.

"But why? That was never part of the plan." He says.

I shrug and feel some sympathy for the person I used to be, "She wasn't strong enough to face the pain in her mind. It was too much for her. I don't have the same memories she tried to deal with. She wanted them gone and allowing me to take over was her only option."

He nods and says, "Bad memories do suck, I have plenty of them. But you can't go through life without them. It's what makes us stronger."

I take my hand away from his and say, "You want her to come back?"

He hesitates for a moment before saying, "I don't know. I liked who she was, but her heart belonged to Ryder and I knew I never stood a chance with that. You want me now and I can still see the part of the girl I met that I really like. Call me selfish, but I wouldn't want to give that up."

"Then I am not going anywhere. And as far as I can tell, that Ryder doesn't stand a chance against you." I reply.

He passes me a smile and reaches for my hand again. He holds onto it while planting a soft kiss against my lips. It turns into something more than just a tiny kiss and our lips stay connected for a long moment.

I close my eyes and let the warmth of his body take the cold away from mine. He places a hand on the back of my neck and I feel something flowing through me that doesn't feel quite right. A strange pinching sensation is roaming in my mind and it's making me very uncomfortable. A face flashes in the darkness behind my eyes and the horrible feeling is too much for me to handle.

I push Jason away from me and scrunch my eyebrows, angry at the pinching still lingering in my mind. My hands are shaking and I stand from the bed and move away from him. I run my fingers through my hair, shaking my head from side to side and I know something is not right. That face in my head was only there for a second, but those hazel orbs burn through me like the sun when it hits my unshielded eyes.

Jason stands from the bed and moves toward me, "Are you okay?" he asks, with concern in his voice.

I grit my teeth and shake my head again and try to get my hands to stop shaking, "I don't know. Something doesn't feel right."

He stares at me with confusion in his eyes. He tries taking another step closer and I quickly take one backwards. My feet move without my command as though my body wants to be far away from the man I am attracted to. If this is some sign that the old me is trying to fight her way back into the world, then she needs to step off. That is a war she does not want to begin because I will win. She knows I am stronger and that she cannot see past the sad memories clouding her vision.

I stand still for a moment, letting Jason's eyes stare at me as he keeps his distance. I take a few calming breaths and soon that pinching feeling in my brain starts to fade into nothing. My hands stop shaking and I finally bring myself to look at him once more.

"What the hell was that about?" he asks.

"Nothing," I reply and take another deep breath, "just nothing."

"It didn't seem like nothing. Once we brought up Ryder, it's like you changed for a second." Jason says, taking a small step closer.

"Trust me, I'm fine. Just a slight headache." I say and force my lips to smile at him.

He nods and slowly closes the gap between us. Gradually, he lifts his hands to my shoulders and calmness instantly takes over me. The longer I stare into his deep brown eyes, the more I feel like myself again and the attraction toward him builds. Now isn't the time to act upon that attraction, but as soon as we get away from this shithole, there will be nothing to stop us.

Not Trevor or his goons and especially not my mind.

* * *

Jason's stomach growls as he lays in the bed beside me. He hasn't eaten anything since some time yesterday and I doubt Trevor will be kind enough to grant him a meal today. It is still very early in the morning and things could always change, but my mind is telling me that it won't happen.

Rain drops hit against the windows of the building and I hear thunder erupting in the sky. The hallway outside the room has been silent most of the night with the occasional cough or small conversation between the two men standing guard.

I sit up and put my feet on the floor. I smooth the hair out of my face and take a look around the dark room. There is nothing in here that would aide with an escape. No pry bar to remove the wood from the door or a gun to kill those men easily. It is going to take a lot more than my bare hands to get us out of here in one piece. I don't doubt that Jason can fight, but with their guns, he'd be dead in seconds.

He stirs on the bed beside me and I glance over my shoulder. He stares up at me with a smile across his lips, then slowly sits up. He stretches his arms over his head and yawns. Our eyes quickly turn to the door when we hear the footsteps stomping through hallway toward it.

"It is too early for this bullshit." Jason says.

"I couldn't agree with you more." I reply, then stand from the bed with him by my side.

The locks on the door are being undone and soon the rusty hinges squeak until the door hits against the wall and Trevor storms inside. Three others are right on his tail and each one has a large rifle aimed for us. I can see that my freedom here has been short lived.

"My people are very upset with what happened yesterday, Bridget." Trevor speaks calmly as he stands in the middle of the room. "They are demanding justice for what you've done or my plans for the future will be nothing more than a failed attempt. Because of what you did, those people would not let me sleep until I agreed to give them what they want."

"So you're going to kill me?" I ask.

He shakes his head, "No, it hasn't come down to that just yet. I promised my people that you will pay for the life you took from them, but I can't give up the cure."

"Then what is it going to be? Are you going to throw me

back in the cage outside? Or perhaps it would be more suiting to torture me like you do with the others that don't quite agree with you?" I ask.

"Those few thoughts had crossed my mind, but I like it better with you in here." He replies with a smile. "I know that you are enjoying your time with your little friend, but if my people aren't happy, then you shouldn't be happy either."

Trevor motions for his men to move and two of them quickly advance toward Jason. Their guns are aimed for his forehead and he raises his arms in surrender so they do not shoot. I try moving to stand in front of him, blocking their aim, but Trevor has already seen that move. He pulls a gun out from behind his back and points the barrel at my head, not afraid to pull the trigger.

"I'm a pretty good shot and my men will kill him if you do anything stupid." He threatens.

I grit my teeth and stand still for the time being. The two large men latch their meaty hands on Jason's arms and pull him away from me. He digs his feet into the floor and they stop with him at the doorway before leaving the room.

"Do you have any idea what you're doing to this boy?" Trevor asks, "That room down the hall is my special little torture chamber, but I'm sure he already told you that. Because of you, he is going back in there and will never be coming out."

"No, please." Jason pleads and the men only hold onto his stronger.

I keep my fists tightly clenched and my lips sealed together.

Trevor keeps his gun pointed at me as he walks the short distance toward me, "Was it worth it, killing Randall yesterday?" he asks.

I smile and words finally find me, "Of course it was."

"It was worth risking his life for the taste of human flesh?" he asks again, pressing the barrel of his gun against my forehead.

"You will never pull the trigger. You need me to cure the people for your army. How else would you take over the world?" I say.

He nods in agreement, "You are right about that. I can't control the world without the cure. But I don't exactly need him and maybe it would just be a waste of time to torture him."

Trevor turns away from me and aims the gun at Jason. He squeezes his finger around the trigger and the world around me passes by in a blur. I leap through the air and tackle Trevor to the floor. The gun flies from his grip, but a bullet has been fired. I don't take the time to see where it landed or who it hit, but I hear a grunting coming from a man in pain.

Trevor growls at me, then slams his elbow against my ribs twice in a row. I roll away from him and grit my teeth from the slight pain in my bones. He is slowly crawling to get to the gun and I see his men across the room changing their aim to me. They let go of Jason and he drops to his knees, clutching one of his legs in pain. The bullet had hit him and the smell of his blood drives the revenge in my unbeating heart forward.

I clench my hands into fists and quickly jump to my feet. One of the men fires his gun and I dart to the side getting out of the way just in time. The bullet smashes in to the brick wall behind me, sending a small cloud of dust floating through the air. I speed across the room, moving faster than either of them could see, and slam my fist against the tallest man's face. He flies backward, crashing to the floor next to Jason and blood pours from his broken nose.

One of them runs into the hallway and the other is fumbling with his gun. The trigger is stuck and his eyes are trained on me instead of trying to fix the problem. I quickly step closer to him and grab his wrist and spin it behind his back until his shoulder pops out of place and the gun falls from his fingers. I kick the back of his leg and he kneels before me.

Finally, I bring my mouth to the side of his neck and clamp my jaw down hard against his skin. It breaks and that amazing warm blood flows down my throat while he screams out in pain.

A gunshot blasts through the air and the man goes limp in my hands. Trevor stands with the gun in his outstretched arm and I let the dead man fall to the floor. I pull myself to my feet and stare into the wild eyes of the man I want to rip apart.

"Maybe you do deserve to die." He seethes.

I shrug and say, "Maybe I do, but that isn't for you to decide."

He lets out a cackling laugh as he speaks, "I own you bitch! I am the only one who gets to decide what happens to you."

Trevor raises the gun and his finger slowly closes around the trigger. Before that blast fills my ears and takes over my mind, I have a flash of something before my eyes. My old life, maybe, a family gathered around a table enjoying a nice meal. It quickly changes to the happiness between two young lovers and I recognize myself in the picture but not the boy I am with. That goes to the hatred I feel for everyone in this building and I am letting the revenge slip through my fingers.

The bullet flies through the air and hits my shoulder close to my neck. I wince from the pain and take a step backward. I press my hand against the wound and fight through it. I see Jason with his arms wrapped around Trevor's legs as they both fall to the floor and the gun slips from Trevor's grip once more. Jason pulls himself to his knees and slams his fist into Trevor's jaw three times until the man's eyes close. He quickly pulls himself to his feet and limps toward me, leaving the gun behind on the floor.

"It's time we get out of here." Jason says, but I stand still.

My eyes are glued to the target lying on the floor. He is barely moving and his eyes are fluttering open and closed.

Blood seeps from the cut on the top of his head and out through the corners of his mouth. I can see his chest moving up and down with every breath he takes. It would be so easy to bend over and grant him the death that has been a long time coming. I could suck the very life from his body while I get to taste the succulent blood that I have been craving ever since the moment I woke up in this form.

"C'mon, we gotta go!" Jason tugs on my arm, but I do not turn to him.

I can't move my eyes away from my prey. I take a step toward Trevor and feel a sharp tug on my arm. Jason pulls me away from the body and drags me toward the door.

"We don't have time for this, we have to go!" he shouts and forces me away from my prize.

There is rage boiling in the pit of my stomach, rapidly flowing through the rest of my body as I leave the nagging reminder of revenge on the floor in that room. My hands are shaking, but my feet move forward with Jason as he leans against me while we walk briskly.

The wound on Jason's leg is keeping him from putting too much weight on it. I shake the revenge from my mind and put my arm around him to help him move faster. He is only focused on getting out of here and will not let me turn back. His arm is wrapped tightly around my waist, pushing me forward with him. Not only is he forcing me to move, but that annoying pinch in the back of my mind has returned and is egging me to get out of the building.

There are three people rushing at us as soon as we step foot out of the classroom. I recognize the two men who always stand guard outside of Trevor's torture chamber. The third one is a burly woman with short blonde hair and dark makeup around her eyes. She carries a sharp machete while the men have guns aimed at us. We stop moving and I glare at each one of them, ignoring their demanding words.

The one standing closest to the wall is shorter than the giant in the middle of the three. The short one's hands are shaking and the gun is wavering in his grip. I keep my eyes on my target and, before any of the three can react, I let go of Jason and lunge through the air. A gunshot erupts around us as I wrap my arms around the short one and tackle him to the floor. The bullet from his gun smashes into the moldy ceiling sending chunks of drywall on top of us.

I grab onto his hair and slam his head against the tiles until a sharp crack comes from his skull and the life is drained from his face. I quickly snatch the gun from his grip and point it at the other man left standing and squeeze my finger around the trigger. I don't have to look to know that the bullet had killed him. The loud thud from his massive body hitting the floor gives that away.

The woman is the only one to remain. She grits her yellow teeth and her eyes dart back and forth between Jason and myself. He is wounded and weak. She knows she could take him down in seconds. She makes up her mind and lets out a shrill growl as she goes for him. The machete is raised above her head as she runs and heated anger fills her eyes. I toss the gun to the ground and take off after her and connect my body with hers, slamming her against the old metal lockers on the wall.

The scream emanating from this woman is louder than a gunshot and it is right in my ears. I grit my teeth and reach for the weapon still tight in her grasp. She tries elbowing me over and over in my chest and stomach, but does not prevail. I latch my fingers tight on her wrist and pin her arm to the wall and she lets out another scream.

"It's time for you to shut up." I seethe and clamp my jaw against her sweaty skin until blood pours out and fills my mouth.

She continues fighting against my grip, elbowing me and clawing against my neck and the back of my head. I keep stealing the very life from her body and my strength only grows while hers is rapidly fading. Her arm slowly goes limp in my grasp and I let go of her wrist. I back away from her, stare at the pale hue overtaking her face until she falls to the floor with her comrades.

I face Jason who is hugging the wall, then I glance to the room behind him. The pinch comes back to my brain and my eyes pull themselves away from the empty doorway and I move to Jason. I put my arm around him and we walk away from the bloody scene and head further away from my room. Further away from gaining my revenge.

We turn down the hallway that will take us to the caféteria and have no choice but to stop moving. Three woman and four men are blocking the way forward. That is the only way I know how to get out of here and backtracking will only slow us down.

One woman with hair as black as the night takes a step toward us, trying not to shoot if she doesn't have to, "We don't want to kill you." She says, but I know she speaks a lie.

I keep my steely eyes set on hers and don't move a muscle. My eyes pass over each of these people and I know I could make it out of here on my own. They would shoot at me and I would possibly get hit a couple of times, but all I need to do is jump over these people and run like hell to the door. Jason would be left behind to face the firing squad or Trevor's torturous wrath, but maybe that is what he deserves for blocking me from making a kill.

"Just listen to us," a man's voice speaks up and I turn my glare to him, "Just calm down and come with us. It doesn't have to end with us killing you."

As soon as those words leave his lips a barrage of bullets fills the air, coming from the hallway behind them and three of them instantly fall to the floor. The other four turn around and return fire, but there are too many bullets flying at them to make a difference. In just a few seconds they are lying in a heap on the floor, blood pouring from the many holes on their bodies, while Jason and I await to see who's coming around the corner.

I recognize Neil leading a small group of three with automatic rifles. One of them is the father I met outside before the zombie attack. He lowers the gun and waves for us to go with them. I nod and hold onto Jason. He limps against me and we make our way to exit the building.

* * *

Dark clouds have blocked out most of the sun, but the brightness of the day is still enough to bring a slight burning sensation to my eyes. I let go of Jason and quickly slip the sunglasses over my nose. Drops of water beads on the lenses but I still see everything out here perfectly.

There are three of Trevor's guards lying dead on the concrete sidewalk beside the door to the school. Each man has a few stab wounds in their chests and the weapons have all been taken from them. Blood has pooled around their bodies, mixed in with the puddles of rain water. I look away from the dead toward the campsite across the yard. The tents are all sealed and no one is outside to keep an eye on things. For a crowd of people Trevor claims to want justice for what I've done, it sure doesn't seem like anyone cared to show their faces to prove it.

"This way!" Neil shouts, pointing toward the tree and the street beyond it. "There are a few others waiting for us outside of town."

I nod, holding onto Jason while we move as fast as we can to keep up with them. He limps against me, but still runs and fights through the pain in his leg. We make it to the street and I hear the first gunshot coming from behind us. I turn my eyes and glance over my shoulder.

Armed men and women are pouring out of the school and chasing after us, shooting wildly in the air. The commotion coming from their guns causes the people in the tents to come outside to see what the hell is going on. I spot one man who has a shotgun of his own and takes out two of the bastards chasing us before ending up with a bullet in his own head. At least he died fighting for something that is right.

Neil leads us to another street a block away from the school and we make a sharp left. By now, people have started coming out of their houses and they stand on their porches to watch the show. A few of women duck back inside when the blasts catch their ears but the men stay put and get their weapons ready.

I look over my shoulder once more to count just how many are chasing us. I spot seven women who move swiftly down the street, darting between the parked cars and debris. Ten men sprint alongside them, grunting as their legs pump furiously after us. There are too many of them and much too few of us.

We turn onto another street and run behind an old grocery store. The others are leaning against the building, loading their guns and catching their breath. I let go of Jason and help him stand up by one of the others. He winces from the pain in his leg and applies pressure to the bleeding wound. The crashing footsteps of Trevor's army are rapidly approaching.

This is not how I pictured things would transpire in this town. I pictured myself killing Trevor as soon as I had gained his trust fully. Killing that man yesterday was part of my plan, but I never expected the people to hate me for it and turn against the cure. I never expected Trevor to treat me as a prisoner again or Jason to keep me from ending Trevor's life.

No, this is not what I was planning at all and everything is falling apart.

"What are we going to do? We didn't anticipate them to

start chasing us." A bald man questions as he looks all around him.

Neil runs his hands through his hair and says, "They were all supposed to be sleeping."

I listen to them trying to come up with a solution to their problem at hand. The father of the little girl is busy fidgeting with the safety on an automatic rifle he took from one of the dead guards. I snatch the gun from his shaking hands and turn the safety off. I then check to make sure it's loaded, then back away from them. There is only one way this thing will end with these people making it out alive and I am going to see that it happens. This is not the way my plan was supposed to go, but now that I am almost out of here, I might as well improvise until all of us are safe.

While listening to the protests coming from Neil and the father, I turn away from them and walk to the middle of the street just in time to see our enemy rounding the corner. I raise the rifle and hold my finger on the trigger, firing wildly at the line of men and women advancing toward me. Five of them go down as blood sprays from their bodies, mixing with the rain on the street. The others are quick to stop moving and dart behind the abandoned vehicles to shield themselves from my rampage.

The gunshots cease and the air goes silent for the moment. I keep my weapon raised and stare at the faces of those still brave enough to face me. My wet hair sticks to my face and my clothes are already soaked just like theirs. It affects them much more than it does me. They wipe the water from their eyes and shake the excess from their fingertips.

A skinny black man steps forward with his arms and gun raised in surrender. From here I can see his teeth chattering from the morning cold. He is not wearing a jacket and his arms are completely bare.

"Listen here girl," he shouts and takes another step closer, "we don't want to hurt you. We just need you to put the weapon down and come back with us."

The others around him are standing their ground with guns aimed for my head. It might not be me they want to hurt or kill, but the few hiding by the grocery store will be dead the second I give up and go back to the school. Trevor won't be so kind to me anymore or anyone who chooses to rise up against him. I am not about to deal with that.

"C'mon, Bridget," the man shouts and takes one more step closer, "just come back with me. I'll make sure no one gets hurts and the others you're with can go free. They can leave this place and go wherever they please. You're the only one that has to stay here."

I keep the rifle raised and say, "I'm sorry, I don't *have* to do anything."

I squeeze my finger around the trigger and three bullets enter that man's body. He crashes to the concrete and the rest of the enemy begins firing at me. I return the favor and let the bullets soar through the air, killing two more in seconds. I feel a pinch in my leg as one of them hits me and I quickly shoot that woman in the head. Another pinch hits my shoulder and I stammer back a couple paces, losing my aim.

I quickly get back in my place, but it is not my weapon that kills another one. Jason is poking his head and arms from around the grocery store, firing a small handgun at the few who are left standing. I smile and take aim once more, ending the lives of those who are left hiding by the vehicles.

The last man crashes to the ground and his gun flies from his grip. The bullets have stopped flying and the only sound I hear now is the pitter patter of raindrops falling from the sky. Neil and his three men quickly run to the dead and grab whatever weapons they can carry. I take a breath and lower the rifle, then turn to walk back to Jason. He leans against the building and lets the gun fall to his side. I am still very upset with him, but knowing he has my back slightly eases that anger.

Movement catches my attention and I look past Jason at the metal dumpster at the far end of the store. A straggler from the enemy we just took out quickly pops out from behind the dumpster and aims his small handgun at Jason and pulls the trigger. I raise my rifle and shoot it at the exact second which he fires his. The man's head flies backwards and he crashes to his back on the wet grass.

I sigh and lower the gun one more time, then keep moving. I turn my eyes to Jason and see the gun fall from his fingers and lands on the grass at his feet. A pained look crosses his face and he slides against the building until he sits on the grass. I let the rifle fall from my grip and sprint to his side. He holds a spot on his stomach and blood slowly seeps between his fingertips.

"No." I say, looking at the wound.

He takes a deep breath and says, "It's okay, I'm fine."

I move his hand away from the gash and more blood pours from a wound I could easily lose a roll of quarters in. I look back to his eyes and forget that he stopped me from killing Trevor and focus only on the need to keep him alive.

"Neil!" I shout. "We need you!"

Footsteps quickly rush from the street until the scientist stops and kneels right beside me. He stares at Jason, then glances to the gunshot wound. Jason moves his hand away and Neil lifts up the corner of his shirt to see it more clearly.

"Can you fix him?" I ask.

Neil studies the gash for a long moment then says, "It looks like the bullet just grazed him. I can fix it up, but not here. We need to get him out of the rain and to a place that's safe. Can you walk, boy?" he asks Jason.

"I think so." He replies.

He applies pressure to the wound then reaches for my hand. He grunts from the pain and I grab the gun from the grass before we get back to our feet. He puts his arm over my shoulder and I carry some of his weight as we walk.

"Let's get moving." I order and Neil leads the way once again.

* * *

The safe place we found is an old barn about a mile out-side of Trevor's community. The roof has a few holes in it, but the building itself is strong enough to hold up. The little girl was waiting with two women when we arrived and she ran to her father's arms. I learned his name was Phil and something about that struck me as familiar. I can't quite pin-point exactly where I would have heard that before. He tried explaining to me, but stopped before he said too much. He didn't want to upset me like he had before. Something else I am glad I don't remember.

Neil managed to get both of Jason's gunshot wounds cleaned and stitched up. He has a backpack with him and a first aid kit inside filled with everything he will need to doctor wounds like that. He even had gauze to cover the stitches and keep it from getting infected.

For now we are safe. We are hidden from anyone who tries following us out here and we have eyes covering every direction beyond the barn. No one followed us here and I don't smell any threat waiting for us on the road ahead. The others want to rest for a little while and eat before we head out again. Neil would like to wait for the rain to stop and the others eagerly agree. I guess I am impatient and would like to put as much distance between myself and that town as I possibly can.

I run my fingers through my dripping hair and spot Jason. He sits on a wooden barrel, his bloody hand pressed against his side as he leans against the wall of the barn. He looks fatigued with tired eyes as he stares at the hay covered ground under his feet. I kick some of it up as I slowly make my way over to him. My sunglasses are still covered with droplets of rain and I take them off to wipe the lenses with the bottom part of my shirt.

Jason smiles at me and pats his hand on the barrel beside him for me to sit, but I refuse. Seeing that he is alive and well has brought back my thoughts about what happened at the school and no longer do I feel the need to shove my feelings inside.

"Are you going to be okay?" I ask, genuinely concerned.

He nods, "I think so. Neil fixed me up as best as could with what he has."

"Good, because I have something to say to you and you need to be alive long enough to feel the regret for doing this."

He scrunches his eyebrows in confusion and says, "What the hell are you talking about?"

"You should have let me kill him." I say loudly and every soul in the barn turns their eyes to me.

Jason seems taken aback and says, "What?"

"You should have let me kill Trevor when I had the chance." I repeat with more anger to my voice.

He shakes his head and says, "We didn't have time for that. His guards were already on the way and both of us would be dead right now if we stayed."

"It would have been worth it." I shout.

He lowers his eyes and holds his stomach, "Forgive me for being selfish and wanting you and the cure to survive. Next time I'll know better."

"Well because of you keeping me from doing what I needed to do, he will never stop hunting us. He knows that we will be heading for the damn city and he'll find a way to beat us to it. All of us here will be killed then and it is all because of you." I argue.

"The city has an army of its own, Bridget," Neil's voice

interrupts us and I feel him approaching, "if Trevor does get there before we do, they will see that he is a threat and will take him out before he has the chance to do the same to them."

I spin around and glare at him, "You're wrong. I have seen what will happen if he gets to the city and get inside those walls. He will destroy it and kill everyone who stands in his way."

Phil steps forward, leaving his daughter to play with her stuffed dog, then asks, "How have you seen it?"

"I am more than just a cure or a freak or the monster that you people like to see. I can do things you humans could only dream of doing and you question it constantly. You people need to believe me when I say that I have seen what he will do and that will bring an end to the life you are trying to save." I snap in response, then turn back to Jason, "You should have let me destroy him."

I turn away from these people and slide the shades back on my face to cover the hate in my eyes. The rain is letting up outside and being in the cold air, away from these people will be much better for me. They don't understand anything I do or why it needs to be done. Trevor has to die. That is the only way to insure the safety of their race, with or without the cure in my blood.

"Where are you going?" Neil calls after me.

"Away from all of you." I reply. "There is no sense in sticking around with a bunch of idiotic humans who will be dead in a matter of hours."

I move quickly toward the old, wooden door and reach for the handle. I can feel the slight breeze creeping in through the cracks in the wood and it feels good blowing through my damp hair and against my skin. The metal of the gun tucked into the waistband of my jeans behind my back is even cold.

"You were human too, ya know." Jason calls from behind me and I stop just before reaching the handle. "Just a few weeks ago, you were a human exactly like the rest of us."

I slowly turn around and see Jason forcing himself to stand from the barrel and take a few pain-filled steps toward me. The group stands at his side with Phil close by in case the pain from his wounds is too much for him to handle.

It's funny how just the other day I found the attraction I had toward him unbearable, yet now, I can't stand the idea of being in the same room with him.

"I know that you say that you have no memories of your human life, but I know they're in there somewhere. And if there is any part of the old you that is left, she will fight against you until you let her come back. She wouldn't stand for this or abandon the people that just helped her escape."

I smile and say, "Then why isn't she here right now? Why did she let *me* take over? That *thing* you used to know is dead. She wanted to forget everything and get rid of the pitiful existence she called a life. I am the only one now who is moving on with the future I want and that does not need to involve humans like you."

I turn around once more and succeed in getting the door to slide open this time. Before I take a step into the misty world outside, a tiny voice holds me back and I stand frozen.

"You were right about what you said when I first met you." The little girl's voice is so innocent as it pierces my ears. "The new cure is just as bad as the old one. Maybe even worse because you aren't a nice person anymore."

I let her words resonate in my mind, not recalling the conversation she claims we had when we met. That was a different Bridget she spoke to then and I have said time and time again that the old me is dead.

I hold on to the side of the door and without looking back at the rest of them I say, "I wasn't created to be nice."

I step over the threshold and walk away from the barn. The ground is mushy and wet under my boots, but the rain has finally come to an end. The clouds are the only thing that remains of the passing storm and soon the sun will shine brightly overhead. The walls of the city lie to the east of here and it would be a straight shot once I get to the road.

I don't think that is part of my plan anymore. Those people in the city will never appreciate the gift I can give them. They will take it and use it for their own purposes then toss me into a cage and leave me to rot.

That is far from the future I want or deserve. I think I will just spend time living in the wild where I feel more welcome. The zombies and vampires will make a nice meal whenever I need one and I don't need the company of humans to make life better. Out there, I could wait while Trevor hunts me down, then get the opportune moment to kill him in the most gruesome way possible.

I head for the road and run my fingers through my damp hair. I don't hear footsteps of anybody following me and I don't care to look back to check. Instead, I close my eyes, put my hands in the pockets of my leather jacket, and take in the amazing scents the world has to offer.

I can smell the rain and the dying leaves on the ground. The wet concrete under my feet and the grime caked on the few wrecked cars on the side of the highway. I can even smell the scent of a different set of humans approaching and I quickly open my eyes and reach for the gun behind my back.

* * *

I fire a warning shot at the oncoming group without thinking. The bullet doesn't hit any of them, but they duck out of my range and hide behind a few abandon vehicles in the road. I hear them moving, which they are probably getting guns out and checking to make sure they are fully loaded. A few of them curse under their breath, confused about the crazy woman standing in the middle of the street all alone.

The sound of the gunshot brought the people from the barn rushing to the highway. They catch sight of the strangers hiding not far in front of me, but none of them act as though they are concerned. I am the only one wielding a weapon and aiming for the people standing in my way.

Phil and Jason cautiously approach and stand a few feet behind me. Phil keeps his gun lowered as he eyes the few weapons scattered amongst the strangers. He moves to stand beside me and raises an eyebrow in my direction.

"Is that Trevor?" he asks.

I shake my head and sniff the air, then say, "Doesn't smell like anyone from his town. These people are different."

"Then why did you shoot at them?" Phil asks with a hint of anger to his voice.

"They are in my way." I reply simply.

"Please don't shoot at us!" a man's deep voice comes from behind a grey truck. "We are just trying to find shelter!"

He speaks as though his words will get me to lower my aim. It is going to take a lot more than that for me to lose focus and trust these people.

"Where are you headed?" Phil shouts as he moves to my side. "There are no safe places around here!"

"We are looking for shelter and food." The man shouts back and I can tell he is lying.

I take a step closer to them and aim for the grey truck. I sniff the air and let their odors drift up my nose. They say that they are looking for shelter, but the nervous tension and fear drifting from them tells me something different.

"They aren't looking for shelter. They are looking for something else." I say quietly.

"You don't know that. They could be friendly and we should help them." Phil retorts, then yells back to the group,

"You should turn around and head for the city. That's the only safe place around here."

"We know where the city is, but we aren't going there!" the man argues. "Just tell her to lower the gun and let us pass through!"

Phil inches closer to me and says, "Bridget, just put the gun down. We don't need to hurt these people. They are travelers like us. We should let them pass."

I shake my head and keep my eyes glued to the back end of the grey truck. I can see the man's feet sticking out from under it and I wait for any slight movement that might prove to me that he is a threat. All I need is one reason to pull this trigger again and I can end the annoyance right now and get on my way again.

"Bridget?" another, younger male voice speaks up and I look away from the truck. "Is that you?"

He pokes his head out from behind another vehicle and I turn my aim to him. I can see his eyes looking at me, his mouth hanging open as he recognizes me. He slowly moves away from the damaged car and I keep my aim, but I cannot pull the trigger. Even as he starts running down the middle of the street, I remain frozen.

"Dammit kid." The man with the deep voice steps out from behind the truck and starts following him down the street.

He catches my attention and I aim for his feet and squeeze my finger around the trigger. The bullet bounces off the concrete by his toes and he stammers backward. He quickly throws his hands in the air and stops moving. Then I turn my aim back to the young man who stares at me and slowly inches his way closer.

"Bridget?" he questions. "What's wrong?"

Footsteps quickly move to my side and I see Jason glaring at me out of the corner of my eye, "Put the gun down." He demands.

I stare at the boy tiptoeing his way toward me. He realizes that my aim is going nowhere and he slowly raises his hands in the air. He is no more than fifteen feet in front of me and I can see him perfectly. His clothes are dirty and wet from the rain. His brown boots are worn out and he has a hole in the left knee of his jeans. His blue, hooded jacket is tight on him and I see his red shirt sticking out from the bottom.

"Put the damn gun down!" Jason orders and limps closer. "Trust me, you don't want to kill him."

The boy moves forward, slowly closing the distance between us. The wind blows through his shaggy, brown hair and a familiar scent drifts up my nose. I don't know how I recognize it or why my hand is beginning to shake as I hold the gun. I move my eyes to his as soon as he is close enough and those hazel orbs stare back at me, begging me to recognize him.

"Please," he begs, "why don't you recognize me?"

I ignore his words and tighten my grip on the gun.

"Bridget, you really don't want to kill him. Deep inside I know you have to realize who he is. Just put the gun down." Jason pleads in my ear and places a gentle hand on my arm. "You don't want to shoot Ryder."

My hand shakes even more at the mention of his name. I don't understand it. If this is the person Jason told me about, then he is supposed to be dead. Jason told me that Trevor had killed him. He was the reason the old me wanted to forget everything and the very reason I feel so much revenge coursing through me.

How do I know that?

The one he called Ryder is even closer to me now and he opens his mouth to speak, "It's me. I'm not dead. You *have* to recognize me."

I shake my head and say, "I don't have to do anything." Even my voice is shaking right along with my hands.

Jason keeps his hand on my right arm and slowly reaches for the gun in my grasp. I can feel his fingertips sliding over the leather sleeve of my jacket and he quietly begs me to give him the gun. I grit my teeth and shake my head from side to side.

My left hand stops shaking and I slowly turn my eyes to Jason. He is paying more attention to the gun than anything else and I take advantage of it. I quickly reach for the collar of his jacket and latch my fingers around the fabric. Before he can get away from me, I shove him backwards until he tumbles to the concrete of the street and hits his back against the curb. He grunts from the pain in his side while Neil quickly runs to his aide.

I turn back just in time to see Phil reaching his hand for the gun in mine and he succeeds. His grip is tight on my wrist and he manages to pry the gun from my fingers. I go for his face as he tries to restrain my other wrist. I'm too fast for him and I leave a nasty scratch across his cheek. The pain doesn't faze him and he is actually stronger than I anticipated. With my right wrist still in his grasp, he twists it around my back and kicks the back of my shin, forcing me to drop to my knees.

It doesn't take much to get out of his grip, but before I can get to my feet I stare down the barrel of not only the gun in Phil's hand but a few others that have quickly crowded around me. The people from the barn scowl, as well as this new group we have encountered.

I stay on the ground and consider my options. I value my life quite a bit to take the unnecessary risk of fighting through this mob and wind up getting shot.

"No!" Ryder's voice shouts and he quickly pushes his way through the gun-wielding men. "Don't hurt her."

He drops to his knees until he is face to face with me. There are those hazel eyes that I saw in my head so many times. They are up close and real right now. He looks at me with a sad expression and shakes his head with what he sees.

"What's happened to you? Why don't you recognize me?" he whispers.

"Don't take it personal. I don't remember anything about

the girl you think I am." I reply.

He reaches his hand out to touch my face and I snap my head out of his reach, "Why?" he says, quietly. "Why would you choose to forget everything? Why would you want to forget me?" he sounds angry now.

I lean closer to him and say, "I did not choose to forget anything. The girl you know wanted to erase you from her mind. She wasn't strong enough to deal with the death she thought you faced."

He shakes his head, "I don't believe you. My Bridget would never do that."

"Deal with it," I retort, "because she did."

Ryder grits his teeth and shakes his head. I watch as he stands and turns away from me. He walks back to the man with the deep voice from behind the grey truck and I can hear their conversation.

"This is the one you were talking about? Your girlfriend with the cure?" his deep voice asks.

Ryder nods and says, "Yeah, that's her. Something isn't right though, she isn't the same."

The big guy turns his eyes to mine and says, "We'll take her to the city like you planned. But it's on you if she goes crazy and attacks one of us." He steps away from Ryder and shouts to those from my small group, "All of you are welcome to come with us to Des Moines. The girl is coming regardless, but you'd be safer there."

I knew he was lying about being a simple group of travelers looking for safety. They were looking for me and now they have me. I am just another prisoner like I was when Trevor caught the old me. Only this time I am not locked in a cage.

* * *

We have been walking down this same stretch of highway for miles. The sun chose to stay hidden behind the clouds that were constantly threatening us with rain, but it never fell. There is a chill to the air and the people surrounding me group closer together to keep warm. Their clothes are too thin for the approaching winter.

Jason leans on the shoulders of Phil as he limps along. The longer I stare at the back of his head, the more the passion I once held for him fades. All I see now when I look at him is the failure he brought me. He lost me the opportunity of killing someone who deserved to die. My mind cannot allow weakness like that to interrupt me from doing what I must to stay alive. Forgiveness is not an option.

I peel my eyes away from him and stare at the road under my feet. The man who was hiding behind the grey truck when we met is walking beside me. He keeps a wary hand close to the strap of his rifle. I learned that his name is Elliot. He doesn't trust me after pointing a gun to them by the barn, but I tend to not trust others too easily either.

Ryder walks a few paces in front of me, glancing over his shoulder every chance he gets. I don't know what his deal is. If he thinks I am going to snap back to the person he once knew, he should consider rethinking things. That girl is long gone. Never to be seen again. Although, I have to say that she has good taste in men. Ryder is a good looking man, not as rugged or strong as Jason, but I'm sure he could hold his own in a fight.

I take a deep breath and look up to the sky. Nightfall will be coming soon and it will be interesting to see how things are out here in the wild when the vamps come out to play. I am sure they are a sight to see.

Those creatures get to live the life I was created for. When they bit me, *the old me*, she didn't do things the right way. She should have allowed herself to transform into the wild being growing in her unbeating heart. I should have been able to come out that very second instead of waiting until the sadness was too much. I can only imagine the things I could have seen or what I would have done. I would be in charge of the cure and not these people leading me to the city. All they want to do is control it and control me. I am not something to be controlled.

I sense Elliot inching closer and I feel the warmth from his body. I look over at him and he wears a constant scowl on his aging face. He walks with strength in every step and determination in his blue eyes. He moves closer until our shoulders almost touch.

"I have to admit, I expected something different when Ryder told me about you." He speaks, interrupting my fant-asies of living in the wild. "I figured we were going to find this young, scared-out-of-her-mind girl, and instead we found you and you scared the shit out of us."

I shrug and say, "I have been known to have that effect on people. Just wait until you see what I can do when a zom-bie is around."

"He's told us all about that. The others in the group I was with thought he was crazy, but I believed him. There's just something about him, his passion maybe, but I knew he wasn't lying." Elliot replied.

"Good for him. I'm sure he told you all sorts of *wonder-ful* stories about me." I say.

"He did. He said how you saved him from a group of really bad humans, how you protected the wall at Des Moines. He told me when you were bitten and everything that happened afterward." Elliot says, then sighs, "That's when we found him. He was barely alive and about to be eaten. We were able to nurse him back to health, then all he could talk about was you."

"Is that so." I reply, not necessarily interested in the story.

Elliot sighs, then rants on, "He told me that you two were in love at one point. After watching you hold a gun to him and threaten to shoot, all I could think of was how twisted one person has to be to do that to someone she cares for."

"The person he is in love with is gone."

Elliot shakes his head, "You're probably right about that, but something kept you from killing him when you had the chance."

"That seems to be happening to me a lot today." I say quietly and turn my glare to Jason's head once more.

I run my fingers through my hair and spot Ryder slowing down to walk with us. He cuts between myself and Elliot and glances between the two of us until his eyes land on Elliot.

"I think we should stop soon." He says, not saying a word about me. "It's getting dark and it'll be too dangerous to travel at night."

Elliot agrees and says, "There's an old house just up the road. We'll stop there, eat, then get some sleep. We should make it to Des Moines the day after tomorrow."

"Good." Ryder says, then looks directly at me, "The sooner we get there, the sooner things will get back to normal. Maybe you'll feel more like yourself once we get back home."

"Home?" I question.

He nods, "Yeah, you know we have a house and friends behind that wall. I'm sure they're all dying to see us alive."

"They'll be dying to see that a cure actually exists." Elliot chimes in.

"Bridge?" Ryder says softly, moving closer until his hand touches mine, "Aren't you happy to be going back home?"

I quickly pull my arm away and glare at him for even thinking about touching me, "Why would I be happy about going to a life that seems more like a prison?"

He shakes his head, "It's not a prison. It's our *home*. The place we fought to get to. Don't you remember any of that? Don't you remember Hatfeld or Dwayne and Sherry or meeting me in that town and killing those zombies with your bare hands? There has to be some part of you that still remembers that."

He sounds sincere but his words mean nothing. The things I remember about my life are disgusting compared to what he wants. I remember death and blood and killing things in order to stay alive. I remember the pain from changing into this glorious creature that I am and that pain was worth it.

I cannot bring myself to think of the memories he wishes me to. The times that drove the old version of myself crazy until she collapsed inside her mind and allowed her world to vanish. Those memories are nothing more than a tiny fragment of time that will never show up in my head again.

"Bridge?" Ryder asks, but I don't bother turning my eyes to him. "I don't get why you chose to forget everything. Some really great stuff happened."

"Then you will have to forgive me for being stronger than the girl you used to know and not allowing those thoughts to keep me from serving my purpose here." I finally say.

Ryder lowers his head and sighs while I watch as Elliot rushes to the front of the group and starts leading them to the small house on the side of the road. It is a shabby brick building with an attached garage. The windows are blacked out but still intact. The front door is wide open so we approach the house with caution.

After a quick but thorough walk-through of the house, Elliot deemed that it was safe enough to stay overnight. There is a fireplace in the living room which is being lit at the moment. The group crowds into the house, scattering through the living room and the very small dining room. Phil helps Jason sit on the old sofa, then goes with his daughter to find some water. Ryder stays by my side, pleading with his eyes for me to recall some memory of him in my life, but I cannot do so.

I walk into the living room while the front door gets nailed shut by two of Elliot's men. Jason is sitting comfortably in one corner of a faded green couch and I pass my angry eyes over him once more. He glances up at me, then quickly turns his attention to the fire sparking to life.

"What do you want?" he snaps.

"Nothing." I reply, still keeping my steely eyes fixated on him.

"Then leave me alone." He demands.

I shake my head and stand perfectly still with my arms hanging at my sides. Ryder steps between us and his eyes dart back and forth from me to Jason.

"What's going on?" he asked. "Why does it seem like the two of you hate each other?"

"I'm not the one who hates anyone. She is the one holding a grudge right now." Jason says.

Ryder turns his eyes to me and says, "Why?"

"He kept me from killing Trevor. This could all be over and the world would be safer if he wouldn't have stopped me." I reply.

"I kept you from killing Ryder too, are you going to hate me for that as well?" Jason snaps.

Ryder ignores Jason's comment and focuses only on me, "You had a chance to kill him?

"I did. I could have ripped his fucking head off, but Jason stopped me. And to think I saved him and kept him alive while we were there."

"You only wanted me alive so you could have something to play with." Jason argues.

"If I remember correctly, you were more than willing to go along with it. You even kissed me back." I say.

A look of shock crosses Ryder's face and he whips his whole body around and stands directly in front of Jason. His hands are balled into tight fists as he glares down at the target of both our hatred.

"You kissed her?" he questions.

Jason shakes his head and says, "She kissed me and wouldn't you know it I'm still alive. If you wanna be pissed at anyone, it should be her."

Ryder still looks shocked and he shakes his head at Jason. He runs his fingers through his hair, then slowly backs away from both of us. I follow him with my eyes and he disappears into another room with a few other humans that are preparing their food.

"Aren't you going to chase after him and beg him to forgive you?" Jason asks, catching my attention. "I'm sure he deserves an apology since I will never be getting one."

I raise an eyebrow and say, "Why should I apologize to you?"

"For letting me think that I had a chance with you. For leaving me after I risked my life to keep you alive. For hurting me even more when I tried stopping you from killing Ryder." Jason rants on. "The list goes on Bridget, just pick one."

I fold my arms across my chest, "There is a small part of me that feels sorrow for bringing you more pain after you were shot, but I am not going to ask for your forgiveness. If these people never came along, I still would have left and you would never see me again."

"Is that what you think I want?" he asks. "I care about you, no matter how much you want to hate me or hurt me, I will always care for you. I want you to be a part of my life. If only you could snap out of it for a moment to see that, you might realize that you want the same thing."

"You want to be around humans and live in that city." I say, lowering my eyes. "That is not the life for me."

"Then what is?"

I run my fingers through my hair and say, "You already know the answer to that. I am meant to be free and live without being threatened by those who are afraid of me. Humans will never be able to accept me for what I am."

"I can accept you for it and you still hate me."

"You want me to stop hating you?"

His dark eyes meet with mine and he says, "I do."

I lean closer to him and say quietly, "I wanted you to let me kill the man who destroyed my life, but we can't always get what we want."

I turn away from him and let my feet guide me through the house. I walk down the short hallway and find a closed door on the right side. I grab the doorknob and push it open to reveal a tiny bathroom with no windows to escape through. I glance back toward the living room and spy Elliot standing at the end of the hallway with his rifle in his hands. I pass him a devilish grin, then walk straight into the small room and close the door.

* * *

The house is almost silent. The only sounds I hear are coming from the living room. It is the constant breathing of those that fell asleep. A couple of them snore and the little girl talks in her sleep, giggling at something running through her dreams. The fire is still crackling and every once in a while I hear someone poking at it with a long, metal stick. Other than the few thin blankets some of them carry, that fire is the only source of heat they have throughout the cold night.

I walk out of the old bathroom and stroll down the hallway to scope out the sleeping bodies. Jason is curled up on the sofa where I left him and Phil sleeps beside him with his daughter on his lap. Two others lay on the floor under one blanket and I find Elliot sitting up beside the fire. He nods at me when our eyes meet and he lingers at me for a long moment before turning back to the fire.

As I move, the eyes of the guard by the front door move right along with me. He tightens his grip on his gun and I pass him a little smile. He could shoot me if he really wanted to. He'd be waking up everyone in this small house as well as drawing the attention of any vampires or zombies within earshot. It would add a bit of excitement to this otherwise tranquil evening. Excitement is not what I am granted and he turns away from me.

I walk away from the sleeping group and go back down the hallway to explore the rest of the house. There are faded squares on the wall to my right where I assume pictures used to hang. Rusted nails jut out from the wall with cobwebs draping off of them. There is a door to my left, across from the bathroom and I peer into the dark area. The window is covered by a piece of thick black plastic and duct tape. The small bed is occupied with a man and a woman. Their arms are wrapped around one another to keep warm while they sleep peacefully.

I turn away from them and walk to the other door and see another bedroom. This one is empty and only dark brown curtains cover the windows. A moldy odor is emanating from inside and I can see the black stuff growing in the corners by the floor. The ceiling has brown spots from where rain water has seeped through and the old, shag carpet is ruined because of it.

I step backwards out of that room and turn around to head for the kitchen. I get one step away from the door, then I feel a tight grip on my arm and get wrenched into the third bedroom across from the moldy one. This person shoves me against the wall, then quietly but firmly closes the door for a private meeting.

Ryder has me pinned against the wall, holding me in place. With the anger from being surprised just now coursing through me, I could take him out in a heartbeat. I actually wouldn't mind doing that. There is something holding me back and it isn't his hands on my arms.

He is seething as he stares into my eyes and his grip is getting stronger against me. There is pain written across his face and a sense of sadness is radiating from him like steam coming from a hot bath.

"How could you do this to me?" he asks, trying to keep his pissed off tone quiet.

"Do what?" I snap in response.

He shakes his head and says, "You know what I'm talking about. Jason said you kissed him. What the hell is wrong with you?"

I raise an eyebrow and say, "There is nothing wrong with me. I am perfectly fine. I think it's you that has a problem right now."

Ryder grits his teeth and his grip on my arms gets tighter, "Don't bullshit with me, Bridge, this isn't you. Whatever the hell happened back there with Trevor, it's over now. You are free and you can be yourself again. You don't need to be this tough bitch that wants to break my heart."

"Who says I'm not being myself? Who says this isn't the version of me that is *supposed* to be here?" I reply, letting my hands tense into fists.

"No, this isn't you. You would never give up on anything, especially not me. You would never want to forget your life." He says, then lowers his eyes. "You would never want to forget me or hurt me like this."

"Then explain something to me," I say and he quickly looks back up, "why did she let it happen? If you know so much about me, why did the old me want to forget everything? What would cause her to shut down and let me have a life?"

He looks away from me for a brief moment to think. His grip on my arms slowly loosens and the pain on his face is spreading. He has no idea why the girl of his dreams wanted to forget all about him, but I do. I could tell him a million times why she isn't here anymore, but he would never want to listen. I can tell by the look on his face that he will never want to believe that she is gone.

His hands drop away from me and a sigh escapes his lips, "I don't know why she would want to do that. I know she had to have a good reason and I wish you would tell me what that is."

I stay pressed against the wall and say, "Is that something you really want to know?"

He nods, then shrugs, "I know you're going to tell me that she wasn't strong enough, but I know she was. She *is* strong enough."

I let out a quiet chuckle, "You have no idea how wrong you are. That girl wasn't strong and she couldn't deal with anything that was going on in her life. She *begged* me to take over so she could forget everything. All she wanted was to be at peace and I showed her a way to do that. I let her disappear."

I see a tear drift from his left eye and fall to his cheek. He quickly wipes it from his face and sniffles back the rest of them. Ryder is much more sensitive of a man than Jason and I can tell that he isn't shy about it. Maybe this is a quality that brought us to fall in love in the first place. He is sweet and kind, a part of me actually feels bad for hurting him just now. The human part of me feels a hint of regret, but he asked and I gave him an honest answer.

He runs his fingers through his hair, then finally looks back at me, "So, since you aren't the same Bridget I fell in love, that must mean you want nothing to do with me. You'd rather be with Jason wouldn't you?"

"I would rather be alone, but I am stuck with all of you at the moment." I reply.

"That's not what I'm asking." He retorts. "Jason said you kissed him. You were too afraid to touch me after you were bitten, because you were afraid that I would turn into something like you. Did you even think twice about that with him?"

"I don't think twice about anything. I am not being afraid to take what I want. She didn't know what we were capable of and didn't know how to handle things. What courses through me will have no effect on humans so long as I don't bite them. My blood is only meant to cure you people."

"What happens if you bite one?" he asks.

"They would die." I reply, not bothering to mention the man with the Mohawk and how amazing his blood tasted.

Ryder nods, but keeps his mouth shut. His eyes seem to light up in the darkness of this room. He walks back to me and I feel his breath on my face. He slowly brings his hand to my cheek and moves some strands of hair away from my eyes. I cannot move to stop him from bringing his lips to mine and stealing a kiss. There is something keeping my legs frozen to the floor and allowing this moment to occur.

He closes his eyes and puts his other hand on my waist, pressing his body against mine. There is so much passion in his kiss, so much love and adoration coming from this one person and I am permitting it to flow through his lips into mine. I let myself close my eyes and drift into the softness of his kiss, the tenderness of his touch as he caresses my cheek and the love that flows from his entire body. I can see him in the darkness of my mind and everything is so familiar.

The way he touches me, the way he holds me, it's as though I have gone through this a million times before. But I haven't done any of this. Not this version of me. I can't let the weakness return to my body and I cannot allow any part of the old me to come back to the surface. Everything about her is nothing more than dead weight.

I run my hands up his stomach and stop at his chest. His muscles are tight under my touch and he tenses his body. He holds me tighter and his kiss gets deeper. I open my eyes and my fingers grip tightly around the thin fabric of his shirt. I give him one quick shove away from me and he stumbles backward falling to his ass at my feet. I pull myself away from the wall and glare down at him as a look of sheer bewilderment crosses his face.

"Why?" he questions.

"You are part of the past. A past that belongs to a dead girl." I reply. "I do not belong to that past or the weakness that devours it."

I turn away and head to the door. I grip the cold knob and twist it until it swings open. Behind me, I hear Ryder scrambling to his feet and rushing to me. He places a hand on my shoulder and I quickly shove him off.

"Bridge, please." He begs, "I know you're still the same person I fell in love with. I know she's still in there."

I pass him a snide glance before walking down the hall and say, "Not anymore."

He lets me walk away from him and I stroll down the narrow hallway, back into the living room to dwell in the silence once again.

* * *

The sun is shining bright in the amazing blue sky. The clouds are scarce and it is relatively warm outside. It doesn't really matter to me what the temperature is, but the humans around me are grateful for the chance to travel in warmth instead of shivering. Most of the rain water from yesterday has even dried up thanks to the sunlight.

My eyes burn as I squint through the tinted lenses of the sunglasses. It is the only thing I have to complain about my life. I can live without a beating heart or eating normal food, but I would love to look up at the morning sky and not be painfully blinded without a pair of shades to protect my eyes. After all, they are a thing of beauty and hiding them is such a pity. They need to be shared with the world at all times of the day or night.

We haven't been walking for very long, maybe an hour or two. Elliot decided to let his group sleep in, then take their time eating breakfast. I think it was foolish of him to do something as time consuming as that. If he was so worried about getting to the city without running into Trevor, we would have left at dawn.

I am honestly surprised that Trevor hasn't caught up with us by now. He has trucks and other means of transportation where all we have is our own two feet. We are a snail compared to him.

I keep to the back of the group staring at those who walk before me. Jason limps with his hand pressed against the wound on his stomach. Neil walks beside him and has been acting rather strange. He peeks over his shoulder, passing me odd yet seemingly hopeful glances. I'm sure he's just glad to be away from Trevor and that life back in the small town, but he is still an awkward fellow.

Ryder walks beside Phil and his daughter. They have been speaking together for a while now. I know they are talking about me. Not because I have the ability to listen in on the conversation, but because Ryder turns his eyes to mine when Phil says something of interest. His eyes are so full of hope that will only be destroyed when he sees that his girl is not coming back.

It's getting to be irritating trying to get people to understand things about me. I am not who they want me to be.

Sure, I might have the same cure that will eventually bring the planet back to life, but I am far from a creature that cares if it actually happens. If we never make it to the city and I find myself living in the wild with the other monsters, I can be okay with that. These people might not be, but it honestly wouldn't break my heart if the cure never goes global. Maybe the humans don't deserve it like they want to think they do.

I sigh and close my eyes as I walk forward. I let the warm air caress my skin and I run my fingers through my hair. Suddenly, my right foot falls into a slight pothole in the middle of the street and I stumble forward a bit. I quickly catch myself and walk straight again. I open my eyes and grit my teeth, angry for that split second of a moment where I wasn't paying attention to my surroundings.

That is how I got into this mess in the first place. If I remember right, I was not paying very close attention to what was happening and that is how the vamp got me first. There was so much pain that came with its bite and I have no idea how I ever made it through it alive.

Wait a second.

Why the hell would I remember that? That was part of the old me. The Bridget that died a few days ago. I shouldn't have her memories, yet somehow that one slipped back into my mind.

I grit my teeth and shake my head. I clench my fists tight, forcing that memory and any other part of her weakness back to hell where it belongs. She can't be here. I can't let her be here. Because of her, I'm in this situation. I am stuck with humans that only want me for the cure then they'll shove me aside like yesterday's garbage.

No!

I refuse to give in to the thoughts that she wants me to think. That old version of me is dead and dead she must remain.

"*I'm still here.*"

I stop walking and stare straight ahead of me for a long

moment. The voice was nothing more than a whisper, but I heard it clearly. I turn my head, glancing at the faces of the people in the group. Ryder and Phil are still gabbing away, not paying me any attention. Neil is taking a drink of water and Elliot is speaking to two of his men as they lead the group. I look to Jason and his eyes are focused on the road ahead of him. It appears that nobody else heard that voice.

I look to the trees of the surrounding woods and see nothing floating between them. This stretch of highway is quiet and barren. The vehicles are empty, other than the remains of the drivers with their hands still clutching the steering wheels. The bones and tattered muscles are left to rot while the world goes on around it.

There is no sign of the voice I heard. I take a deep, calming breath then begin moving once more. I stare at the ground under my feet, then look up to the backs of those in front of me.

"You really think you can get rid of me?" once again, that voice enters my mind and I am the only one who can hear it.

I keep moving and run my shaking right hand through my hair. I can't pretend that I did not hear her voice in my head. That annoying sound rings in my ears and all I want to do is scream at her for coming back.

I shove my hands in the pockets of my jacket and force my feet to move onward. I walk a little faster to catch up with the others and soon I am right behind Jason. He moves slower than I do, so I have to ease my pace a bit. He notices that I am near him and he steps to the side and allows me to walk beside him. I feel his eyes staring at my disheveled face and he raises a questioning eyebrow.

"Are you okay?" he asks.

I pass him a slight nod and say, "Just a little hungry." It isn't exactly a lie, I just don't want to explain the annoying voice rolling around in my head.

"There's not a whole lot I can do about that to help you." He says.

"It doesn't matter." I reply.

"Can you tell if there's a zombie around? Maybe you can snack on that." he suggest rather snidely.

I scowl and sniff the air, trying not to let the human scents interfere as I search for anything that might be undead. I strain my ears and listen for any groaning that could be coming from a zombie either in the woods or on the road ahead. Other than the smell of the corpses in the cars and the chatter of the rest of the group, there is nothing that would appease my hunger.

"Unfortunately I do not smell one." I reply.

"Then I guess you'll have to wait." He states. "We're out in the open now, we're bound to run into something before we get to the city."

"I truly hope you are right about that. I don't know how much longer I can handle this."

"Handle what?" he asks.

I shake my head, "Nothing. Just keep your eyes peeled for a zombie."

"We're out in the middle of nowhere, I can almost guarantee we'll run into something soon. That is how you found me." He states.

"Not quite in the middle of nowhere. There were houses around." I add, not thinking about the words that came out of my mouth.

He raises an eyebrow and says, "Hmm, I thought you said you don't remember anything about your past life. I guess you were wrong about some things."

"What?" I question, but he does not answer.

I grit my teeth once more and squeeze my hands into fists. This can't be happening. The longer I am around him and the rest of these people, the more I can feel her creeping up my spine and entering the darkest corners of my mind. She is like a leech trying to suck the normalcy away from me.

"I'm not going anywhere." Her playful tone whispers a threat into my mind.

I haven't been out here long enough for this to be happening. This *shouldn't* be happening. She is too weak to fight against me. There is no way she could win any war I throw at her. I need to end this before she has the chance at trying.

I glance around, searching for anything that might make her voice leave me alone. I don't think shooting myself will cause her to disappear. I could bite into one of these humans. There is a decent possibility that it would work, but I risk the chance of being shot down for doing so.

I turn to Jason and stare at him for a long moment. I glance to his lips and a thought pops into my mind. Quickly, I grab his arm and turn him toward me, forcing his feet to stop moving. I press my lips against his and steal a kiss that might drive her back to where I put her.

I close my eyes and put my hand on the back of his neck. Slowly, the blackness behind my eyes takes over and I can feel myself relaxing as that voice and the person behind it fades away.

Jason fights against me and breaks away from the kiss. He stares at me with disgust and confusion across his face.

"What the hell are you doing?" he shouts.

The humans in front of us have stopped walking and turn their attention to me. I feel their eyes staring me down. Elliot pushes his way through them with his gun out and ready for use. Jason moves away from me and goes back to Neil's side.

"Everything okay back here?" Elliot asks with tension in his voice.

"We're fine." Jason snaps.

I roll my eyes and turn away from Elliot as he keeps his stance before me. He stays put for a little while before backing away and joining his men at the front of the group. I catch Ryder's hateful eyes glaring at me for witnessing a stolen kiss from a man he now despises.

I shrug him off and walk onward. My mind is completely blank and my hands no longer shake. I feel like I am in control once again and the world belongs to me.

"You'll have to try harder than that, monster." That voice destroys the sanctity of my blank mind and the rage boils through me once again.

* * *

We walked until the sun was at its highest point in the sky, then Elliot chose a nice spot on the side of the road to stop for lunch. There is absolutely nothing around. No abandoned cars or old buildings rotting away in the earth. The trees occupy the other side of the four lane highway and this side is a barren wasteland. The grass and weeds are dying from the oncoming winter and, even with the sun shining brightly, the land looks depressing.

For their meal, Elliot and his small group of soldiers provided vegetables and water. It doesn't seem very nourishing, but the humans eat it like it's their last meal. Jason nibbles on the upsetting food, not enjoying it as much as the others, but he's eating it with a brave face. I'm just glad they didn't offer any of it to me.

I stand in the middle of the street while they munch on their small meals and rest for a few moments. The air is calm and the sun beats down on us. I adjust the sunglasses on my face to cover more of my eyes, but the sun still finds a way to slip through the sides and it burns a little. I'll be glad when night comes again.

Jason sits on the curb beside a few others. Phil sits not far from him while his daughter, Sarah, plays with her stuffed toy in the dead grass. Elliot is keeping an eye out as he takes a sip from his canteen and the rest of the group is just plain quiet.

I turn around and face the line of trees across the street. The leaves are almost gone from the branches and they look dead like the rest of the world. Birds fly from them and flutter to the sky, chasing one another in a game only they can enjoy.

"You used to be afraid of the woods, ya know." Ryder says as he steps to my side and joins in my stare. "When I first met you, neither of us would even think about walking through the trees or getting anywhere near them. Damn vampires ruined that part of the world."

I can tell he is trying to get me to remember something with this small talk of his. He sounds sincere and calm, not at all worried about the kiss he saw between myself and Jason. I am only worried about his words bringing the voice back to irritate me even more.

He takes a side step closer and smiles, "I remember after we first met and we were walking on this very highway to get to Des Moines, you told me that after what we went through in Hatfeld, it was going to take a lot to scare you. I think you were right about that."

I nod, taking in the words that mean so much to him as he speaks. I feel his hand brushing against the back of my own and I glance down to see his fingertips wanting to grasp onto mine. I take a breath through my nose and stuff my hands in the pockets of my jacket.

"There used to be a time when you would actually want to touch me or kiss me the way you kissed Jason back there." He says, keeping his eyes focused on trees, while I pick up something odd floating on the air. "I know this is something that I'll just have to deal with, but I don't want to."

I keep listening, but take another inhale smelling the odor drifting this way. It seems to be coming from the woods, but I can't see anything stumbling amidst the trees and Ryder's voice is stopping me from focusing on other sounds.

"Bridge, you have to know that I'm going to fight to get

you back the way you have always fought for me. I don't care how long it takes or what I have to do, but I'll get you to remember me and how much we love each other. Whatever this is with Jason, it's nothing compared to what we have."

I raise an eyebrow and turn my attention to him for a moment, "And just what do we have?"

"Love." He replies simply. "Real love that isn't just a fling because the monster that's taken over you wants something different. What we have is much stronger than that and I know we'll have it back someday."

"You really believe that?" I ask.

He nods, "Of course I do. It's going to take a lot more than you kissing Jason or shoving me away to keep me from being in love with you. You'll change back to the girl I know is still in there and we can have our lives back to the way they were."

I roll my eyes and say, "How many times do I have to tell you that she's..."

"She's not dead." He argues before I can finish the sentence. "You can say it a thousand times and it will never be true. When I kissed you last night, I could tell that she is still in there and she will fight her way back to me. Then you will be the one who's dead."

Something snaps in the trees and I whip my head around and take a step forward. Ryder heard it as well and puts his hand on the gun at his waist. I sniff the air once more and let the smile come across my lips. It feels like months have passed since I've tasted the flesh of a zombie and here comes one stumbling between the trees, ready for me to have a snack.

It isn't just one zombie, there are two of them coming for us. Another one walks close behind the woman and my smile grows wider. I lick my lips and listen to the sounds of the people behind me jumping up to prepare themselves. I shake them off and move forward.

"You people want to see how the cure works?" I say and

hear a few mumbles in response. "I think it's time you see it firsthand."

I stroll across the pavement and step into the rocky median. Brown grass sticks out between the gravel and is waiting for Spring to come to grow green and tall. I cross into the other lanes of highway and the two zombies stumble through the trees. I get a closer look at them and take in another whiff of their scent.

The second zombie is a man. He's wearing a thick green sweatshirt and his jeans are muddy to match his shoes. The woman's hair is a mess and the glasses on her face are crooked and cracked. Her blouse is ripped and the bite mark on her right arm looks fresh. The mark on the man's neck appears to be fresh as well. They are much cleaner and less rotten looking than zombies I've met in the past. These two were probably trying to find safety and had some unfortunate, yet recent bad luck.

I keep moving forward, staring at the walking meal in front of me. Their arms sway back and forth as the monotonous groaning comes from their raspy throats. Something on the woman's left hand glimmers in the sunlight when she trips over the curb onto the street. It's a wedding ring. A symbol of humanly love binding them together for all of eternity. I spot the same symbol on the man's hand as well and realize these two are married.

I stop walking and tilt my head to the side. From what I know of this ritual, marriage is the one thing people do to cement their love to the never-ending status. I don't feel that way towards Jason. It's more about the strength and the passion I feel when we touch. Not the soft, mushy feeling that love brings with it. That's more of what I felt when Ryder kissed me last night. That feeling was very familiar to me.

"I told you I'm still here." That voice is in my head once more and I grit my teeth and push those horrible feelings from my mind.

I clench my hands to fists and leap through the air,

tackling the woman to the concrete. She shouts at me and claws her nubby fingertips against my back. Her feet kick wildly at the ground and she thrashes her teeth at me. I stare into her pitch black eyes, seeing my own reflection staring back and wrap my hands around her destroyed blouse.

I lift her torso from the ground and bring her face closer to mine. She claws at my face and neck, reaching behind me for the true prize in her eyes. I bring my teeth to her neck and chomp down hard, breaking the skin and letting that dead blood rush into my mouth. This is to bring an end to that voice in my head and the constant feelings of weakness and emotion that seem to be making an appearance in my life.

I slurp down as much of her blood as I can until she stops grasping at the air behind me and her arms fall limply to her sides. I carefully let her body fall to the ground and rise to my feet. The other zombie has completely ignored the fact that I just saved his wife and is quickly making is way across the median.

The humans he is walking toward all have their guns raised and aimed for the zombie's head, but none of them fire a round. I guess they believe that I have the cure and it would be unfair to this man if they allowed him to die. I quickly walk up behind him and grab onto the hood on his sweatshirt, stopping him from taking another step closer to Ryder.

I bite down on the back of his neck and he tries walking away from me. He takes a step, dragging me with him as I suck the dead life from his veins. This one tastes even better than his wife lying on the ground behind me. I can feel myself getting stronger and the last hint of the old me is gone entirely this time.

Once his body goes limp, I let go and he crashes to the ground. I wipe the remainder of his blood on the back of my hand and smile down at my handiwork. It won't be long before these two wake up and add to the number of humans I am stuck travelling with.

I stare at the others who are gawking at me. It's like they

have never seen a thing like me attack zombies. I guess that's true for most of them. I'm sure it is a sight to witness the miracle of giving life back to the dead. If only there were two of me, then I could witness it as well.

That first gasp fills the air and an astonished Elliot aims his gun at the woman lying on the ground. She starts coughing and hacking, trying to catch a breath of fresh air. Neil grabs his backpack and rushes to her side. I turn around and walk backwards toward the rest of the humans. Neil helps the woman to her side so she can breathe, then he feels for a pulse and smiles.

"Where am I?" she asks in an ever pleasant tone.

"You're safe and alive now." Neil replies as she sits up. "Do you remember who you are?"

The woman nods and says, "Yes, my name is Amanda. My husband and I were on our way to the city and we were attacked by zombies and...oh no." her eyes find her husband on the ground, still waiting to wake up.

She quickly scrambles across the street to be with him. She holds his head in her hands and rocks him gently back and forth. Neil slowly walks up behind her and as soon as his feet stop moving, the man sucks in a heavy breath and opens his eyes.

"Richard?" Amanda speaks quietly. "You're alive. Oh thank God."

He coughs and holds onto his wife. I glance to the others around me and see that all of them are smiling. I don't know if they are happy about seeing the cure or about the love that has been reunited between those two. Either way, it's annoying. We can't waste time admiring my miracle every time I give it to someone. It's old news and soon it won't be news at all.

As I stare at them, something creeps up into the back of mind. These two can go back to the life they were given the day they were born. They can be happy when we make it to the city and start a family or do whatever they do to feel joy.

Where does that leave me once the whole world has the cure? I will be just another part of the apocalypse that will fade throughout history until I am forgotten. I don't quite like the idea of that. This cure and these creatures that kill human beings are my only future. It saddens me to think that I will be nothing without them.

I run my fingers through my hair and shake my head as I turn away from their happiness. Elliot and his people are helping the two cured ones by giving them water and telling them about our plan of going to the city. I meet with Jason on the curb and he pulls himself to his feet.

"You did a good thing just now." He states. "You know that, right?"

I nod without saying a word.

"Then why do you look so unhappy about it?" he asks. "This is why we're going to the city, ya know. You'll be able to cure the whole world once we get there."

I sigh and look away from him, "I'm sure that would be a good thing."

"But..." he says.

"I don't plan on staying once we get there." I confess.

He turns his shocked eyes to me and says, "What are you talking about? You can't just abandon the world and let this pandemic continue. The world will need you, just like those two needed you."

I shake my head, "They won't need me for long once they have what's in my blood."

He rolls his eyes and turns away from me, "What's your plan then? Leave and never look back?"

"I will help all of you get to the city and I will make sure that if Trevor attacks I get to kill him. But once you're safe on the other side, you will never see me again." I state, staring straight ahead of me and feeling absolutely certain. "I can promise you that."

He looks down to his feet and shakes his head, "You know they won't let you leave once they see that the cure exists. They will force you to stay there."

I shrug, "Then I guess they'll just have to fight me for it."

* * *

Once again, I am left to walk alone behind the rest of them. They keep a watchful eye on me, simply to make sure I am not going to take off. As much as I know things would be easier on my own, I made a promise to get these people safely to the city. Once that task is accomplished, I am the only thing I need to worry about.

Jason doesn't quite agree with my new plan, but I am not about to change it. I can't let the people in that city use me for what's in my blood then shove me aside. I know that's what will happen and I am not meant for that. The old Bridget wasn't meant for it either. It was the only thing we had in common.

Neither of us wanted to be locked in a cage.

We have turned onto another highway that should take us straight to the city walls. According to Elliot, we will get there sometime tomorrow afternoon and all will be well. I am still counting on Trevor catching up with us. In fact, I *want* him to find us. His pathetic army could come at us this very instant and it would be absolutely perfect. Our guns would slow them down and I would finally get this vengeful feeling off my back and eliminate him from existence. I could taste the blood under his tanned skin and enjoy every second as I watch the very life fade from his eyes.

That thought is making me hungry again. Zombies wouldn't be enough and vampires aren't out just yet. The sun still has a little ways to go before it disappears completely and by then, we will be safe in some building where they cannot harm us. I don't want either of those things anyway. A human is what I crave. They have a flavor that cannot be matched by anything else on the planet and there is a small group of them ripe for the picking a few paces in front of me.

I just need one of them. The weakest one perhaps. That little girl up there is small and not strong enough to fight anything off. She wouldn't be very filling and I would be longing for more the second her blood hits my lips.

I pass my eyes over the others and they are all pretty healthy. Their flesh is pink and luscious, probably a bit tough to bite through even. Most of them appear strong enough to fight back, except for one.

He limps next to Neil and still holds onto the wound on his stomach. The scent of his blood catches my nose once in a while and I can almost taste him. It wouldn't take much to render him helpless. He's halfway there right now and I just need one quick bite and the rest would be over.

Who am I kidding. I could never hurt Jason like that. Our relationship might not be perfect or even intact at the moment, but he is still important to me. The type of important that needs to live on for as long as he can without me there to threaten it.

That's why it won't be good for me to stay in the city. Not like this. I am stronger out here and that is where I must stay.

"*Not without Ryder.*" There is that voice I *love* so much.

I guess that bitch can hear my every thought as it roams through my head. I hate to tell you, but Ryder is not for me. Sure, he's handsome and has a sweet voice, but that's not what I want. I need someone equal to me. If I knew how to do it, I would find the perfect match and turn him into another creature like me.

"*No,*" the voice whispers in my head, "*We want a cure for this.*"

"There will never be a cure for this. Don't you see that?" I argue quietly, catching the attention of no one.

"*You don't know that.*" she says.

I grit my teeth and clench my fists. She isn't supposed to be in my head and here she is telling me about some *magical* cure that's going to take care of all her problems and make her human again. She would get rid of me in a heartbeat and I am not going to let that happen. She can live in my head and haunt me all she wants, but she will never have this life back. She gave that up when she chose to be weak and forget about everything she cared for. Her family, her friends, Ryder, she wanted those memories to go away and I did that for her. She just needs to shut the hell up and thank me for ending her pain.

"*I was wrong.*" She says.

"No, this was the best decision you ever made. I just wish you would have made it sooner." I snap.

One of the humans glances over their shoulders after hearing me argue with the air. The older woman with her hair in a tight bun on top of her head raises a confused eyebrow and I glare right back. It's none of her business if I am yelling at the voice in my head. She can just turn around and go about her day until we get to the city.

"*You can't just leave them there. You have to give them the cure.*" This voice is driving me crazy.

"You are not in charge so you don't get to tell me what to do." I reply.

"*It's the right thing to do. It's what I would do.*" She states.

"Well you're not here!" I shout. "You wanted to give up on this life and you willingly gave it to me. So just shut the hell up and leave me the fuck alone!"

I look up from my feet and see the entire group staring at

me. Elliot has a hold on his rifle and he looks at me with worry in his eyes. Jason has his mouth hanging open and his eyebrows raised in surprise.

"What?" I snap at them.

One by one and very slowly, they turn around and start moving again. Amanda and Richard keep their distance as they hold hands. Phil lifts his daughter and carries her over his shoulders. Jason doesn't bother looking back and Elliot slows down to be closer to me in case I lash out again.

Ryder moves to my side and matches my pace. He is the only one that doesn't seem to be judging me and actually has a stupid smile on his face.

"You okay?" he asks.

I shove my hands in the pockets of my jacket and say, "I'm fine."

"It doesn't seem like you're fine. It seems like you're at war with yourself right now." He states, that smile still glued to his lips.

"No, I'm at war with an idiot who lives in my head." I retort.

The smile on his face grows wider, "That idiot happens to be the old you trying to make her way back. I told you she was still there."

I scoff at him and move a little faster to get ahead of him. Of course that doesn't keep him from matching my brisk pace and he stays by my side.

"Will you please just leave me alone." I seethe.

Ryder shakes his head and says, "I'm not going anywhere and you can't stop me from walking with you. With this being the end of the world, I can pretty much do whatever I want."

Those words sound very familiar to me. I turn my eyes to him and stare at the annoying smile on his face and it's like I have been in this moment before, hearing those exact words.

"That's what he said the first day we met." The voice chimes in, answering my unasked question, she sounds a bit

snobby this time.

"Oh my god, just shut up already." I say.

"What?" Ryder asks, turning his eyes to me and the smile on his face goes away.

"I wasn't talking to you." I reply. "Although you can keep your mouth shut too."

Again, he passes me a ridiculous grin and keeps walking next to me. Sure, I have the option to run as fast as I want to get away from him and the rest of these humans and a small part of me wants to do that. However, when I look back at his smiling face and stare into those hazel eyes, I find myself wanting to stay. Maybe it's the voice in my head that won't let me run or maybe I want to see that these people get to the city without getting caught up with Trevor. Whatever it is, it's annoying and pathetic.

* * *

The next few hours of walking were very uneventful yet the time seemed to rush right by me. Elliot found a spot under an overpass to stop for a short meal. There isn't a house or building anywhere near here, so we'll have to risk moving in the dark in order to find a place. The sun hasn't set just yet, but the sky is getting darker by the minute.

I stand just out from under the overpass and stare at the long stretch of highway we still have to cover. There are cars and trucks scattered about the road, most of them are smashed beyond repair. I notice dead bodies belonging to zombies and even a few vamps are piled on the grass on the side of the road. The stench from their decomposing bodies is repulsive, but the humans still manage to eat through it.

I glance down at my feet and eye a smear of dried blood on the concrete. The stain has settled into the pavement and there is something about this spot that strikes me as familiar. I can see the violence and bloodshed that occurred here and can almost hear the screams of people shouting for help. Whatever happened here was sad and horrible, I can feel it straight through to my bones. My hands are shaking as I look away from the blood and turn back to the pile of dead creatures.

"I hoped I'd never have to see this place again." The voice has made a comeback to interrupt the already annoying thoughts in my head.

Out of sheer curiosity I ask the voice, "Why? What happened here?"

I look around the place and listen to her answer, *"This is where you were created."*

She sounds so upset in my mind, I can almost picture the weak girl bawling her eyes out by being in this spot again. She is stuck reliving the memories of the worst day in her life, yet it happened to be the best day in mine. I might not remember it as she does, but I have no reason to hate the vampire and zombie that bit me and granting me life. I glance down at the blood stain by my feet and feel my lips curling into a smile.

"This wasn't a good thing, monster." She argues with me. *"This was the worst thing to ever happen to me."*

"I find that hard to believe considering how we got the cure with what happened here. This should be named as a historical landmark in my name." I reply.

"You don't understand." She says solemnly, *"I lost everything because of what happened."*

I feel my head turning toward Ryder and my eyes linger on him for a long moment. He is sitting beside Elliot, talking about something that has to do with the city. He notices my stare and our eyes meet. He passes me a smile and I quickly look away from him.

"Love gets in the way of things. If you would have noticed that a long time ago, you wouldn't have erased it all from your mind." I say. "That's why I'm here. I know how to survive a hell of a lot better than you."

"*You're wrong.*" She retorts. "*Love is the best feeling in the world. If you were able to look past the hatred in your eyes, you'd be able to see that.*"

I grit my teeth and shake the voice from my head. There is no sense in arguing with her when I know I am right about this. She let me out so I can live a life where nothing will get in my way. I won't feel the sadness that she does nor will I ever do something as foolish as allow myself to be captured like she had done when Trevor got a hold of her. I am not that stupid.

A set of footsteps approaches and I don't need to see who it is to know that Ryder is standing right next to me. He has a very particular scent that stands out above the others and I could pick him out of a crowd filled with hundreds. He stares at the oncoming stars and lets out a sigh.

"Never thought we'd be back here again." He states.

"Apparently you're not the only one." I say.

"Is she talking to you again?" he asks.

I nod and say, "It is getting to be rather annoying. I'll need to find a better way of getting rid of her."

"I don't think you should do that. You need her around." He states.

"No, *you* need her around. I am fine living with the emptiness in my head."

"Then stop thinking so much. I've warned you about that time and time again." He says with a smile. "Thinking only gets you in trouble."

I scowl and turn my eyes to the sky, passing over the few fluffy clouds floating above us. I know Ryder is enjoying how the voice is annoying me. By the look on his face he wants it to continue happening. I hate to break it to him, but the moment I find a way to get rid of her forever, I'm taking it.

There is movement coming from behind us. I peer over my shoulder and see that the rest of the group is getting their gear together and packing up their water bottles to hit the road again. Elliot puts his bag over his shoulders and keeps the gun in his grip as he leads the group away from the overpass.

I walk with Ryder and Jason soon joins us. His hands are shoved into the pockets of his jeans and he tries to smile apologetically at Ryder.

"I'm sorry." He says quietly.

Ryder shakes his head and says, "Don't worry about it."

"I did kiss her back and I wanted to, but that was only because I thought you were dead and even then I knew it was wrong. I'm sorry about it."

I listen to the two of them talk calmly back and forth as though their conversation means something. Jason speaks like he wants me to hear his sorrow as he explains everything to Ryder. Humans and their constant need to feel better about themselves is a feeling that eludes me. I don't feel rueful for anything that has happened thus far and I probably never will.

"I hope we don't run into any vamps out here." Jason says, their conversation drifts on to small talk.

"Me too. We can't afford to slow down if Bridget wants to bite them." Ryder comments.

"If we had a dart gun it would be easier. That's what I used to cure Trevor's vampires." I say out loud instead of keeping that thought in my head.

"Unfortunately none of us have one of those." Ryder says.

"Then we'll just have to kill them. It's not like it will matter anyway," Jason says, "Bridget doesn't plan on giving up the cure when we get to the city, so the whole world will still be dead."

Ryder snaps his eyes in my direction and seems confused

as well as upset. He shakes his head and runs his hands through his shaggy hair.

"What is he talking about? You *have* to give them the cure. That was always the plan." He argues, keeping his voice down to not upset the rest of the humans.

"Plans change." I say. "She planned on keeping me bottled up inside forever and look how that turned out."

"Well you can't change this plan. You have to cure the world and give people another chance." Ryder pleads. "Why wouldn't you want to do that anymore?"

"Why would I want to be a prisoner inside the city walls? Do you really think they'd let me be free once they know what I can do and what I have done?" I ask.

He raises an eyebrow and says, "What do you mean? What have you done?"

I glance to Jason who keeps his mouth shut. It is best to maintain the secrecy of my human snacks in order to keep myself as free as I possibly can. Elliot seems like the type of man that would put me in shackles if he found out that I have a desire for fresh blood as well as that which belongs to the undead.

I shake my head at Ryder and say, "Nothing. I am just referring to the zombies and vampires I have bitten. Something tells me they would see that as a threat and lock me away."

"You're not the monster you like to think you are." Ryder says and I turn my eyes to his once more. "You can tell yourself that you are freak or a demon as much as you want, but I know the truth. I know you would never be seen as a threat once they know that you hold the key to surviving the apocalypse."

"*That's my Ryder. He always knows what to say.*" The voice chimes in and I roll my eyes.

"I have never once said that I am a monster." I say to both Ryder and the voice in my head. "I embrace that part about me. That old version, the fucking voice in my head, she is the one who believes I am a freak. The humans in that city will see me in the same light that she does. That's why I don't want to give them the cure. If they cannot accept me the way I can, then why should I give them what they want."

He sighs and says, "Because it's the right thing to do."

"Well, sometimes the right thing to do isn't always the best thing to do." I reply. "At least not for me."

Neither of us have anything left to say. The voice even keeps her mouth shut and grants me the peace of a blank mind. Those empty thoughts are short lived and I am left to ponder every action I wish to make.

My life was simpler when I walked out of that barn yesterday and was headed for a life of complete solitude. I knew what I wanted to do and knew that I could conquer anything that crossed my path. My mind had been made up and I was ready to spend eternity completely alone, in fact I was going to embrace it. Listening to Ryder speak his nonsense about curing the world and it being the right thing to do and I can't stop the weak thoughts from entering my mind.

I can feel them creeping into every crevice of my brain and taking over the very blood under my skin. The old version of myself wants to cure the world. I can feel her fighting against my plans in order to make hers come back to life.

If I let that happen, I'm dead. I will be shoved back into the blackest pit of her mind, never to see the light of day again. My hands are shaking at the very thought of that.

* * *

There is nowhere to hide out here in the middle of the

night under the cover of the stars. The moon refused to show itself tonight and the lack of shelter put a damper on the plans of staying safe while the humans sleep. Most of them can't seem to get their eyes to stay closed. I hear them shifting where they lay, shivering both from fear and the coldness taking over their bodies.

We can all hear the vampires out there. Their footfalls are hard when they hit the crunchy grass and their raspy breathing isn't something to be missed. They stand amongst the trees and watch us. I see their pale faces in the darkness and their grey eyes that blend in, It gives them a hideous mask that would render even the strongest man to have the most treacherous nightmares.

Our fire light is dimming and the smoke rising from the ashy logs is beginning to dwindle. Elliot stands alert with his large rifle in his grip. He can see the vamps staring at us as well and is waiting for them to make a move. His feet are planted a few feet from me and two others are watching the other side of camp.

If the fire goes out, the humans will be blind. The vamps are stealthy enough to move swiftly around in the darkness without being seen, especially when the light is scarce. But I can see them. That is the glory of having these special eyes.

A short one pokes her head around a tree and stares at me. She's a young vamp, maybe a teenager, too young to have her life taken away from her. She moves away from the tree entirely and takes a step into the barren field. Elliot holds the rifle tighter and takes aim. He stares through the scope and I'm sure he can see the same face I see staring back at us.

Another vamp steps into the field and Elliot is trying to decide which one is more threatening. If he could see the other faces peering out through the trees, he could clearly see that we are outnumbered. The few guns these people have won't be enough and I can't stop them all. I might be strong, but I count over fifteen of them in the trees and they would render me useless after just one bite.

The second one that came into clearing is an older man. His tattered clothing and muddy shoes make his ghastly appearance seem worse. He inches through the field, steadily getting closer to us. Elliot cocks his gun and readies his finger on the trigger. The vampire stops when he hears the click of the gun and he tilts his head to the side in confusion. The young girl at his side does the same, then turns her eyes back to mine.

"What the hell are they doing?" Elliot asks, quietly. "Why aren't they attacking us?"

I wish I had an answer to his question, but I honestly don't know. The vamps have no use for a thing like me, but these humans are more than appetizing. Their smell has got to be driving those creatures into a frenzy they can't contain. They have no reason not to attack them and enjoy their feast in the process.

A soft groan catches my ear. It's coming from the trees where the vamps are standing and I hear the stumbling of feet in the woods. I take a step forward and squint my eyes to peer through the darkness.

"What do you see?" Elliot asks.

I watch the trees for a long moment, listening to the footsteps and the groaning is getting louder. I sniff the air and smell the wretched death emitting from their bodies.

"Zombies." I say quietly.

A few gasps come from behind me and people are rustling to get their guns ready. The branches of the trees sway back and forth as the zombies drag their feet into the field and stand with the vampires by their side.

It truly is a sight to see. Over a dozen vampires are standing amid a small cluster of zombies and they aren't even that far from us. I could throw a stone and be able to hit one of them in the head.

Ryder comes to my side and stares at the horde of beasts by the trees. A gun dangles from his hand and by the look on his face, he believes that we are utterly screwed.

"We can't even make a run for it." A woman's voice comes from behind me. "The vamps would catch us and let the zombies feed on us."

The rest of the humans are wide awake and on full alert now. I take another step closer to the beasts and stare at their serene faces. The dead eyes of the zombies stare right through me, but they don't seem to want to attack. The vampires stand their ground, side by side with zombies and not a single one of them is moving.

"*They're hesitating.*" the voice in my head chimes in and I raise an eyebrow at her assumption.

"What do you mean?" I ask. "Vampires don't hesitate and zombies are stupid."

"*Look at them, monster,*" she commands, "*they aren't moving or rushing at the group. They want no part of the humans. How else can you explain this?*"

I take another look at the undead creatures on the other side of the field. My eyes scan over each one of them and see the same uncaring expressions on their faces as they look over the humans behind me.

For once, the voice might actually be helpful.

"*The vampires can talk, ya know. Go find out what they're up to.*" She states.

I let the devilish grin cross my lips and stick my hands in the pockets of my jacket. I stroll through the field, hearing the sounds of protests coming from Ryder. His footsteps come next, but he keeps a safe distance away. I don't have to glance over my shoulder to know that he has the gun ready to shoot in case something goes wrong.

I approach the horde and stop a few feet from them and Ryder stops a few feet behind me. Their eyes are telling me nothing, but the way they maintain composure with a human so close to them, I know something isn't right with these things.

"What do you want?" I ask.

The teenaged girl steps closer then stands completely

still. Her eyes are blank and her hair is a faded shade of red. Her once pink nightgown is now a blood stained rag barely covering her body. Her bare feet are covered in dirt and scratches and her pale legs are bruised and veiny.

"You...dead." she speaks softly.

I nod and say, "Sort of. Why aren't you attacking the humans back there?"

She doesn't even look past me as she says, "Don't...want to."

I raise an eyebrow and ask, "But why? That doesn't make sense."

"You are...cure." she says and the zombies begin to groan.

"How do you know that?"

She sniffs the air as well as a vampire standing behind her, then she says, "Smell different. We...want."

I look over my shoulder and Ryder seems to be just as confused as I am. Vampires are supposed to be these blood thirsty creatures that roam the night, enjoying the mass killing of humans that cross their paths. They shouldn't be going soft and asking for the cure.

"Give us...cure." She sounds demanding this time.

I turn back to her and say, "It's not that simple."

"Bite us." She says and takes another step closer.

I shake my head and reply, "I can't do that. If I do, I'll black out and there is a good possibility that a lot of bad things will happen to you and the humans back there."

She advances toward me and I have no choice other than to back away from her. She reaches her hand out for mine, but I'm quicker and stay out of her grasp. Another vampire comes at me too and reaches his claws out for my skin.

"*We can't let them bite us, monster. We can't afford to pass out right now.*" The voice says.

"Tell me something I don't know." I argue.

She says nothing and another vampire along with two zombies are heading right for me. It's clear now that they have no desire to hurt the people behind me. I am their target and for some strange reason, they are craving my blood.

"Give us...the cure." The little girl says again and I see the anger in her grey eyes.

"I can't do that." I reply, louder.

Her eyes turn to Ryder who is still standing behind me. In a flash, a tall lanky vampire leaps through the air over my head and lands on the ground directly in front of Ryder. He knocks the gun from his hand and wraps his fingers around his throat and leans his face close to his neck.

"No!" I shout, feeling the sudden urge to keep him safe.

I reach out for him and move my feet closer to the vamp hovering over his neck. A zombie stops me from getting too close and I'm forced to watch Ryder struggle against the vampire's grip. He fights for breath as he claws at the vamp's arms, but the thing never unlatches its grip. The humans standing by the fire all have their guns raised, but maintain their safe distance from these creatures.

"Cure us!" The girl says again and I keep my eyes on Ryder.

Why are they begging for this and threating to kill him if I continue to say no? This isn't the way it's supposed to be. I am the one that has to be in control, but these damn beasts are about to overpower me in a way I can only associate with weakness.

The zombie standing in front of me growls and her body sways back and forth. The vampires reach out for me, getting too close for me to be able to stop them all from biting me and stealing the cure. My eyes are focused on Ryder's face and I can hear him gasping for breath.

"*Please don't let them kill him.*" the voice begs me.

"I'm trying." I snap a response.

An odd sensation fills my mind and my eyes turn to the zombie in front of me. Her black eyes stare right through me and the low groan coming from her throat has advanced to the point of utter annoyance. I grit my teeth and lunge at her. I grab the collar of her disgusting shirt and let her claw at my back. I clamp my jaw against her neck and let the dead blood and skin slide down my throat. I don't take more than I need and toss her slowly dying body to the ground.

The other creatures keep coming for me, their arms outstretched and they are begging for a taste. One of them gets in my way and his claws nearly get my face. I back out of the way just in time. I spin away from him and focus once again at the vamp still gripping onto Ryder. His eyes are bloodshot and he cannot breathe at all. I clench my hands into fists and push myself from the ground, flying through the air, and tackle the damn thing to the ground.

His hold on Ryder quickly releases and he falls to the ground beside me. He lets out a painful cry, but he can finally breathe. I pull myself up and help Ryder to his feet and we stand together, facing the mass of zombies and vampires still calling out for the cure.

We slowly back away from them, keeping just out of their reach. By the feel of things we won't be making it to the city with these damn things constantly on our tail. I won't be able to stop them or cure them all. We would need a better plan, a dart gun to do it safely so I won't have to go hours in the shrilling blackness of my mind.

"I will cure you!" I shout and a few of them stop moving to listen.

What am I saying? I can't cure them here.

"*Let me speak for a minute.*" The voice demands and she takes over, my lips begin to move and it's her words coming out. "We are going to the city. I can't cure all of you from here, but I can when we get there. They will have a better way to do it. You just have to let us get there and trust that I am speaking the truth."

So that's what the old me was good for. Coming up with smart plans that I disagree with.

The vampires and zombies standing before us come to a complete halt. They stop reaching out for me and their eyes no longer burn with rage over wanting the cure. The young girl pushes her way through the others and plants her feet right in front of me.

"The city?" she questions and I nod. "If you lie...we kill...him." she points at Ryder, then leads the cure-hungry creatures back to the woods.

I breathe a sigh of relief and hear Ryder wheezing behind me. I wait until the creatures are completely hidden by the trees again, then spin around and see the others walking up to us. Elliot still has his firearm aimed at the woods and rushes our way. Ryder is still wheezing and his hand grips at a spot on his neck. I move closer to him and eye a tiny hint of red glistening in the starlight.

"No." the voice whispers, but I speak right along with her.

I reach for his hand and move it away from his neck. Sure enough, there are two long scratches deep in the skin where that vamp held onto him. The damn thing dug its claws into him. It doesn't need to bite him in order for its disease to spread. A simple scratch will do the trick.

* * *

"You can stop this right?" Elliot asks as he puts more logs on the fire to rebuild it.

Ryder sits on a tree stump, keeping a rag pressed against his neck to slow the bleeding. His breathing is raspy and slow. His hands are shaking and his eyes are wide open in fear. It will take a few days for him to change if the world allows that to happen. He will go through a severe amount of pain as his body slowly dies and he is forced to be awake through it all.

"Bridget." Elliot says louder, grabbing my attention, "Can you fix this?"

I kneel in front of Ryder and slowly take his hand and the rag away from his neck. The fire is getting brighter as two others poke at it with long sticks. The shadows of the flames dance across his blood-soaked skin and that over appealing scent drifts up my nose. I stare at the crimson liquid of my desire, but don't feel the craving for it like I have with humans before. The sight of seeing Ryder's blood has a part of me feeling something other than weakness or hatred toward him.

Jason comes to his side and examines the wound as well. He turns to me with sad eyes and shakes his head.

"You can't bite him." he says, kneeling beside me. "He's still human, you'd kill him." his voice is quiet so only Ryder and I can hear him.

I nod and say, "I know."

"How do you know that?" Ryder says with a shaky voice.

Our eyes meet, but I cannot tell him what happened, "I just know."

He tries to smile and trusts me with his eyes. Every person in the group is watching us, waiting for me to save the day with the miracle in my blood. I don't even know if it will work this soon. He was just scratched and is still human.

"*Let him drink our blood.*" The voice suggests and I raise an eyebrow.

"How do you know it won't kill him if I do that?" I ask and instantly get strange looks from those around me.

"*Just trust me on this. You might not remember things, but I do.*" She says.

I sigh and reply, "Whatever you say, but if he dies it's all on you."

Ryder goes pale at those words and says, "What are you talking about?"

I shrug, "She told me to have you drink the cure. I'll need a knife or something."

I hear shuffling coming from behind me. A bag gets unzipped and things get ruffled through before someone quietly says "yes" then comes to my side. A young woman hands a small pocket knife to me and I quickly take it. I pull the blade out and admire its sharpness. The metal reflects in the fire behind me, then I bring the tip of it to my arm.

Before I break the skin, the worst possible sound we could hear right now erupts through the air around us and the group once again goes on high alert. A stick breaks and footsteps stomp through the dry grass. I hold my breath and look away from Ryder. They aren't vampires and they certainly aren't zombies.

"Well, well, well," a man's voice breaks through the silence of our group, "look what we found."

I get to my feet and stare at three men dressed all in black to blend in with the night. Elliot has his gun drawn and the others are quickly getting theirs out and aimed for the strangers. I take a whiff of their skin and catch a familiar scent mixed with it.

"Trevor will be so happy to get his hands on you again." A dark skinned man steps forward with his eyes focused solely on me.

I step away from Ryder and say, "Where is my old friend?"

"He's not too far behind us. We were sent to scout ahead and thank god we did. You certainly are a prize, especially this time of night."

"A prize?" I ask.

He nods and comes closer, "You think you're gonna get away from us again?"

"I know I will get away from you." I say and my group

has their weapons trained on these men. "You are more than outnumbered and I can easily take you out without their help."

He laughs and the sound of other footsteps surrounds me. A dozen more of his men come out from nowhere, doubling our number and our guns. All of them have huge automatic shotguns and their aim is dead on with the barrel pointed at each person's head who stand behind me.

"You are coming with us." He speaks again. "We'll even let these people live if you come willingly."

I run my fingers through my hair and let the devilish grin cross my face, "There is just one thing you don't know about me, I never do anything willingly."

The first gunshot is fired, coming from Elliot and a member of the enemy goes down with a thud against the grass. At that instant I leap through the air and plummet the dark skinned man to the earth. He slams his fist against my side, hitting my ribs and I wince from the pain. He hits me again and I am forced to roll away from him.

Another gunshot blares through the air and is quickly met with a few more. The people in my group are scrambling around to find a safe place to hide while Trevor's men shoot at them wildly. I can't tell if anyone has gotten hit and I don't have the time to waste in order to check.

I pick myself back up and face my enemy once more. He is slowly getting to his knees and I slam my foot against his back, sending him to the grass for a second time. He gasps for the air that was stolen from him and I rush to pin him to the ground. He reaches for the small gun at the waistband of his jeans, but I grab his wrist and twist it sharply. The snap fills my ears and he screams bloody murder.

As his scream flows through the air, I notice the rest of his men are letting out terrified shrieks as well. They are shooting wildly at something running after them and I take a short second to look over my shoulder. The zombies and vampires from the woods are rushing at them, taking a few of them out and killing them instead of biting them. Some take bullets to the chest and others get hit elsewhere on their bodies, but they come to our rescue.

I brush off their help and look back to the man pinned on the ground. He swings his arm through the air before I could stop him and I feel a sharp pinch in my shoulder, close to my neck. He rips the serrated knife out of me and I more than wince from the pain caused by it. He grabs my jacket and throws me off of him then he gets back to his feet. This time he is able to get the gun out and aims it at me.

I press a hand to my shoulder and press down for a moment until the pain is more tolerable. My angry eyes glare up at him and the rest of the world fades for a moment. The sounds of screaming disappear and all I hear is this man's breathing as his chest heaves in and out. I want that movement to stop.

I want his heart to stop.

I take my hand away from my shoulder and thrust myself from the ground. He fires off a round that completely misses me and I plow myself against his stomach until he crashes to the grass one final time. I straddle over him and rip the gun from his grip and throw it somewhere I do not see. I take a handful of his hair and lift his head off the ground, then bring my face to his neck.

He digs his fingers into my back as I sink my teeth into his skin. The taste of his blood flows down my throat and my chin. I hold his body tight and allow myself to suck the life out of him. I rip away more of his skin, tearing through the muscles that connect his neck to his shoulder and take in more of this great tasting thing. He struggles for a few moments but I hold him still until his body goes limp and the weight of the dead human is heavy in my grasp. I take one last slurp of his warm blood, then let go of him and allow the world around me to come back.

Everything is silent and still. The screams that came from the enemy are over and we have won this round. The zombies and vamps who helped here tonight are retreating back to the woods.

I feel the eyes of the humans leering at me and I slowly get to my feet and turn around. I wipe the blood from my chin and stare at the barrels of the guns aimed right for me by the very humans I intend to keep safe.

Ryder comes out of nowhere and rushes to stand in front of me. His arms are raised in hopes of protecting me from their bullets, but they still keep their aim.

"Get away from her, Ryder." Elliot demands. "She's clearly not something to be trusted."

Ryder shakes his head and says, "That was the enemy. She's not going to hurt any of us."

"Prove it." Elliot says.

"We've gotten this far, haven't we? If she wanted to take us out, she could've done that already." Ryder replies. "You have to trust me on this, she is not going to hurt us and you can't hurt her either."

Elliot comes forward, his rifle still aimed straight ahead of him, "You don't know that. She killed a human. She tasted his blood and enjoyed it. There is no saying when she'll do it again or how many of us will have to die because of her."

"You can't kill the cure." Ryder says.

"I don't want to." Elliot states. " But she is a threat to us now and I can't risk our lives any more than we have to."

He holds the gun up high and motions for Ryder to move out of the way. I take a deep breath and glance over to the vampires who are still standing nearby. They look pissed off and their eyes seem focused on Elliot. They won't let the cure slip through their fingers like that. The teenaged girl lets a shrill scream come from her throat and she lunges for the gun in Elliot's grip. He fires off a round, sending the bullet soaring through the air above our heads. Ryder ducks and I quickly grab his hand and pull him away from the group.

We run through the night, jumping over the dead bodies of our enemy and two of our own. I don't look back as I hear

Elliot screaming and a few gunshots echoing through the air. We just need to keep running and stay alive. That is the only plan now.

* * *

Ryder and I made it back to the long stretch of highway and we keep going until we no longer see the flickering light of the fire in the field. I strain my ears to listen for sounds of footsteps chasing after us or shouting coming from the humans we left behind. The wind rustles through the remaining leaves on the trees and a bat flutters through the air somewhere above us, but there is nothing that threatens our getaway.

The highway is dark, almost pitch black with the only light coming from the scattered stars above. I stay close to Ryder and guide him down the concrete path, being his eyes and pulling him with me. He is panting heavily and slowing down, but we have to keep moving. Outside of the humans that now want to kill me and the hesitating zombies and vampires, we still have Trevor's army to worry about. Those men said he wasn't far behind and if that's true we need to cover as much ground as we can.

Our hands remain clasped together and we pump our legs for a long while until I know he can't go on anymore. He lets go of my hand and forces his body to a stumbling stop. We have to be over a mile away from the group in the field and this road seems never ending in the darkness.

Ryder bends over with his hands on his knees trying desperately to catch his breath. I stand a few feet from him and glance in every direction. The scattered trees are hiding no threat and the woods across from us seem empty at the moment. I don't see or smell any signs of humans chasing us and the pavement we just ran on is empty of any living or unliving being. It feels safe enough to take a breather.

Ryder's wheezing grabs my attention so I turn to face him. He is still bent over and a few droplets of blood fall from the scratch on his neck. They splatter to the ground at his feet and I stare at the long scratches on his skin. He is bleeding quite a lot. If we don't get it taken care of soon, there is the real possibility that he could bleed to death and then turn into a vampire. We have come too far and gone through so much for me to allow that to happen.

I spin around and spot a totaled car sitting in the middle of the street. One of the windows is smashed and shards of glass are clustered together on the ground. I could use the glass to cut myself enough for him to drink. I walk to the car and break off a piece of the window. We might as well get this over with while we have a few moments to catch our breath.

"What are you doing?" he asks between breaths.

I lift the sleeve of my jacket and walk back to him, "I have to cure you."

He shakes his head and straightens his spine, "We can't do that yet."

"Why? If we wait too long you will either turn or bleed to death first. The voice in my head won't allow that to happen." I reply.

"I'll pass out. That's what happened to the last one that had just been bit. That kid was out for almost a day. We need to get to the city and be safe, then worry about me." He states.

So there *are* things the voice in my head knows more about this life than I do.

I lower my arm and the sleeve falls back to my wrist. I

toss the piece of glass to the street and it clanks against the pavement. I take a deep breath and look at his wound. The scratches are deep and the blood continues to seep through it.

"I have to do something to stop the bleeding. We won't make it very far if we don't." I say.

I turn around and take a step closer to the car. I poke my head through the open window and search around inside. The previous owner of this vehicle is not in here rotting, but there is a bloody stain on the drivers' seat that suggests he did not make it out of the accident alive. The front windshield is also cracked and the hood is crinkled up with the rest of the front end.

I reach for the glove compartment and pull on the handle. It falls open and a thick book slides out and hits the floor. I ignore it then turn my eyes to the backseat. A garbage bag filled with old clothes sits open on the seat and I reach for some of the fabric lying on top. I let two, small children's shirts fall to the floor and keep only the thin, grey shirt that seems large enough to make a bandage. It isn't much, but it might slow the bleeding enough so we can get to the city.

Ryder has a hand holding the side of his neck and I walk up to him with the shirt, "What are you doing with that?" he asks, nodding toward the cloth.

"Trying to keep you from bleeding to death. Move your hand." I demand.

He lowers his bloody fingers and I stretch the shirt out and wrap it around his neck like a scarf. I make sure to cover the scratches, pressing the shirt against that part of his neck and he winces. I tie it gently, but I also make sure it's tight enough to stay in place.

"Can you breathe okay?" I ask.

He takes a few breaths and nods slightly, then lifts the hood of his jacket over his head which masks the appearance of the shirt bandage. I try to smile then look back down the road just to make sure no one has caught up with us.

"We should keep moving." I say, "The faster we get to

the city, the faster I can heal you."

He sighs then says, "So you do care about me."

I turn my eyes to his and reply, "The voice in my head cares about you enough to drive me insane if I let anything bad happen."

He nods in agreement then moves closer to me. I stare into his eyes and listen to the breaths escaping between his lips. He stands before me and reaches a hand to my face, tucking a few strands of hair behind my ear. As much as I want to back away from him, my feet remain motionless and I simply stare at him.

"Why can't you just accept that the Bridget I fell in love with is still in there and she wants to come back?" he asks.

I shake my head and say, "She can't come back. Not if we want to survive."

"She was more than capable of keeping us both alive long before she was bitten. You might not remember it, but it's in your head somewhere."

I step away from him and say, "I don't care. Let's just keep moving."

We walk instead of run and he stays by my side not saying a word. The stars are still shining brightly overhead and the sun will be rising in a few hours. The wall surrounding the city is on this road somewhere and I know once we get there, it will be a battle just to get through the gate.

* * *

The morning sun is starting to peak over the horizon and I slide the sunglasses over my eyes. We have been walking for hours now and I can smell humans coming from every direction. I don't know if we are nearing the city or if Trevor's army is right on our tail. We move as fast as we can, walking down the middle of the highway and hope to get to the city before it's too late.

Ryder is fading. His breathing is raspy and he shivers every few seconds despite the beads of sweat on his brow. His hands are shaking so he hides them in the pockets of his hoodie. He cannot hide the paleness of his skin though. He refuses to stop no matter how much pain I am sure he is going through. He keeps insisting that we don't stop walking.

I love his strength and persistence, but there is a limit one man can take. Soon he will either succumb to his fate and become a vampire or we will make it to the city walls and they will shoot us both. The nagging voice in my head refuses to let either of those things happen and I don't quite know how to shut her up. Her worrying is seeping right through to me and I cannot stop myself from checking on him every chance I get.

I watch him now. He rubs at the shirt around his neck, wincing from the pain when his hand grazes the wound. That portion of the makeshift bandage is spotted with blood which still seems to be bleeding more than I want it to.

"Are you sure you're okay enough to walk the rest of the way to the city?" I ask.

He nods slowly and says, "I'll be fine. We've been through worse."

"I can't imagine what would be worse than getting scratched by a vampire." I reply.

"Almost losing you is worse than anything." He says and rubs at his neck again.

I don't know what to say to that. I know he still loves the version of me that isn't a monster who kills humans by biting them. *Who knows*, maybe he loves me for that too. Jason looked past it pretty quickly, but that was as far as it went with him. The more I think of it, the more I know it wouldn't have worked out. He stopped me from doing something I would have enjoyed so there was never a guarantee that he wouldn't do something like that again.

Ryder gasps as he scratches at the wound and he quickly pulls his hand away from his neck. Blood covers his fingertips and he starts shivering again. I glance to his hand and watch as he wipes it on his already stained jeans.

"You need to hurry." The voice finally makes an appearance.

"You think I don't know that." I snap, turning my head away from Ryder. "We are moving as fast as we can."

"That's not good enough." She replies. *"He'll die if you don't make it there soon."*

"Can you not see the amount of pain he is in right now? He can only move so fast without hurting himself." I argue.

"I never should have given up." She sounds aggravated now. *"I should have just kept going with it and dealt with the pain instead of letting you take over. He wouldn't have gotten hurt if I was there. This is all your fault, monster."*

"How is it my fault that those creatures showed up last night and threatened me or that Trevor sent those bastards out to kill us? Like I'm supposed to be a fortune teller mixed with the rest of this shit I have to deal with. You couldn't handle any of it." I shout.

Ryder stares at me and listens to the argument I'm having with the voice in my head. I sound like a crazy person yelling at thin air, but she is driving me insane. She has no idea how to handle anything life throws at her. That is why I am here. She gave me this life to help her escape everything and I am doing a damn good job at it. If she would just stop popping up in my head, I could do even better.

"Hey," Ryder says, taking my hand and holding it tight, "stop thinking about whatever is going on up there." He motions to my head, "We'll get to the city and everything will be okay."

"She blames me for what happened to you."

He shakes his head and says, "It's not your fault though. I was in the way."

"But you wouldn't have been in the way if I would have just left the vamps alone. I allowed my weakness to show through and bad things always come with that."

He nods as though he agrees with me. I have a feeling the old me has let something bad happen due to her weaknesses and the love she feels for him. I can only assume that she has or else she wouldn't have gotten taken by Trevor. After all, Ryder did almost die under her watch and she got Jason kidnapped right along with her. I believe that I wouldn't have let that happen.

We keep moving and I keep a tight grip on Ryder's cold hand. His fingers are shaking and his teeth start to chatter. I squeeze my eyes shut tight and force the upset feeling back down into the pit of my stomach.

When I open my eyes again, a noise catches my ears. I look straight ahead of me, expecting to see a mass of humans or other creatures staring us down, but I see nothing. I glance over my shoulder and see the same emptiness taking over. The sound comes again and I sniff the air, taking in the human scent that comes from all directions.

We aren't alone out here and we have nothing to shield us from the enemy's sight.

"I really hope we make it there soon." Ryder speaks slowly.

I agree, but it isn't my words that are the response to his statement. The deafening sound of footsteps are approaching and I focus my hearing on where they are coming from. They are on the road, kicking up pebbles as they walk. There are a lot them and not a single human says a word.

Ryder notices the sound right along with me and he starts looking for the people heading our way. I let go of his hand and turn around, still waiting to see Trevor's army on our tail.

I squint my eyes and see the faint shadow of humans stomping on the concrete as they walk down the highway.

"How much farther until we get to the city?" I ask.

Ryder takes a breath and answers, "Not far, maybe a mile."

I take a step away from him, a step back the way we came and the humans are steadily coming into view. Dozens of men and women ready to fight a battle that they do not intend to lose. Their weapons look fierce, some carry swords while others have handguns and automatic rifles. They look pissed off and some are wearing war paint on their faces. They have black lines drawn under their eyes and across their forehead. They look ridiculous and menacing at the same time.

I scan their faces searching for the only one I want to see in that group. His bruised face from Jason's punches will be just what I need to smile as I rip him apart. But I don't see him. He is not walking at the front of his group or even mixed in with them. I wouldn't expect him to walk in the middle of all his men. He is the type of leader that needs to be at the front of the line to witness the show up close and personal.

By now, Ryder has turned around and is staring at the army coming after us. He reaches for my hand and tugs at it slightly. I turn to face him and see worry in his eyes.

"I think we need to keep moving." He states.

I nod and we start walking backward a few paces. He turns around first and I am quick to follow. The smell of humans is getting stronger the closer we get to the city and it is masking my ability to track the scents that belong to our enemy. I need to keep on the lookout for Trevor and it is next to impossible to hone in on his odor.

I focus my eyes on the road, ignoring the potholes and debris that lie in our way. We rush past the trees of the surr- ounding forest and the abandoned cars left to rust on the sides of the highway. Ryder wheezes as we jog and he struggles to maintain a brisk pace. I keep my fingers laced with his and listen to the voice repeating the same thing over and over in my head.

"*Please make it in time.*" She says. "*Please don't let him die.*"

I am doing my best. I swear on whatever life that flows through me that I will keep him alive. I know she can hear my thoughts and she has to know that I will try to do as she wishes. I might hate that girl in my head, but she has the same desire to keep Ryder alive that I do and together we cannot fail.

The footsteps are getting louder and sound more rushed than before. I strain my ears and listen to the voices that are speaking above the falling of their feet. They have spotted us. Each and every person chasing after us can see exactly where we are and they are picking up the pace to catch up.

I pull Ryder with me, willing him to run faster, a task he is simply too weak to go through. His breathing is becoming more and more labored, his heart is beating rapidly, meaning that the vampire's poison is flowing faster through his veins. He could drop to the ground right now and endure the terrible transformation right before my eyes. Still, I tug on his arm and he moves his legs as fast as he possibly can.

We pass by a dark green truck sitting crooked in the middle of the road. As soon as we run by the tailgate, a gun-shot blasts through the air and bounces off the old metal. The bullet came from somewhere ahead of us and we force our legs to stop pumping. I hold onto Ryder's sweatshirt as we stumble to a halt and stare at the empty road.

"Shit." I say, then look over my shoulder.

A good majority of Trevor's army is catching up and they are slowing down as they close in on the green truck. They have guns aimed and swords raised over their heads, ready to fight to the death for a future that should not have to exist.

I turn to the path leading to the city walls and I finally see the oncoming threat that fired the first shot. Many of them crouch low to the ground with guns pointed directly at us and the army coming their way. The men guarding the wall wear green camo outfits and look more like an army than Trevor's ever could.

"We're surrounded." I whisper, although Ryder can already see that.

He nods and says, "What do we do?"

I glance back and forth between the two armies. The one from behind has us completely blocked in. Some of them are trailing into the woods, hiding amongst the trees to keep that way secure as well. I scan the faces of those that are close enough to see and I finally spot the one man who needs to die. He slowly walks through the crowd of men, a smile crosses his face and a gun is dangling in his right hand.

I shake his face out of my mind and turn to the men in front of us. The wall is not far away from them, I can see it poking above the tops of trees. We were so close to making it and now we have completely failed.

A familiar looking tall man with olive colored skin steps through his people with a few of them following close behind. Each one has a gun trained for Ryder and I, leaving us with no room for error.

Ryder's question lingers in my mind and for the first time in this short life of mine, I have no idea what we are going to do to get out of this mess alive.

* * *

Another bullet flies through the air, passing right by us on its way to Trevor's army. The group protecting the wall can see the threat behind us and they are ready to take them down. The bullet struck an older man in the gut and he falls to his knees, shouting out in pain. The others around him ignore his cries for help and Trevor steps over him as though he is nothing. He nods to one of his own who fires a return shot at the city army, but that bullet misses its target.

"Stand down!" a male voice comes from the city army, shouting orders that will never be obeyed by Trevor.

Trevor keeps walking, inching his way to the front of his group and his eyes stay focused solely on me. I fire my glare right back at him and keep a tight grip on Ryder's hoodie.

"I am ordering you to stand down!" the man's voice shouts again. "We will open fire on you!"

Trevor laughs and keeps moving. He brushes those orders right off his shoulder and he takes that final step out in front of his people and breathes in through his nose. Accomplishment crosses his face as he stares at me and the gun hangs at his side.

"Looks like I found you, Bridget." He shouts to me. "I can see that your boyfriend didn't die after all." His eyes turn to Ryder and I move to stand in his view.

"Bridget?" a confused voice comes from a man behind me, but I don't turn my head to see who it's from.

Trevor advances and Ryder and I both take a step backward, "You might as well give up and come with me. You did it so easily the first time, it shouldn't be that difficult now."

I grit my teeth and ball my right hand into a tight fist. My fingernails poke into my skin and rage boils beneath it. I stare at his face, still bruised from his encounter with Jason back at the school. This wouldn't be happening if I had killed him then. We would be safe right now.

"Stop dwelling on what could have been and focus on what's happening now, monster!" the voice shouts at me, snapping me out of the regret in my head.

The faint sound of a gun being cocked echoes through the air from the people guarding the city. Trevor stops moving and his eyes turn to those of the army behind me. He seems annoyed at the fact that someone is getting in his way and making things harder than they have to be.

"This is your last chance to put your guns down and get the hell out of here!" the man from the city shouts again.

"Or what?" Trevor replies. "Are you going to open fire on us and risk killing these two kids standing in the way? I hope you'd realize just what you'd be killing if you pull your triggers."

I hear angry footsteps stomping across the pavement behind us and I steal a quick glance over my shoulder. The tall, familiar man, steps closer with a rifle aimed out in front of him. A few of his men follow close behind and prepare themselves for what's about to come.

A war is about to break out between these two armies. Dozens of people will die because one man has the sick fantasy of taking over the world and will stop at nothing to get what he wants.

"We have to stop this, monster." The voice says and I couldn't agree with her more. *"You have to stop this."*

"It doesn't have to be this way, Trevor." I finally open my mouth and take my hand away from Ryder. "There doesn't have to be a war and you know that."

He grits his teeth and spits as he talks, "War is the only way. That city belongs to me."

I take a step away from Ryder and say, "No. You can't kill them because of me."

Trevor smiles and says, "I can do whatever the fuck I want because of you."

He raises the gun in his hand and fires a round at the group behind me. He nods to a few standing close by and they do the same. I quickly grab Ryder and pull him closer to the truck and we duck down by the tailgate. The city's army is returning fire, sending a barrage of bullets into the men and women following Trevor's every command. I smell the blood of those that have been shot and listen to the sounds of their bodies hitting the concrete when they die.

"Come on you can stop this." The voice is pleading with me now. *"You can't let Trevor take over the city. You are strong enough to stop this. Be the monster I created and do what you are meant to do."*

Those are the first encouraging words she has ever spoken to me. I *am* strong enough to bring an end to this before it goes too far. There doesn't have to be a war or meaningless death of hundreds of humans. I think I might know exactly what to do.

A bullet crashes into the bed of the truck and Ryder jumps at the sound of the ping. He is breathing quickly and his eyes are stricken with fear. I put a hand to his face and stare into his calming eyes for a short moment.

"I know how to stop this." I say.

He quickly shakes his head from side to side as though he knows what swims through my mind, "You can't go out there."

"It isn't the best plan in the world, but it is the only way." I reply.

"You could die." He states.

"I know, but it is worth it. You and the rest of the world will be safe and Trevor's army will fall."

He shakes his head and his eyes turn bloodshot and teary, "I can't lose you again, Bridge. I love you too much to watch you die."

I stare into his eyes for another moment and say, "Then don't." I press my lips against his, stealing a long kiss from his soft lips.

I let this moment linger longer than I planned. He puts a hand on my back, gripping onto my jacket, never wanting to let go. I feel myself never wanting this short moment to end. There is something in this kiss that is more than just familiar. It is warm and filled with a kind of love I know I'd never find with anyone else. But I have to let it go and do the one thing in my power that will end something horrible.

I pull myself away from him and push off the ground. Before he can protest, I am out of his line of sight, ducking between bullets that constantly slam into the green truck. There is something clogging my throat and my eyes are heavy with tears, but I push my legs to keep moving and ignore the sad feelings growing inside of me.

My eyes scan the faces of Trevor's men, ignoring those that fall to their death as bullets pass through their bodies. They are scattering about, dodging bullets and firing more shots into those that guard the precious city. I quickly move away from the truck and spot the man of my evil desire standing tall beside a few of his men as he kills those who are in his way.

He wears a smile on his face and I let that image drive out the revenge boiling in my heart. My hands clench into fists and I move my legs faster than I ever have before to clear the space between us in a flash. I knock the man standing to his left out of my way and he flies to the ground, smashing his head on the concrete.

A younger woman steps in front of me, raising a small sword to my throat. I lift my arm and wrap my fingers around her wrist faster than she could ever anticipate. Her fingers unlatch the hilt of the sword and it falls to the ground at my feet. I grab the collar of her shirt and toss her out of my way. She lands on her back and rolls into the legs of one of her comrades. He trips over her body and slams to the ground with his face hitting the concrete. I smile a little more, then focus solely on the angry eyes of Trevor.

He lifts his gun and fires off a round. I move to the left and the bullet soars right by me. He pulls the trigger again and the bullet grazes my arm as I send my body into his. I wrap my arms around his waist and tackle him to the ground. The gun flies from his grip and slides out of his reach.

"Let go of me you bitch." He seethes and sends a sharp

blow to my ribs.

I grunt and roll away from him. That gives him the time to move to his stomach and push himself from the ground. I get to my knees and wince at the pain in my side. He stands behind me and I listen to his footsteps moving closer. I can feel the heat from his body as he reaches his arm out for my hair. I quickly spin out of the way and kick his legs out from under him. Once again, he crashes to the pavement and his elbow cracks against it.

He gasps for breath and I move to him. I reach for his jacket and force him to sit up and face me. His eyes are bloodshot and filled with the same amount of rage I can feel flowing through my veins.

"You tried to steal my life away from me." I say over the sounds of gunshots.

He smiles and wraps his left hand around my wrist, then leans closer to me, "You have no life."

I failed to see the dagger in his right hand and he thrusts it into my stomach, just below my ribs. My jaw drops and I can't breathe from the pain coursing through me. He shoves the dagger in deeper until I feel the hilt against my skin. He leaves it in its place and grabs my throat, pulling my face closer to his.

"You see," he says, "I will always win. You will *always* belong to me."

The pain in my gut is wrenching and my hands are shaking uncontrollably. I manage to keep my grip on the collar of his shirt and force myself to stay strong. The voice in my head is quiet, unable to help me through this horrible moment of weakness and bad judgment.

The smile on Trevor's face grows and he speaks so only I can hear, "I told you, you have no life. You might as well give up."

My eyes meet with his as his words resonate for a brief moment. I tighten my grip on his shirt and calm my breathing.

"I have no life, huh?" I ask, not waiting for an answer. "Then I will just take yours."

His smile fades and he raises an eyebrow in confusion. In a blur, I swipe his arm away from my throat and move my mouth to his. I close my jaw on the skin of his throat and bite until he bleeds. The warmth of his blood as it caresses my tongue and enlightens my taste-buds, has been a long awaited treat. It dribbles down my chin and my eyes fall shut and I allow this moment to consume me. Even as Trevor claws at my back and tugs at my hair, there is nothing to stop me from sucking the life from him.

I pull some of his skin away, spit it on the ground, then continue ripping through the muscles. He screams at the top of his lungs, digging his fingers deeper into the skin of my back and I take in those sounds escaping him. The screaming is music to my ears.

The life I take from him is for the revenge that has been burning through to my core ever since I woke up a few days ago. It is for the pain he brought to Jason when he locked him in that torture room back at that school. It's for Ryder and the many times he tried to kill him and thankfully failed. Trevor's death belongs to those humans he destroyed and the millions of lives he ended without even thinking about it.

Most importantly, this is for the voice in my head. He was the reason for her pain and weakness. He brought her a kind of sadness that no one should have to go through and I hope she is enjoying this moment just as much as I am.

I take in more of this succulent meal. I want to savor this part of my life although it is a short lived moment. His body goes limp in my hands and his fingers no longer dig into my skin. I uncurl my fingers from the collar of his shirt and take the last sip of his blood. I open my eyes and let his lifeless form crash to the ground at my knees and glance to his eyes that will never open again.

It is at this moment that I realize the fighting and gun-shots have come to an end. The eyes of the humans around me, stare at me in wonder and fear. Those from Trevor's army are actually starting to back away. They toss their guns to the ground and slowly head for the trees. Their leader has fallen and can no longer give them orders or even the will to fight for the false hope they once believed in.

The strength I got from drinking Trevor's blood is starting to fade and the pain from the dagger still sticking out of my stomach is making its way back to the surface. My hands start to shake and my knees are growing weak.

"C'mon monster, don't fade on me now. I need you to save Ryder." The voice pierces my ears, but my body cannot respond like she wants me to.

"I'm sorry." I whisper and drop to my hands.

I try holding myself up for as long as I can but I feel my arms wanting to fall out from under me. I can't even move my hand to pull the knife from my stomach and it is the only thing causing me to lose strength right now. I grit my teeth and squeeze my eyes shut tight, then fall to my side right next to Trevor.

"Bridget, no!" Ryder's voice screams through the air and I hear his footsteps rushing to me.

He comes to my side and holds my head in his hands. I open my eyes and stare up at him, gazing into those hazel orbs that have haunted my thoughts. Others from the city army are crowding around us, keeping a wary eye on me and a hand on their guns.

"You can't die on me. That's not how this ends." Ryder pleads and holds my hand in his.

"Then how does it end?" I say, feeling weaker by the second.

He tries to smile and squeezes my hand tighter, "It ends with me and you being together forever. With the world finally safe and no threat of anything to split us apart. You can't leave me right when things are going to get better."

"I'm sorry." My voice is quieter now.

He runs his hand through my hair and I take in a deep

breath through my nose. The shirt is still wrapped around his neck and the red blood seeping through the fabric is there to taunt me as I wait for death to take me.

I lift my shaking hand and wrap my fingers around the thin shirt and gently pull it away from his neck. The scratches are deep red and bruises cover the skin around them. The few people standing nearby gasp at the sight of what happened to him. The tall, dark skinned man who seems so familiar to me steps behind Ryder and passes us a look of despair.

"*Cure him,*" the voice in my head is raspy and fading, "*while we still have the strength to do it.*"

Just one bite will do the trick. He's already going through the transformation and the worst that would happen is that he would die. We could be together in the afterlife, whatever that may be. Slowly, I lean my head toward his neck and take in another inhale of his sweet blood. I bring my lips closer to the wound and feel a coldness escaping his skin. I open my mouth and gently sink my teeth into the soft spots on the marks and feel new rush of blood flowing down my throat.

Ryder grunts from the pain and holds me tighter against him. He clutches the leather of my jacket as I continue letting my saliva transfer into him to fight the vampire's poison. I pray that this works and he will wake up later on as a human.

The longer I keep steeling the blood from his body, the more I feel myself fading. My eyes fall shut and something warm grazes my cheek and slides down my face. This is what sadness and death feels like. I had hoped I'd never get to meet those two demons, yet here I am, standing on the doorstep of a fate that has been awaiting me since I turned this way. At least I will die in the arms of the man I love and bask in those beautiful eyes for all of eternity.

* * *

The air around me is cold and silent. A soft breeze kisses my cheeks and ruffles through my hair, sending an eerie shiver along my spine. I move my hands on the surface beneath me, feeling a glossy floor that ripples under my fingertips. Behind my eyes, I see only the blackness of my mind, yet I am afraid to open them and look at the world I will be stuck calling my new home.

I picture this place as a land of misery and hatred. The blackest parts of the mind I was once trapped inside. I will be imprisoned here with the old me and despise the fact that I allowed us both to die. I will never know the joys of living free in the wild that the earth had to offer or know what it truly meant to find happiness. The cure will never find a place in the world and humanity will still be lost.

This is what it means to fail at everything.

Dying is the ultimate ending to the life I have tried to lead. I believe it was a good one during the few days I was granted with it. I saved a few people along the way and I got to meet the one person who changed my life from the very beginning. Before I became this mess of a monster, Ryder was there for me and I am starting to see the good times we shared together.

I can recall everything about him now. The night kissing in the rain or staying up all night just talking about what we wanted to do in the future. It's funny how those things come back to me now that I know I'll never get to have him. He was the only thing that made sense in this otherwise tormenting world and I've lost him forever.

I run my hand along the slick floor one more time, feeling the ripples of the surface flowing against my palm. It is so peaceful in this place and the quietness doesn't bother me so much. It is quite embracing actually.

I squeeze my eyes shut tight and shake my head from side to side. I don't want to embrace this world that I have been sent to. This is not what I want or where I deserve to be. My life belongs outside of the blank space my death has sent me to.

I quickly open my eyes and stare up at the glass-like ceiling. A dark blue shade has taken over the space with tiny white dots spread out to create an array of stars. They seem to be flowing against the canvas above me, dancing in the sky that doesn't seem to exist yet it is still there.

"I know this place." I say quietly.

"Of course you know this place." The voice whispers in my ear and I feel her presence not far from me.

I hear her footsteps easing across the rippling floor and the stars stop moving for the brief moment as she makes her way to my side. I push myself from the floor and sit up for a second before completely standing. When I turn around, I stare into the eyes of the girl I replaced and finally the voice belongs to a face. Her clothes are the dirty rags which I replaced at the school with Trevor and her hair is a tangled mess. But it is my face that I see staring back and she scowls.

"I was hoping I'd never see you again." I say to her.

"I told you I wasn't going away." She replies.

"Well, we're both stuck here now so I will have to get used to being around you." I say, glancing around this peaceful world.

She nods and looks up to the swirling sky, "Yeah, it is very unfortunate. I wish you would have tried harder."

I raise an eyebrow and glare at her for saying such a thing, "I did better than you could have ever dreamed. Did you not see everything that I have done for you? I saved that boy you love so much and I got him safely to the city. You never could have accomplished any of that."

She nods and passes me a small grin, "Maybe you're

right. Maybe I couldn't have done any of that the way you have, but I have gotten Ryder to the city before and we were safe once we got there. I actually cared about doing it though. You only care about yourself."

I shrug and tilt my head to the side, "I was not created to care about anything else."

"And that's why you're dead." She snaps.

She turns away from me and the floor ripples as she walks. She is angry with me, I always knew she was, but this time it's different. I've only heard her voice in my head and now that I see her face, I know that she only holds hatred for me in her heart. But we are one in the same. If she hates me, she hates herself and I do not believe that she truly wants that.

I pick up my feet and begin to follow her. I move quicker than she does and grab onto her shoulder, forcing her to turn around to face me once again. She rips her arm out of my grip and stammers back a pace, then waits for my words.

"We are both dead and you have to accept that. You have to deal with the fact that you failed and in result of that failure, we wound up here together. There is no way out of this and you cannot hate me for anything that you gave me permission to do. Don't you remember the words you spoke me not long ago? Don't you remember what you begged me to do?" I argue.

"Of course I do, but if you honestly think that I am going to spend the rest of my time locked in this cage with you, then you are completely out of your mind." She retorts. "I made a mistake by letting you out and I will never do something as ridiculous as that again."

"What are you talking about?" I question.

She takes a step closer to me and places a hand on my shoulder. A cold sensation flows from her hand and into the very blood under my skin. A smile crosses her lips, one that I only recognize as my own.

"I learned something while I've been here, monster," she says, then turns away from me, "I've learned that in order to accept the things I hate to deal with, I have to remember them and think about them whenever I get the chance. You might think that is no way for a person like us to live, but it is the only way I *want* to live. And after seeing Ryder alive again, I have to get that back."

"But we are dead. Can you not see that?"

Again she nods, "I can see that *you* are dead. I can also see that you are afraid of this place and you're especially afraid of what I can do to you while you're here."

I take a step closer to her, ready to fight my way out, "And just what do you think you can do to me? You are weak and pathetic. The very existence I was trying to get rid of."

"If I am so weak, how was I able to find my way back into my mind and break you down until you did what I asked? How is it that I am the one in charge here?" she argues with her back to me and her voice is getting louder. "If I am so pathetic, how am I able to lock you in the same cage that I was locked in with Trevor?"

The very instance she turns around, bars fall from the sky, surrounding me in a tight box. Before I can jump over them, a steel roof gets added to the mix and I am completely stuck in this cage without a door to break through. I rush at the bars and wrap my fingers around the cold metal, pulling with all my might, trying to break free.

She approaches the bars and smiles at her handiwork. Her eyes move up and down the length of the bars, scanning them to make sure they are completely secure so I cannot get through. Then her eyes meet with mine and she places both of her hands on top of my fingers and holds on tightly.

She leans closer to the bars and the cold feeling creeps up my arms and into my shoulders and neck. I remember this sensation from the moment I took over her life and became my own person. It appears that she wants to do the same thing and knows how to get it done.

"I just want you to know that I appreciate everything you've done for me." Her voice speaks, growing stronger

with every word. "You took me out of my mind when I needed it the most and you saved me from a life I know I'd hate. I
love you for that."

"Then why are you locking me in here?" I ask, seething
with anger.

"You don't deserve to be free if you don't plan on giving
my cure to the rest of the world. You want to keep it all to
yourself and live without the idea of saving humanity. That's
not what I want which is why I came back so soon. The moment you changed your mind was the exact moment I got to
see things through your eyes and I was sickened by it." she
states and holds my hands even tighter.

Another bout of coldness rushes from her skin through
mine. My knees begin to shake and I can feel my legs
wanting to give out. I feel that the only thing holding me in
place is this woman keeping me pinned to the bars of the
cage.

"You can't do this. You need me!" I shout.

"I thought I did, but not anymore. I only need myself and
the person I love most in the world. With him, I can conquer
anything." She replies, then releases her grip on my hands.

She pulls herself away from the bars and I drop to the
floor. It splashes as I crash and tiny droplets of black water
caress my skin. It doesn't drip away or fall back to the floor.
Instead it lingers and soaks into the very skin on my hands.
The coldness gets stronger and I slam my fist into the floor,
sending more of this black water to splash. The blackness is
taking over, covering every inch of me that was once the silky
white skin I had grown to love.

Quickly, I wipe my hands on my jeans, trying desperately to get the water off my skin. The rubbing only causes it
to spread faster until I feel it creeping up my arms and
flowing over my chest under my shirt.

"No!" I scream and cover my face with my hands. "Stop
doing this!"

"I can't help you. This is how I've always seen you and

this is what you truly are. The blackest parts of my mind that never should have seen the light of day." Her voice rings in my ears and a slight pain emanates with her every word. "I'm sorry it has to be this way, but it is the only way."

I shake my head from side to side, the blackness is drifting up my neck and quickly covering my face. I scream as loud as I can but the pain coming from this transformation never ends. That girl I took over will never let me be the person I am meant to be.

I slam my fists against the floor again. There is no sense in caring how much of this liquid I get on my skin or my clothes. She will not let me out of here and I am doomed to roam forever in this cage and she is the only one with the key.

My time has come to an end and I have no choice but to accept it.

Part Three

The ground is soft beneath me. It feels like I'm lying on some plush thing that's both comfortable yet annoying at the same time. My head is resting on an overstuffed pillow that has a hint of a bleachy smell to it. I take a breath through my nose and sniff the air. It stinks of formaldehyde and some type of cleansing product.

My eyes flutter open and I stare up at a white, tiled ceiling above. There are tiny holes poked into the tiles and an unlit light fixture hangs in the middle of the room. I turn my head to the left and find a large wooden door with a silver handle to open it. A sink is against the wall beside the door with a good sized cardboard box on the counter next to it. The paper towel holder nailed to the wall is empty and a single blue towel is folded on top of it.

I move my eyes away from the sink and pass across the room in front of me and the bed I'm on. A flat screen TV hangs from the ceiling above a wall of cabinets and another counter is underneath them. There are white sheets and a pile of clothes on the counter and I squint my eyes to see them. The clothes are black and familiar. I don't exactly remember putting them on myself, but I recognize them from what the monster was wearing. The leather jacket is hanging from a hook on the wall beside the cabinets.

Since those happen to be my clothes folded neatly on the countertop, I glance down to look at my body. A thin, white sheet covers my stomach and legs, hiding the fact that I am wearing an ugly hospital gown. I roll my eyes and keep checking out the rest of the room.

To my right, there is a window with black-out curtains blocking the glass. The sun peaks through the bottom of the fabric, creative shadowy waves on the floor. I squint from the slight amount of light as it hits my eyes and quickly turn away from the window.

A couch is pressed against the wall next to the window and a figure is sound asleep on top of it. His back is to me and a thick blanket covers his body. I take another whiff of air through my nose and let the familiar scent overtake me.

"Ryder?" My voice is groggy as I speak.

It wasn't loud, but my voice was still able to wake him from his slumber. He pulls his head away from the small pillow and pushes the blanket away from him. He stretches his arms over his head and sits up, then turns around to face me. A smile crosses his face and he stands from the sofa and walks across the room. He sits on a portion of the bed and stares at me.

"It's about time you woke up." He says.

"How long has it been?" I ask.

"A little over a week." He replies.

"What happened?"

He takes a deep breath and says, "Well, after that whole incident with Trevor, you sort of died for a little while. I was only awake for a few minutes after that, but it was long enough to convince Dwayne to bring us back here. I woke up the next day and he believed every word I had to say about you. The entire city did."

"Trevor's dead, right?" I ask.

He nods, "Yeah, you killed him. Don't you remember that?"

I remember bits and pieces of what happened while the monster had her fun. I saw Trevor and could hear his voice, but there were times when she was able to completely shove me from my mind and not let me see a thing.

"The monster killed him." I reply.

Ryder smiles again and takes my hand, "She did and then she cured me. I'm glad that I have you back though."

"I'm sorry I ever left. I don't know what was going on with me, but losing you was too much to handle."

He squeezes my hand tight and says, "Don't worry about it. You did what you had to do and we wouldn't be here right now if you hadn't."

"Where are we?" I ask. "I know we're in a hospital, but where?"

"The city." He states. "Dwayne brought us both here. A few others managed to get here a couple days ago too. Jason and some scientist guy, Neil, and that man and his daughter."

"Phil and Sarah. I'm glad they made it."

"Me too."

I run my fingers through my hair and lift myself off the pillows and sit up. My head feels light and my muscles are stiff. That's what I get for being dead for a week. I take a deep breath and run my fingers through my hair. It's soft and tangle free and the skin on my face and neck is still so smooth.

I turn my eyes to Ryder's and let them linger on those beautiful hazel orbs staring back at me. For the longest time I thought I'd never see him again. And here he is staring back and me with the same look in his eyes that I fell in love with the first time I saw him. I've been waiting for this moment for a while now.

I put my hand on the back of his neck and bring his face closer to mine. I press my lips against his and close my eyes, letting the wonderful sensation flow through me. Knowing I can kiss him without consequence is by far the best thing the monster could have ever taught me.

"I've missed you so much." I say as I pull myself away from him.

"So have I," he replies. "I hope I never have to lose you in any way ever again."

"You never will. The monster is never coming back and I ain't going anywhere without you."

He smiles and runs a hand through my hair, "I don't want to rush you, but Dwayne wanted me to bring you downstairs as soon as you woke up. They wouldn't let me go to the house, but they did wash your clothes. I even made sure they kept those boots and that jacket you had on. I don't know what it was, but I really didn't want to keep my hands off you when you were dressed like that."

I smile and roll my eyes, "I guess the monster had other things to say about that, huh."

"Yeah, she was a little hard to get, but I broke through in the end. About the time you started coming back, I knew I had her." He jokes.

"You always did."

He kisses my forehead, then stands from the bed. I push the blanket away from me and stand beside him. My knees pop and my ankles are very stiff as I move them. They limber up slightly by the time I make it to the counter and sift through my clothes. My trusty shades are sitting on the counter beside the clothes and I let the smile creep across my face.

* * *

I got dressed quickly, then let Ryder lead me out of the room and into a dimly lit hallway. One of the fluorescent lights above us flickers and buzzes and a few others are out completely. I notice that this entire section is empty. There are no humans or living beings at all. I sniff the air and I can smell them nearby, but the rooms around us are empty as well as the hall.

Ryder takes my hand and we turn left away from the room. I slide the sunglasses over my eyes and we walk to the end of the hall, then turn another corner heading for the stairs on the right. The sun is shining brightly through the tall windows and I squint in order to see as we descend the winding staircase. The number three is plastered on the landing between the sets of stairs and we have two more to go before we make it to the lobby.

"Everyone is waiting for you. Dwayne's been checking in ever since I woke up and now he can stop bugging me." Ryder explains.

"Is he the only one that's been asking about me?" I ask.

He shakes his head, "No, that Neil guy came in a lot, with some other doctors. As much as I told them to wait until you woke up, they insisted on taking your blood. They were able to reproduce it so they won't have to steal the cure from you anymore. That was two days ago and you won't believe what all has happened since."

"I can't wait to find out." I say, utterly relieved and shocked that things have happened so fast.

I assumed it would take months for anyone to reproduce my cure so I won't have to bleed myself day after day after day. I never expected things to transpire this quickly and have the world change before my eyes right after I wake up from a week long death.

We make it to the first floor landing and I hear voices

coming from a room not far from us. They are loud and happy, filling the hospital with laughter and jokes about life. My hands start shaking and the smells of human life drift up my nose and it is just as intoxicating as before. The sweet scent has me drooling over them and I can remember just what my monster did when I let her take over.

I remember the man with the Mohawk. He was the first one and his blood was the tastiest. Then the few others I took when Jason and I were trying to escape. They were just as good as the first. Then there was Trevor whose blood took things over the top because I knew I craved it more than anything else. The revenge made his taste like candy and killing him was the only way I could end the thirst I felt for it.

At the bottom of the stairs the scent gets stronger and I feel myself slowing down. If I walk into a crowd of humans and they see me as something that is capable of killing them, they will lock me in a room from which I will never be able to escape. They will see me as something only nightmares can create and I will always be yearning for the blood that flows under their luscious flesh.

I stop walking and let go of Ryder's hand. I can't face the people that deep down inside I want to devour. I run a hand through my hair and shake my head when Ryder turns to face me.

"What's the matter?" he asks.

"I don't think I can do this." I reply.

"What are you talking about?" he takes a small step closer to me.

"I don't know if I can control myself around them They already know what I can do. They know what I have done and they saw me kill Trevor the way that I did. What's to stop them from locking me away?" I ask.

Ryder moves closer to me and places his hands on my shoulders, "You're crazy, you know that. The people out there could care less about how you killed Trevor. The moment I woke up and told them what happened, they fell in love with you and the cure. They were even happier when Neil was able to make more of it and none of them can wait to see you. Dwayne has already cured so many of them and is constantly bringing more here every day. You have nothing to worry about."

He smiles and I stare at his lips for a few seconds. All this time I thought the world would only see me as the demon who was bitten by a vampire and zombie. I never thought they would accept me for this.

I guess I was wrong.

I take a deep breath and say, "Then let's go out there."

He takes my hand again and we walk out of the stairwell and into a short hallway. Our footsteps echo slightly on the marble floor and we walk into a large room with a receptionists desk facing a wall of windows at the front entrance to the hospital. A couple dozen people are grouped together by the old and closed up gift shop. I recognize Keith standing amid the group and he is the first one to spot us.

A wide smile crosses his face and he takes a step away from the other members of the security force. He claps his hands together and shouts my name in praise. The others soon join him and they smile as they move toward us. This is a much warmer welcome than I ever could have expected.

"Glad to have you back, Bridge." Keith exclaims, patting me on the shoulder when he gets closer. "The team was lost without you."

I smile and nod my head, "I'm sure they were."

He laughs and the others with him laugh as well, "Dwayne is waiting for you outside with the rest of them. Go enjoy this. You deserve it."

"Thank you." I say and walk with Ryder to exit the building.

My hands are still shaking as Ryder pushes the glass door open. We walk through it with Keith and the others following close behind. The human smells are getting stronger with every step I take out of here and my hands won't stop shaking. Ryder can feel it and he squeezes my hand tighter. He nudges me with his shoulder and we walk through the second door in the foyer and step outside into the cool Autumn air.

* * *

A crowd of people have grouped around the hospital. They are dressed in warm clothing and foggy breath emits from their mouths. There are too many of them for me to count and every single one of them is here to see me. Some of them I know are citizens of Des Moines and others I don't recognize. Their pale skin tells me that they have recently been cured and I couldn't be more grateful to see them all here.

We walk further away from the doors and I spot Jason standing with Phil and his daughter Sarah. Our eyes meet and he tries to smile, but it is forced. The smile across my lips is forced as well. Things will never be the same between us. I remember the few moments that monster used him to destroy me and it worked. She was able to hurt a friend while tearing my heart right out of my chest whenever she kissed him.

I shake those thoughts from my mind and turn away from him and the others. More familiar faces come into my line of vision. Rose and George are standing with Katie and Adam. Annah stands with that little boy I saved from the truck stop and each one of them turns their attention to me.

Something warm hits my cheek as I stare at the friends I

saved not long ago. Each one of them is alive and safe in the city while my cure is being sent across the country. I wipe the stray tear away and smile at them.

"Bridget!" I know that loud voice.

I turn my head and see the bubbly Sherry running through the crowd, cutting across the pavement just to get to me. She leaves Seth and her father to stand with Isaac and her nephew Dillon. They wave and cheer for me and soon the rest of the crowd joins in.

Sherry runs to me and throws her arms around my shoulders. Ryder's hand slips out of mine and I stammer back a couple paces from the force of Sherry's hug. I wrap my arms around her and hold onto my best friend for a long moment. I make the mistake of sniffing her and smelling the warm blood under her skin and I have to pull myself away.

"You are so lucky you're alive. I was ready to come after you and kill you for leaving me like that." Sherry states, speaking fast and loud just like always.

"I'm sorry you didn't get the chance." I reply.

She shrugs, "It's okay. I forgive you this time."

We both smile and another familiar face approaches us. Dwayne doesn't wear a smile as he walks this way and a small crowd of guards walk close behind him. I eyeball the pistols hanging at their waists and the smile fades from my face.

I knew this moment would come. They have to be cautious and keep this city safe. I'm not human after all, but I am not a threat either.

Dwayne steps up to me and takes a deep breath. He plants his feet firmly on the ground so his body blocks my view of the crowd behind him. I hear their cheers and words of praise, some shout my name and clap their hands, but the expression on Dwayne's face doesn't match their happiness.

"Thought you were dead." He speaks slowly.

I nod, "So did I."

"You should be dead after everything you went through.

I heard the story and could hardly believe a word of it. Then Ryder woke up and Neil convinced me to let him do an experiment. A group of zombies and vampires showed up two days after you got here and I watched each one of them come back to life because of you." Dwayne explains. "I don't know how this is possible, I don't know how this happened nor do I want to know. The only thing that matters is that this cure is possible and good things can happen."

Finally he smiles and I breathe a sigh of relief. For a moment I thought he was going to treat me as a prisoner and take me to the small jailhouse in the center of the city. I'm glad that didn't happen and I feel a strange sensation taking over my entire being.

A heavy burden has just been lifted from my shoulders and the world is saved now. Humans have another shot at survival and can take the world back from the undead. It will take years to cure everyone and get things as close to normal as it ever can be, but it's possible now.

Dwayne turns away from me and faces the crowd as he speaks, "A lot has changed over the last ten days. That group that came here to be cured wasn't the only ones we've gotten to. While Neil was working on reproducing it, I sent troops out to gather others and bring them back here to receive it. Some even went pretty far south just to get them. They were mainly looking for their families that they lost along the way and some have managed to find them, but we got a lot more as well."

He steps out of the way and I scan the crowd one more time. There are faces of people I have never met before mixed in with plenty that I have. Young children all the way up to old men and women, stand together as they catch a glimpse of the thing that saved humanity. They clap their hands and cheer, inching closer to me but keeping their distance at the same time.

I move closer to Ryder and wrap my fingers around his hand once again. The smiles crosses my lips and I couldn't have hoped for a happier ending to this story. The human race has a future in the world again and I was able to be a part of that. A big part of it actually. But it's in their hands now and it's up to them on getting it global.

"I told you no one would see you as a freak." Ryder says, squeezing my hand gently in his.

I shake my head and say, "I know."

"Are you happy?" he asks.

"Of course I am." I reply.

He nudges me with his shoulder and leans closer to me, "I mean, are you happy that they have a cure even though you still don't?"

Slowly, my head bobs up and down in response as the words fall out of my mouth, "I think I can be okay with it. Who knows, maybe one day Neil will find a cure for me. If not, I'll be okay like this."

"Me too, no matter how disgusting your new diet might be." He says and we both share a laugh.

* * *

Another two weeks has passed since I woke up. The cure has now been spread to every corner of the country and they are working on finding ways to get it overseas. Neil and the rest of his team work day and night, producing as much of the cure as they possibly can. I'm happy to say that they don't need me for it. I actually don't care that they will never come to me for more samples of my blood.

More and more of the undead are being brought here every day to be cured as well as troops are being sent out to distribute the cure to villages across the nation. They travel all over the place, scooping up stragglers along the way and letting Neil work his magic in the basement of the hospital. New faces come out of that place with a brand new life to lead and no idea where to start. Dwayne feels that the city is good place, which is why most of them are brought here.

Ryder and I are back at our small house next door to Sherry. It's empty and annoying without Carter being here to make me pick up after myself. We remember him and think of him every chance we get. Ryder even prays before he eats his dinner now while I listen to his words and keep my thoughts in my head.

Our lives in this house are coming to an end. We have made plans and neither of us want to stay in the city. This isn't meant for us and, now that the wall will soon be coming down, we want to go out and explore the rest of the country. We will be safe with the cure still in my blood and I can see firsthand the many zombies and vamps that get brought back to life. I feel useless being here and both of us want to start another chapter of our lives doing something that will make us happy.

We are leaving in the morning. Ryder is upstairs packing up anything he feels is important to him. Mainly clothes and water, but there are a few books and things he wants to have with him. Life on the road will get boring at times and a good book will keep us entertained for a while. He tried conning me into bringing that damn cat with us, but I put an end to that and promised Phil and his daughter could keep it when they move into this house after we're gone.

I think I'd eat that cat after a while anyway. It would be more like a treat to me knowing that annoying little life of his would be over.

I walk through the kitchen with the sunglasses covering my eyes. The windows are wide open and the sun shines in, cutting through the bare branches of the trees outside. Since winter is almost here, our first destination is somewhere down south where the weather will be warm and the snow will be scarce. It will be easier to get around in warmer climates and Ryder will be happier.

The car we managed to get a hold of sits on the street and I eyeball it as I step into the living room. I can see it through the bay window and smile. I've never driven before and I am more than looking forward to doing so. The car is pretty nice too. A small blue sedan with tinted windows and a sunroof. Dwayne filled up the tank and put two gas cans in the trunk that are completely filled as well.

I hear Ryder's footsteps on the floor above me. He is stomping around up there as he goes through our things. I turn to face the stairs and slowly let my feet take me to them. As soon as I step on the bottom step, a knock comes from the front door.

Sherry is out to lunch with Seth and her father. Phil and Sarah won't be here until after we are gone tomorrow and everyone else should be busy at the wall. The Mayor and the rest of the security force plan on having it down as soon as they can. Dismantling a steel structure like that will take time and a lot of their effort for the next few months.

I move to the door feeling slightly on edge about not knowing who is on the other side. I sniff the air, catching a tiny hint of familiarity coming from the other side. It isn't a strong scent and I slowly move across the hard wood floor under my leather boots. I run my fingers through my hair, brushing a few strands away from my eyes and reach for the knob. I take another inhale as the visitor taps on the door one more time. Still, I can't pinpoint why this scent is familiar.

I twist the knob in my hand and slowly pull the door open. I start at the man's feet and eye his brown boots. His jeans cover the laces, dragging on the floor from being too long. The shirt he's wearing is a thick button down with a light jacket over top. He breathes fast and nervously, the same as I do. I move my eyes to his face and my jaw drops and my eyes open as wide as they can.

I think back to the last time I saw this man and can't possibly believe that he is really standing here in front of me. He *shouldn't* be here. He shouldn't be alive. I saw the hole in his chest and he was not breathing. The bite mark on his arm was bruised and deep and he was sure to turn to a vamp if he never pulled the trigger on himself.

But, as I stare into his eyes, the eyes of a man I haven't seen in over a year, I begin to question everything I saw that day. Did the bullet really hit his heart? Was he really dead or simply stunned from the gunshot? Or am I dreaming right now and I'll wake up feeling depressed and alone without him?

I might never know the answers to these questions, but I really don't care. I stare at him with a dumbfounded look on my face and I know he must think I am more than confused. The look across his face reads the same.

Footsteps come from the stairs behind me and I hear Ryder's voice calling to me as he heads my way, "Who's here, Bridge?" he asks.

I don't bother turning to him to answer his question. He walks down the stairs and approaches me, but I never turn my head away from the man standing in the doorway. My hands are shaking at my sides and I've never actually been speechless before.

"Bridget?" Ryder asks, stepping up to my side and eye-balls the man in front of me. "Who is this?"

Finally, my mouth forms the only two words I can muster and my voice leaves my throat, "My dad." I can hardly believe it myself, but he is standing right in front of me with a smile on his face.

Dad glances to his hands and I do the same. He is carrying a small, brown paper bag with hardly any weight to it. His fingers are wrapped tightly around the crinkled edges of the bag and I wonder what's inside. We can get to that later. I move my eyes back to his and feel myself getting choked up on the rock clogging my throat.

"I thought you were dead." I say. "You shot yourself."

He nods, "I guess I missed."

"That's good to know." I reply with a small smile.

"The man who cured me told me all about you and what you've become. I didn't want to believe it at first, but the more he spoke about you, the more I couldn't wait to see you." Dad says then lifts the bag and hands it to me, "After I told him who I was, he gave me this to give to you. He said it would mean more coming from me."

I take the bag from him and say, "What is it?"

"Something he knew that you'd want." Dad replies.

Confusion fills my mind and I slowly open the bag. I look inside and notice something shiny staring back at me. Light reflects off the silver surface and I reach in and pull out a syringe filled with a yellow liquid. I raise an eyebrow, staring at the needle then back to the strange liquid. My eyes catch a piece of Scotch tape with my name written on it in black letters. Under my name are two measly little words that have completely taken my breath away.

I feel Ryder looking over my shoulder and he asks, "What is that?"

I gently hold the syringe in my hand and let the bag fall to the floor. I can hardly believe what I am holding. This tiny object houses something I never thought possible, but Neil was able to do it. Having my father alive again was more than I could ever ask for, but holding this in my hands takes things over the top.

My eyes stay focused on the liquid and my mouth finally finds an answer to Ryder's question, "It's my cure." I say and I know the next chapter in my life is only just beginning.

The End

Acknowledgements:

I would like to thank my family for always being there to encourage my writing. I thank my friends for making sure I never give up with things. A special thanks to my husband, Brad, for always listening to my crazy ideas for my books and never allowing me to give up. Lastly, I thank my fans for all the amazing reviews my work receives.

About The Author

Born in 1988, Tahnee Fritz is the youngest of four and grew up in the small city of Burlington, IA where she still resides her husband. She studied creative writing and English before graduating from Southeastern Community College with her Associates degree.

Other works by Tahnee Fritz

The Human Race: Book One
The Fighting Chance: Book Two of The Human Race

Crazy For Love

www.trfritz88.wordpress.com

www.ingramcontent.com/pod-product-compliance
Lightning Source LLC
Chambersburg PA
CBHW071146170626
46809CB00002B/793